Praise for South to South: Writing South Asia in the American South

To a region much inclined to look backward, the American South, Khem K. Aryal's anthology offers a vision as contemporary as it is vital and varied. These stories and essays assemble the conflicts and collisions (often literal) of cultures to explore and expose the traditions, mysteries, and wonders of Atlanta and Mobile and Houston and all points in between that South Asian populations have transformed. These writers, of Bangladeshi, Sri Lankan, Nepalese, Pakistani, and Indian descent, are all ones you'll want to know further as soon as you shut the cover of this magical and necessary book.
—Tom Williams, Author of *Among the Wild Mulattos and Other Tales*

A stellar and much-needed anthology that illuminates a part of American life that has gone unacknowledged for too long. Gloriously written and contextualized in a well-researched introduction, this contribution to South Asian immigrant literature not only brings to life the experience of the writers and characters in the sixteen essays and stories, but offers with breathtaking clarity a vision of the American South from a vantage point that makes an old landscape new.
—Joanna Eleftheriou, Author of *This Way Back*

South to South is a wonderfully varied collection of work, subversively curated to showcase writers inventing their own traditions as they resist and complicate how we imagine South Asia and the American South. If you thought anthologies were here to generalize, let this one prove you happily wrong! With a range of nuanced, surprising essays and stories from voices originating from Nepal to Georgia, this book offers what I'm looking for in any writing about South Asian Americans: ferocious wit, elevation of historically marginalized voices, and a lively interest in critique of society and self.
—V. V. Ganeshananthan, Author of *Love Marriage*

T0283691

South to South

Writing South Asia
in the American South

Library of Congress Cataloging-in-Publication Data

Names: Aryal, Khem, editor.
Title: South to South : writing South Asia in the American South / edited
    by Khem K. Aryal.
Description: First edition. | Huntsville, Texas : TRP: The University Press
    of SHSU, [2023] | Includes bibliographical references.
Identifiers: LCCN 2022022499 (print) | LCCN 2022022500 (ebook) |
ISBN
    9781680032963 (paperback) | ISBN 9781680032970 (ebook)
Subjects: LCSH: American literature--Southern States--South Asian Ameri-
can
    authors--21st century. | South Asian Americans--Southern
    States--Literary collections. | LCGFT: Essays. | Short stories.
Classification: LCC PS508.S67 S68 2023 (print) | LCC PS508.S67 (eb-
ook) |
    DDC 810.8/08914075--dc23/eng/20220927
LC record available at https://lccn.loc.gov/2022022499
LC ebook record available at https://lccn.loc.gov/2022022500

FIRST EDITION

Front cover image courtesy: licensed via Shutterstock.com
Cover design by Bradley Alan Ivey

Printed and bound in the United States of America
First Edition Copyright: 2023

TRP: The University Press of SHSU
Huntsville, Texas 77341
texasreviewpress.org

South to South

Writing South Asia
in the American South

Edited by Khem K. Aryal

TRP: The University Press of SHSU
Huntsville, Texas

CONTENTS

INTRODUCTION

The impetus for this anthology came from the 2020 annual conference of the Association of Writers and Writing Programs (AWP) held in San Antonio, Texas. Along with four other authors coming from South Asia, I proposed an event, titled "South Asian Experience in the American South," a reading of fiction and creative nonfiction, to showcase not only the experiences of the people of South Asian heritage living in the South as depicted in the panelists' works, but also the panelists' own interpretation of the American South as it pertains to literary production. Due to COVID-19, not every author on the panel could make it to the reading. But the session drew a sizable audience and generated quite a lot of interest, especially among writers from South Asia. Some even shared their work impromptu. Out of this came the realization that an anthology comprising the best of contemporary fiction and nonfiction by South Asian American writers could not only cater to the interest of the readers of the American South but also help spotlight the literary work that is being produced by the South Asian diaspora in America. This anthology is that dream come true.

As the data from the United States Census Bureau and other sources show, South Asian Americans are one of the fastest growing immigrant groups in the United States,[1] their population increasing from 2.2 million in 2000 to 4.9 million in 2015. It is estimated that about one third of South Asian Americans live in the American South, nearly tripling in number between 2000 to 2017, to 1.4 million.[2] This wave of South Asian immigration has brought in people from all walks of life, not only professionals like doctors, engineers, professors, and journalists, but also Amazon warehouse pickers, Walmart associates, gas station servers, and writers and artists. Showcasing some of the unique immigrant experiences of the South Asian diaspora, this anthology highlightsan impressive literary intervention by authors of South Asian heritage in the U.S., particularly in the South.

The South Asian diaspora in the American South, like anywhere else, represents a rich and a vastly diverse literary tradition. "[T]he literatures of South Asia," writes Sheldon Pollock in the introduction to *Literary Cultures in History: Reconstructions from South Asian*, "constitute one of the great achievements of human creativity.[3] Pollock continues, "In their antiquity, continuity, and multicultural complexity combined, they are unmatched in world literary history and unrivaled in the resources they offer for understanding the development of expressive language and imagination over time and in relation to larger orders of culture, society, and polity."[4] This is not to mean that the South Asian writers in the U.S. write fully in those traditions, but the current generation of writers—either born and raised in South Asia or raised by parents born in South Asia—are bound to have some level of reflection of, some level of connection to what they were grew up with. Although it is too early to assess and establish definitively the literary tradition of South Asian writers in the American South, it is never too early to examine what the immigrant communities with roots in those rich and diverse literary cultures bring to the United States, and what South Asian experiences get expressed, and how they get expressed, in the works they produce.

While it can be tempting to oversimplify what South Asian experiences are, it is necessary to acknowledge that there's no such thing as *the* South Asian experience. South Asia, home to about one-fourth of the world's population, is anything but a homogeneous entity. The diversity found within a single country of the region—consisting of Afghanistan, Bangladesh, Bhutan, India, Maldives, Nepal, Pakistan, and Sri Lanka—can be staggering. Cultures, languages, and foods in Northeast India, for instance, are very different from those in South India. Even in a country as small as Nepal, there are 123 different spoken languages (some 780 languages in India), and in terms of the overall lifestyle, people living in the northern Himalayan region can identify themselves with Tibetans while those living in the southern plains, less than two hundred miles apart, with North Indians.

People from that vastly diverse region have moved to the United States under equally varied circumstances. Some have come here as students and then settled for the rest of their lives. Some others have entered the country as short-term professionals and adopted this land as their new country. Some others arrived as Diversity Visa winners. Even others have come here as refugees, and some others have entered the country without papers and made it their home. Some have arrived here via a third or even a fourth country—such as the people of Indian origin who had settled in African countries, like Uganda.[5] For a new generation of South Asians, this is the only country they know as their own.

With this experience come issues of colonial legacy—though not every South Asian country was colonized—caste hierarchy, and religious differences. It is imperative to consider these variables as they interact with the ways of life in the American South and what experiences they stoke for the transplants. The politics and the socioeconomic realities that the immigrants have left behind, and the ones they encounter in this new land, are bound to shape their experiences differently. The works included in this anthology reflect that reality and make it a rich collage of immigrant experiences, which have not only have to do what they bring with them to the region but also what they have left behind.

The American South has been traditionally "measured," James Charles Cobb and William Whitney Stueck contend, "against its longtime nemesis and counterpoint, 'the North,' which was actually a partly imagined regional embodiment of the overarching American legends of success, enlightenment, virtue, and innocence."[6] This traditional lens of processing the South through and in relation to the idealized North does not necessarily reflect the way South Asian immigrants, or any immigrants for that matter, experience the region today.

Similarly, these new writers in the South today, unlike the writers before the First World War—when, as Michael O'Brien explains in *The Idea of the American South*, "words had to be altered, new connections made within the Southern tradition so that audiences in the South would not bridle at the naked power of the new capitalism"[7]—are free of the burden of the past, although the influences of existing literary traditions cannot be undermined. It is equally pertinent to remember that South Asian immigrants' experiences tend to be different from those of many other Asian immigrants because of their late arrival in the United States. As Bakirathi Mani explains, "South Asians didn't participate in large numbers in the civil rights and ethnic studies movements of the 1960s and the 1970s," because many immigrated to the U.S. only after 1965, the year of the abolition of National Origins Act. Similarly, South Asia didn't have a direct historical connection with the U.S.,[8] which they had with European empires. This is bound to define their experience of the South uniquely, and it is reflected in the works included here.

The eight short stories and eight narrative essays in this anthology do not weave a homogeneous South Asian story in the American South, and that is not the aim of this project. It is meant, rather, to present local narratives as windows to the world of transnational exchanges that are made possible by migrations of various kinds. They, like most all immigrant writing, expound a sense of being in two places but being hardly entrenched in any one of them—the proverbial displacement. Notwithstanding how they may have left their countries, either by choice or by necessity, the immigrants often live euphoric dreams for the future. But there's always a sense of loss in tow, a sense of longing for what has been left behind, or what has been brought along without the same flavor it had in a different geo-cultural setting.

In "The Immigrant" by Chaitali Sen, Dhruv witnesses the disappearance of a little boy at a restaurant in Austin. But he is unable to talk about a boy because he feels "as if he were trapping the boy with his story," as if the lost boy's story were his own story of getting lost in a foreign country. Hasanthika Sirisena's "Pine" tells of one Lakshmi, who must walk a tightrope to satisfy her seven-year-old son's demand for a Christmas tree. The tree that she initially considers as "only a pine tree with decorations thrown on it" becomes much more than that when her ex-husband lets her know he is converting to Christianity, "to fit in" and "to get ahead in this country." Following Christmas, the pine becomes "a simple pine tree again" as Lakshmi tries to stand it against a trashcan as if it were going to come back to life despite being rootless.

In his essay "Gettysburg," Kirtan Nautiyal broods over the ever-fascinating question: how can an immigrant claim ownership of their new country's history? An immigrant child is brought to America or is born here to parents who have had no engagement with the country's past, but as a citizen of the country, he needs an association with the country's history in order to live in the present. What will bind him to this new land? His father had, writes Nautiyal, "come to make a little more money than he could have in India, that was all. I wondered if his desire for just a little more was enough to bind me to this land." In "Fresh off the Plane," Jaya Wagle recounts the story of her arrival in America as a newly married Indian woman and a barrage of missteps, such as an accidental call to 911, and the anomalies she encounters as she settles and makes adjustments to not only her arranged marriage but also the climate, food, language, transportation system, and all the demands of a new country.

Nafisa Ali, in Aruni Kashyap's short story "Nafisa Ali's Life, Love, and Friendships, Before and After the Travel Ban," is a new arrival in the U.S. But the timing of her arrival is less than ideal. Will her husband, who is still in India, be able to join her? How will she find love and friendship in his absence, in an America where the 2016 election has just taken place? In Anuja Ghimire's "Mail and More," a young student from Nepal struggles to reconcile with the harsh realities of being an international student in America, having to work illegally at a store, the owners of which, themselves immigrants from South Asia, are undergoing their own family issues. Niva, notwithstanding her worries about her studies as well as her parents in Kathmandu, must bear witness to the store owners' woes that she doesn't quite understand.

In "Drinking Chai to Savannah," Anjali Enjeti is "the clueless audience for conversations rattled off in Hindi, a language I don't understand," since she was born in the U.S., unlike the others in the group she's traveling with. How do those born in the U.S. experience America differently than the ones who were born abroad? Of the small-town experiences in the South, Enjeti writes, "[M]y friends probably can't decipher because they grew up in countries where their brown skin and names did not summarily mark them as outsiders." Sometimes the lack of knowledge provides a sense of security. How ironic is it, that those who were born here experience racial discriminations *more* than those who were born and brought up elsewhere? Tarfia Faizullah shares similar experiences of racial bias in her essay, "Necessary Failure." "I just have to ask," a lady asks her politely, "what are you?" Is "Homo Sapiens" an answer? For how long do you have to be living here not to be seen as the other? Will the amount of time spent in this country, or the amount of Diet Coke consumed, change that dynamic?

Sindya Bhanoo's "Nature Exchange" is a story of a grieving mother who has lost her son to a school shooting. Veena obsessively visits an exchange at a local nature center hoping to, one day, trade-in enough objects to accumulate points to claim the antlers her son had his heart set on. But will that heal her wounds? The story looks at the harrowing reality of gun violence in America from a rare angle of those who have no "interest in activism, in fighting publicly against gun violence or school shootings," but must bear the brunt and deal with the consequences in their own ways, nonetheless. Ali Eteraj's "Encased" follows one Saba Muhammad, born of Pakistani parents in Alabama, whose casual sharing at her birthday party that she has "more than one mother" leads to revelations of her father's secrets that she had not imagined. Unable to live with the harsh truth about her father, she leaves home and builds her American life on her own. But will she ever be able to break away from the "case" she so despises? Will the taweez with the verse by a leading Pakistani poet, "We, for whom there is no idol, no god, beside the way of love," save her?

Sayantani Dasgupta, in her essay "Rinse, Repeat," reflects on getting "evacuated from home" in the context of an impending hurricane in a southern state. What does it mean to leave a place even before you have settled enough to call it home? What is involved in being settled and then uprooted by the need to flee a storm? In her essay "What I Found There: Transcendence through the Blues and Two Books," Shikha Malaviya recounts her days in Tampa, the "Suitcase City." She's been married for less than two years to a man she hardly knew before marriage, and the couple hasn't felt any more settled than an Indian man walking aimlessly with a suitcase, crying, because his wife has kicked him out of their home. How does a new place, an alien socio-cultural reality, treat a newly married couple? She won't be able to get the "Hindustani Thumri" in Tampa, but the "blues seem the American equivalent" of it for her. Malaviya contemplates how "we discover things so gloriously different and make them our own" through what we already possess and who we are. In a similar vein, Rukmini Kalamangalam, in her essay "Slow Fruiting," finds that no matter where you move, no matter how far away from your original place you settle, "there are some things that don't change." Bangalore's jamun, Houston's chikoo, or Monroe's nartanagi all blend in one as the garden becomes "our way of connecting and collecting."

Jenny Bhatt's "The Weight of His Bones" tells of a man from Mumbai and his son born here in the U.S., both of whom going through a rough time in

Texas. Deepu, the son, is an autistic teenager, but the father fails to understand him and to provide for his needs because he has his own issues. The father imagines the moment after his death when the son is being asked to go back where he came from, despite being "Texas born and bred." "Laxman Sir in America," by Khem K. Aryal, is a story of a Diversity Visa winner, who works at an Amazon warehouse in Memphis and misses the social standing he used to enjoy as a teacher back in Nepal. His story depicts an immigrant's struggle to forge a sense of belonging and selfhood by reconciling what he has with what he has left behind.

The final piece in the anthology, Soniah Kamal's essay "Writing the Immigrant Southern in the New New South," adopted from her keynote address to the Red Clay Writers Conference, in Georgia in 2019, and first published in *The Georgia Review*, contemplates what it means to be an immigrant writer in the American South, and in a way sums up the experiences of many of the writers in these pages. "Can one be in two places at the same time?" Kamal asks as a writer. Indeed: where do we write from, and what is the location of our writing? What have a writer's "emotional coordinates" to do with it? "What is foreign for one is home for another," she continues, "and when the two combine, it turns out it's just a hot nourishing meal on the table, and this is writing the immigrant Southern in the New South."

Stories are a way we develop relationships to places. While stories help us understand, define, and create a place for ourselves, the place in turn defines our stories. Sheldon Pollock writes, "To understand literature in relationship to a place … is as much a matter of understanding how literature can create places as it is a matter of understanding how it is created by them."[9] Pollock further writes, "[L]iterary representations can conceptually organize space, and the dissemination of literary texts can turn that space into a lived reality, as much as space and lived realities condition conceptual organization and dissemination."[10] This anthology is an attempt, as is much of our writing, to organize our lived experiences in a new country, to create, define, and claim a place of our own as South Asian immigrants in the United States. It is also a study in how the South has defined us, as South Asian immigrants in the American South. Since this is a new field, this anthology is the first of its kind, and I believe that it will serve as a companion and a gateway reader to the work of not only the writers included in these pages but also to the many other South Asian immigrant writers in America.

Khem K. Aryal
February 2022

Notes

1   "An Introduction to South Asian American History," *South Asian American Digital Archive*, https://www.saada.org/resources/introduction

2   Sabrina Tavernise and Robert Gebeloff, "How Voters Turned Virginia From Deep Red to Solid Blue," *The New York Times*, November 9, 2019. https://www.nytimes.com/2019/11/09/us/virginia-elections-democrats-republicans.html

3   Sheldon Pollock, Introduction, in *Literary Cultures in History*, ed. Sheldon Pollock (California: University of California Press, 2003), 2.

4   Ibid.

5   David M. Reimers, "Asian Immigrants in the South," in *Globalization and the American South*, ed. James C. Cobb and William Stueck (Athens: University of Georgia Press, 2005), 100-134.

6   James C. Cobb and William Stueck, Introduction, in *Globalization and the American South*, ed. James C. Cobb and William Stueck (Athens: University of Georgia Press, 2005), xi-xvi.

7   Michael O'Brien, *The Idea of the American South*, 1920-1941, (Baltimore: Johns Hopkins Press, 1979), 7.

8   Bakirathi Mani, "Becoming South Asian in America," *Swarthmore*, n.d. https://www.swarthmore.edu/news-events/becoming-south-asian-america#transcript

9   Sheldon Pollock, Introduction, in *Literary Cultures in History*, ed. Sheldon Pollock (California: University of California Press, 2003), 11.

10   Ibid, 27.

The Immigrant

Chaitali Sen

THE IMMIGRANT

D hruv found this faux French restaurant—a restaurant of sorts but perhaps more of a cafeteria—off the bypass road of a highway called Research Boulevard, close to his hotel. There were many of these restaurants all over the southern and midwestern states to which Dhruv traveled for work, and he had eaten in most of them. On a Wednesday night he was having a late dinner of something they called chicken friand, a square puff pastry stuffed with chicken and gravy and smothered in a thick, gummy mushroom cream sauce. As always, he ordered it from the counter and watched it plucked from its home under a heat lamp where it had been kept warm for an undisclosed length of time. This was one of the better ones, still somewhat moist and flaky. Sometimes the corners were so dry and hardened he couldn't get his fork through it, yet he took his chances on this dish every time he came.

He had to admit the concept here was well executed, a testament to the power of objects. Mounted on a brick wall across from his table, a decorative iron hook held a long-handled copper saucepan. The hook's baseplate was a pleasing silhouette of a rooster, a motif repeated throughout the restaurant, on a teacup, a ceramic jug, and a porcelain plate. A fireplace divided the two dining rooms and on the broad mantel rested a giant iron lid and a bellows. Dark wooden beams stretched across the plaster ceiling, and some of the walls were paneled with the same coffee-colored wood. The few segments of wall not made of brick or covered with wood were accented with framed pictures—maps of France, still life paintings, and sketches of ruined castles on riverbanks. The music was baroque.

He never dined idly anymore. During this meal he wanted to get a letter written to his parents. "I am sitting in a quaint French-style restaurant," he wrote, in English. His old friend Tuli had once joked that his parents did everything in English—they shopped in English, they ate in English, they even made love in English. Picturing Tuli's jolly, white-toothed grin, Dhruv sighed deeply before continuing his letter. He tried to describe the rustic décor and how it was meant to evoke the French countryside. This would mean little to them since neither he nor his parents had ever been to the French countryside and his parents had no appreciation for the charm of old things, no nostalgia for simpler times. They lived in India surrounded by old things, and their lives had always been relatively simple. Among the three of them, only Dhruv would have fallen victim to the manipulations of this interior. This dining room, reproduced hundreds of times in hundreds of cities, somehow awakened heartfelt pastoral yearnings, as if he'd been a French farmer in another life.

He wanted to write about a woman he loved but couldn't begin for many reasons. For one thing, she had not yet returned his feelings, and for another, she was a Muslim, though not devout in the least. In fact, she was a heavy

2

drinker. He believed he could fix that if she would give him the chance.

He was easily distracted from his letter. Outside in the parking lot, an old Asian man was shouting at an Asian woman, presumably his wife. Dhruv studied the man's behavior, the angry spasms of his mouth and his arms flailing theatrically under the eerie orange street lamps. He wondered if something justifiably outrageous had set him off on a public tirade, or if he was just prone to tantrums.

Dhruv looked away momentarily to see if anyone else found this scene riveting, but the only other person facing the window was a woman sitting alone a few tables down. Dhruv had noticed her when he sat down with his tray because she was dining alone and reading a book, and he was always curious about people dining alone. He tried to guess at her situation. She could not have been on a business trip. She was too much at home, with an unhurried air of self-possession. She looked to be in her mid-forties, not unattractive but not overly concerned with her appearance. His powers of deduction led him to conclude merely that she was an avid reader who had wanted to get out of her house. She did not look up to watch the man with the loose temper. Her book, whatever it was, held her unfailing attention. Every few pages she would lift her glass of white wine and take a sip, and that was her only distraction.

The Asian man threw his car keys on the ground and took off walking while his wife, somber with her head bent, remained by the car. After a moment she picked up the keys and drove away.

Then Dhruv saw a tiny boy wobbling around the restaurant with a giant laminated menu in his hand, smiling at anyone who was interested and tilting the menu vaguely in their direction. He was a beautiful child, with thick black hair and shining black eyes. He came to Dhruv's table. "Are you the waiter?" Dhruv asked him.

The boy froze and stared at Dhruv's mouth as he spoke.

"Would you like to give me a menu? Is there anything good to eat today?"

He finally stood up to look for the boy's family. He did a kind of dance with him, herding him toward the adjacent dining room, where a large party had joined together many tables to accommodate everyone. An elderly gentleman saw them and came over, snatching the boy up and giving Dhruv a brief, grateful glance. As the boy was carried back to the table, he cried and dropped his menu, causing him to cry even louder and thrash about in the old man's arms. The old man quickly dropped the boy into the lap of a young woman, surely his mother. Like the boy she was strikingly beautiful, with high cheekbones and deep-set eyes. She pressed the boy's head against her chest, quieting him down, and a man who must have been the boy's father picked up the menu, while still engaged in animated conversation, and put it

3

absentmindedly on another table. Dhruv didn't recognize the language they were speaking. Not Spanish. Portuguese? They were all dark haired and fair skinned.

Since he was up, he decided he might as well go to the pastry counter to get a chocolate croissant and a cup of coffee. He didn't want to go back to his hotel room just yet. When he returned to his table, which had been cleared of his dinner tray, he began to write what was foremost on his mind: Ma, Baba, I have met someone. Before he could get very far, the woman with the book made a remark. "No one is watching that boy," she said.

At first Dhruv didn't understand what she meant.

"He's wandered over here at least ten times," she said, seeming stunned that Dhruv hadn't noticed him earlier.

"Aah," Dhruv said. "Well, we are all watching him, aren't we?" He turned back to his letter, shrugging off the strange admonishment. At least he had returned the child to his family, while she sat there with her nose in the book.

As he wrote about Mahnoor, he knew he would never send this letter. He had seen her nearly every weekend for over a year through a small circle of Chicago friends who gathered frequently, yet he was at a loss for words to describe her. He listed the facts. She was a pediatric oncologist with a broad smile that turned her cheeks into two crescent moons. Long, wispy bangs grazed her eyebrows. She had a habit of brushing them aside with her fingers to reveal a narrow triangle of forehead that he found very attractive. He knew the group gathered during the week as well, in his absence, and when he returned on the weekends she always looked surprised to see him. "You're back," she would say, and he could never tell if she was disappointed or relieved. She had a distinct American accent that her friends said was a Southern drawl. Drawl was a word he found difficult to pronounce. She had grown up in Georgia.

Last weekend he had given her a ride to her apartment in Highland Park because she got drunk, extremely drunk, and wanted to go home before her roommate was ready. In the car Mahnoor confessed that she was thinking about distancing herself from this group of friends, that they had become too dysfunctional and incestuous, and lately she felt her life had become all about work and drinking. She needed some quiet time. She needed some time to read and travel and visit museums and learn something new, to learn how to do something new. She'd always had an interest in carpentry, in making things with her hands.

"You know," he had said to Mahnoor, still thinking about the word incestuous, "I like to do all those things." He had felt a rising panic threatening to choke him. He did not know how he could see her if she left the group. He and Mahnoor had never done anything on their own, until this drive.

4

"You like carpentry?"

"Well, I've never tried it, but I have assembled a lot of Scandinavian furniture."

She laughed and laughed and laughed. He laughed too.

"I've never seen your apartment," she said. "Why don't you ever have us over?"

"I'm hardly ever there."

"Have you decorated it? Does it feel homey?"

"No, I haven't done anything with it."

All he could say about his apartment was that it was impressively clean. It had a brand-new kitchen that had seldom been used, and polished wood floors, and a bedroom set that matched. The walls were bare and the shelves were empty. He saw so little of it because the consulting company he worked for shipped him anywhere they liked for the workweek. When he first got the job, he thought it would be interesting, traveling all over the country, going to business lunches, getting to know all kinds of people. He had planned to experience the culture and beauty of every place he visited, but in two years he had not seen anything but highways and business parks, and often he could not even remember where he was. The company flew him in on Monday mornings and flew him back to Chicago on Thursday evenings. Every week he was in a new city, sitting in a new cubicle in an office building that looked like thousands of others, and it didn't matter where he was, really.

"I was talking more about the travel, and the visiting museums," he said to Mahnoor, gathering the courage to ask her out on a date.

"You like to visit museums?" she asked doubtfully.

"I love art. Paintings, sculpture, design."

"I would never have guessed," she said. She sounded delighted.

But she fell silent after that. The mood changed so rapidly he knew it would be a mistake to try to return to their previous conversation. Something must have happened earlier, some heartache that kept coming back to her despite her best efforts to remain cheerful. He kept looking over to see if she was crying or feeling sick, but she was perfectly composed, yet melancholy.

Once they got out of the car, she was unsteady on her feet. He stayed close beside her as they walked along the path to her apartment building and up the stairs to her second-floor apartment. On the steps, suddenly, she stumbled and fell into his arms. She stayed there for a moment, looking up at him with her pearly black eyes, but then her eyebrows twitched and she pulled away. She thanked him for the ride, politely but with an unmistakable finality. He waited on the landing while she fumbled for her keys and clumsily opened her door. She said goodbye again, without looking back, and slammed her door shut.

He was sure he had not done anything wrong. He had only held his arms out to keep her from falling down the stairs, but now that some time had passed he thought he knew what had troubled her. She had been attracted to him, there on the steps, and imagined briefly being with him before she came to her senses. The reason for her rejection was not that he was a Hindu and she a Muslim, or that she saved children's lives while he traveled around the country as a programming consultant, or even that she was beautiful and he was . . . not bad. It all rested on the immutable fact of his Indian-ness. No matter what he wore or how he styled his hair, he would never carry himself with the easy confidence of American men. His American-born friends taunted him about this. They told him to not to be such a FOB. "Don't be fobbish," they often said, when they perceived him to be too Indian, too foreign, and he never could quite get their meaning. He never could quite understand what he had done to offend them.

He had filled three pages of onionskin paper with this drivel about Mahnoor. He put his pen down and massaged his neck, and thought about tearing up the letter and starting again back in the hotel room, or at the airport tomorrow. He would have plenty of time in the next twenty-four hours to write a more sensible letter.

The family in the adjoining dining room was making a racket as they prepared to depart, giving him his cue that he should leave as well. They were calling out the little boy's name—Rafael—and Dhruv looked around, expecting to find the boy nearby. The woman with the book had gone. The restaurant was about to close. The heat lamps had been turned off, the counter was dark, and a girl in a burgundy apron packed the salad greens into plastic tubs while another employee brushed dust off a ceiling beam with a mop he held upside down. The dust fell, like dirty snow falling from dirty clouds, onto the food counter before the girl had finished packing away all the salad greens. Dhruv watched them, wincing.

He stood up and prepared to leave, but something about the family looking for the boy, something in the volume and pitch of their voices, kept Dhruv from walking out the door. They had recruited an employee to help them look for the child in the kitchen, behind the counter, and in the party room, which the employee agreed to unlock, despite the implausibility of the boy getting into that room through a locked door. Dhruv approached the old man who had taken the boy from him earlier. "Can I be of some assistance?"

"Rafael," the man said, but clearly his English was not good enough to explain the situation. The man called over another male relative, a boy of about twelve or thirteen who spoke perfect American English. He told Dhruv they were looking for his baby cousin. Last they saw he had slipped under the table to hide, and everyone assumed they would still find him there when they were ready to leave.

"Does he hide often?" Dhruv asked.

The boy shrugged. He did not seem as alarmed as the adults, and Dhruv took this as a good sign. He tended to trust the instincts of children, even children as old as this one, whose body language suggested this was not the first time the whole family had gathered forces to find the errant toddler. Still Dhruv was moved by the mother's panic. She had become distraught in the last few minutes and could not be comforted. Her cries were becoming increasingly desperate. She called out her son's name in a way that might have made the child feel too frightened to come out.

Dhruv decided to take a quick look outside before he headed back to his hotel room. He was not eager to become further involved in this rising drama, but he suddenly remembered the woman reading. What was it she'd said? No one is watching him. Dhruv couldn't help but wonder if the woman had taken the boy somewhere, perhaps out of the restaurant but somewhere close, just to make a point. She seemed like the didactic type.

Dhruv hurried out of the restaurant and circled the building. An employee with a flashlight and another member of the family were already surveying the parking lot, which extended far out along the length of the bypass road. Behind the restaurant there were ten or twelve other shops, all connected to each other in one long concrete strip. At the far end of this shopping center there was a movie theater with a full and expansive lot. There were a million places to hide. A million places for a woman—who might be slightly mad, now that he thought of it—to take a child and still keep an eye on the scene unfolding at the restaurant. He headed for all of those places, looking around corners, columns, and bushes, out as far as the movie theater. He ran through every row of the theater lot and then ran back to the restaurant, thinking the boy must have been found by now, but as he came around the corner he saw two police cars parked by the restaurant.

Dhruv took out his cell phone. It was past eleven. They had been searching for more than an hour.

* * *

Outside the restaurant he gave a statement to the police, but all the while he imagined the interview being cut short because the boy was right there inside, slumbering in a shadow, somewhere they'd looked a thousand times without seeing him. The family was huddled together in silence at a patio table nearby. The police took a long time with the interviews and every now and then the father implored them to cut the questioning short and keep looking for his son. Dhruv tried to be quick with his details, but he wanted

7

to be thorough. As expected the officer was interested in the woman with the book. Most of the questions were about her, and when Dhruv was asked if he saw the woman leave, he shook his head guiltily. "I was writing a letter. I didn't notice she had gone until I heard them looking for the boy."

He heard the officer discuss the woman with his partner. "Let's hope she used a credit card," he murmured. Dhruv was a little taken aback by how firmly the woman had become a suspect based on his testimony. He hoped he had just given the facts and not misrepresented anything he heard or saw, but if the woman was innocent, the most this would cost her was a few hours of her time and some humiliation. If she was guilty, if she had indeed snatched the child, Dhruv felt at least she wouldn't harm him. He found himself hoping that his suspicions were correct. If Rafael was not in the restaurant, the best alternative was that he was with a bookish, middle-aged woman with poor judgment. Any other scenarios were far more sinister.

When he was a child, this happened all the time. Children went missing for a while until they were discovered at some neighbor's or relative's house. He himself was lost during Kali Puja when he was about five years old. He happily sat for hours with an old man who fed him sweets and told him stories. He did not even go home that night. An aunt and uncle he didn't recognize found him and took him to their house. The next morning his family's driver, Santosh, came to retrieve him, and at home he was lightly scolded for wandering off.

The officer told him he was free to go.

"I'm going back to Chicago tomorrow," Dhruv said. "Is it possible for me to get news from someone when the boy is found?"

As he put the officer's card in his wallet, he realized he had left his letter pad at his table. He was embarrassed by the thought of someone finding it and reading it, but it seemed inappropriate, petty somehow, to ask if he could go back into the restaurant to retrieve it. He said goodbye to the family and told them how sorry he was that this had happened. "I'm sure you'll find him," he said, "soon." The men shook his hand. The women bowed their heads, except for the mother, who was staring at the road, lost in a waking nightmare.

When he turned to go to his car he was surprisingly disoriented. He couldn't remember where he had parked, and although he stood for a long time staring at the silver Hyundai that was his rental car, he had been looking for his own car, parked in the basement garage of his apartment building in Chicago. Without any recollection of driving this car over the past week, he took the key out of his pocket. He pressed a button, heard the click of the car unlocking, and opened the door. He was tired and overstimulated. He would go home, not home but back to the hotel, take a hot shower, and fall into bed.

* * *

Back in the hotel room he was still awake at three in the morning. He had not even changed out of his clothes or turned out the lights. He did not turn on the television or read a book. He just sat on the edge of the bed and relived his evening in the restaurant over and over, trying to uncover something he might have missed. After a while his mind started playing a game with him, like one of those *Where's Waldo* books his nephews liked so much. Where's Rafael? He is by the fireplace. He is under the copper saucepan. He is there in the framed picture of a ruined castle.

Suddenly Dhruv covered his eyes. A rush of tears fell into his palms. His chest heaved. A groan escaped from his throat. He was sobbing like a little boy, his body expelling some kind of liquid anguish. He had never cried like this before, not even when his beloved grandmother died. He sobbed until he was exhausted. He got into bed, thinking he would fall right to sleep, but as soon as his head sank into the pillow he was wide awake.

He took out his phone and studied his contacts list. Who could he call at this hour? He could call his parents, but on a cell phone the expense would be enormous and they would worry about him. He had friends in California, but it was late even for them. He came to Mahnoor's number and stared at it, wondering what would happen if he pressed the call button. He did it without thinking. His mind was an empty vessel.

She picked up after two rings. He hung up.

His phone rang. He answered it.

"Dhruv?"

"I'm sorry. I dialed you by accident. I've woken you up."

"No," she said. "I was awake."

"Are you on call?" he asked, certain he must have disturbed something in her schedule.

"I couldn't sleep. Then you called . . . by accident," she said, and he understood that she was teasing him. "Where are you?" she asked. She sounded sleepy. He imagined her lying in her bed.

When he tried to answer he could not for the life of him remember where he was. In his mind he could clearly see the building where he'd worked that day, the on- and off-ramps of the highway, the shopping center, the restaurant, the parking lot, his hotel. This litany of images did nothing to help him recall his location. It only prolonged the silence. He thought of France.

"Dhruv?"

"One moment," he said. He looked for clues on the bedside table. There was a breakfast menu, directions for ordering movies, and even a booklet

9

with dining and shopping options in the area, but not a city name to be found. I'm nowhere, he thought.

It came to him at last. "Austin," he said. "Austin, Texas."

He paused, wishing he had not called her, but wanting desperately to keep her on the phone. "I've had the strangest night."

"What happened?" she asked. Her voice inflected in a way that suggested genuine curiosity, even concern. He would tell Mahnoor everything about the missing child.

"I was sitting in a restaurant, trying to write a letter," he began, but he felt mournful and guilty, overcome with an uncanny sense of anxiety, as if he were trapping the boy with his story, as if the story itself could make him lost forever.

Pine

Hasanthika Sirisena

That year Lakshmi yielded and bought a Christmas tree. In sixteen years of living in the States and eight years of marriage, she had never seen the need. If asked why, she explained this was a tradition with no place in her home. But now she could not keep one more thing from Sareth and Aruni—not after everything they had lost. So when Sareth, who was seven, asked for a tree, as he had for the past three Decembers, she said yes. It was after all, only a pine tree with decorations thrown on it. Still, karma has its effects, and, when she recognized her uncle's voice on the phone, she felt as if he had caught her out.

"Lakshmi, I need a favor," her uncle said. "The Sri Lanka Buddhist Society has a priest from the temple in Atlanta coming for a dana. He's flying into Raleigh-Durham this afternoon. I was supposed to fetch him, but I'm on call tonight. Can't you pick him up, darling? He can stay with you tonight, and I'll come by tomorrow morning."

"It's Christmas Eve, Vijay-mamma." "What's that got to do with you?"

"Is it okay for a priest to stay with me? Isn't it against his vows to stay with a woman alone?"

"He's almost doddering, Lakshmi. I doubt he'll do anything to you, and I equally doubt you'll want to do anything to him. It's hardly fodder for a scandal. You have time for us, no?"

"I'm not trying to put you off. It's just that Nimal is coming tonight. He has some kind of request to ask in person."

"Isn't he your ex-husband now? Doesn't he have a new wife?"

"No, she's just his girlfriend."

"The priest is flying in at two. Won't that give you enough time?" He paused. "It will be good for Sareth to meet a priest. Don't you think?"

After they finished speaking, Lakshmi walked into the living room. In Sri Lanka the Christmas tree wouldn't have mattered to her. Every December, her parents had kept a small, plastic one on top of the refrigerator, and she had exchanged small Christmas gifts with some of her Christian friends. She had loved how the Colombo shopkeepers had decorated their facades with colored lights until the war put a stop to that. But here in America the Christmas tree seemed a time waster, an imposition of someone else's culture and tradition. Now, amid the devil-bird masks with hissing cobras wrapped around sharp beaks, the brass plates engraved and pierced with scenes from Sinhala mythology, the batiks depicting dancers with arms flung wide and legs bent in traditional poses, the small pine tree—only a head taller than Lakshmi herself—looked out of place.

At the abandoned lot turned boreal forest, she had surveyed the felled trees tethered together and displayed like carcasses in a butcher shop and felt dismayed by the waste. When Lakshmi bought the tree, the salesperson informed her, after she had asked how she was supposed to make it stand, that she would have to purchase a tree stand, a tree skirt, and a humidifier to keep the needles from becoming brittle and dry.

And she had to find decorations. At the local Kmart, she scoured rows of Santa Clauses, gaudily painted reindeer with red noses, crèches, and stars all which she deemed too holiday specific, before she settled on a box of silver and gold globes, tinsel, and colored lights.

She and Sareth decorated the tree while her two-year-old, Aruni, sat and watched, clapping her hands and reaching for the glistening ornaments. When they finished decorating, Lakshmi stepped back to assess their work. The tree sagged under the weight of its tinseled finery and with lights blinking—red, yellow, green, red, yellow, green—it lost any resemblance to its natural form. But Sareth didn't see it that way. Her heart tightened when she noticed him standing there, his dark, beautiful face radiant and warm like a piece of coal in a fire. He turned to her and smiled, "Amma, isn't it amazing?"

Two days later, he returned from school with a small package wrapped carefully in newspaper. He held it in front of him and walked gingerly, as if he were an unsteady waiter balancing a tray of glasses.

"What are you carrying?" she asked.

He held it out to her. "Open it, amma."

Lakshmi unwrapped the paper. A misshapen papier-mâché star, the size of her hand, covered in tinfoil and decorated with glass beads, lay inside. "What is this?"

"It's the star of Bethlehem. When I told Mrs. Pratt we got a Christmas tree she was so happy she helped me make it. She said that we have to wait and put it on top of the tree on Christmas Eve."

"You shouldn't have told Mrs. Pratt we have a tree."

"All the kids have Christmas trees," he beamed. "Now I'm like them." Lakshmi rewrapped the star and gave it back to him.

"Then why don't you keep it in your room until Christmas Eve."

He wrinkled his nose. "Aruni will eat it. I'm going to keep it here, where everyone can see." He unwrapped the star and placed it on the middle of the kitchen table. After a few minutes consideration, he placed the newspaper wrapping underneath the star. So it would not get hurt, he told her.

She felt as if she lost him little by little each day.

*　*　*

That had been over a week ago. Now the tree looked even more pathetic. And, as if it were registering displeasure at its fate, a thin carpet of pine needles surrounded its base despite the stream of cool, moist air provided by the humidifier. She tried to keep the floor clean, but a new layer reappeared within minutes. There was nothing she could do about the tree now. She would just have to hope the priest would not notice it.

She took a back road to the airport to avoid holiday traffic. The rural landscape was barren and lonely; swaths of black and ochre stretched toward a sunless sky. A rare, early winter snow had fallen two nights earlier. Much of it had melted the day before and refrozen during the evening. A hard sheath covered the ground and trees. The patches of ice were cloudy and dense in the formless light of the gray December afternoon, and the landscape appeared trapped under a fragile coating of glass. As she drove, Lakshmi imagined reaching out and shattering the brittle world with just one warm touch.

Lakshmi arrived early at the airport so she could grab a smoke. She had tried to quit a couple of times since the divorce, without success. She had managed to reduce her habit to the occasional drag while sitting in the car just before work. The stress, however, of the impending visits by the priest and her ex-husband, Nimal, proved too much. The pack of cigarettes and the silver cigarette lighter with her initials engraved on the side—a gift from Nimal—now sat on the car seat beside her like faithful friends. She was not sure why she kept the lighter when she had packed up and stored everything else that reminded her of him. After months of trying to get her to quit, he had given it to her with the admonition that, if she were going to kill herself, she might as well do it in style—a bad joke. Still, the lighter reminded her of a time when they were able to laugh at each other's choices.

They had met during her sophomore year in college. Lakshmi had moved to the states when the Sri Lankan government closed the universities in order to crush student-led opposition. The shutdown, which was only supposed to last a few months, appeared as if it might, like the civil war, go on indefinitely. Her family had decided she shouldn't wait. So, at eighteen, she enrolled in a small college outside of Winston-Salem with the expectation she would go back home when she finished school.

In Sri Lanka, she had grown accustomed to the war; the fatalistic acceptance of a life attenuated by violence had become routine. But once in North Carolina, surrounded by the pristine Appalachian landscape, she had recognized the perversity in that existence. Then, she had met Nimal at a Sri Lanka Society party. A business student at Chapel Hill, Nimal had lived his whole life in the States, the child of immigrant parents who believed their son would succeed only if they pushed him to be as American as possible, without the influence from their Sri Lankan culture. When she met him, Nimal had just started to explore what he referred to as his roots.

When Lakshmi reached the terminal gate, the Buddhist priest was already waiting for her. She placed both palms of her hands together and started to drop to her knees. He stopped her before she could reach the floor. "It will make all these people jealous seeing such a beautiful woman kissing the feet of an old man."

The monk was tall and fleshy. Wire-rimmed spectacles balanced precariously at the tip of his bulbous nose; they seemed flimsy and ludicrously useless dangling in the middle of the priest's expansive face. He wore a black wool coat over his yellow robes; a black wool cap covered his shaved head. His left arm shielded a small bag that hung from his shoulder, and in his right hand he clutched a metal cane, though he did not seem to need it. In fact, he moved so quickly Lakshmi, who was much smaller, had trouble keeping up.

At her car, she opened the back door, but he waved his hand in protest and opened the front door instead. He paused when he noticed the pack of cigarettes and the lighter on the seat. Lakshmi reached around the priest and placed both objects on the dashboard. Great first impression, she chided herself.

*   *   *

During their marriage, Lakshmi created for Nimal an ideal of what it meant to be Sri Lankan. She cooked for him—kirri-bath, string hoppers, chapatti—all the food he had never tried. She took him to temple. Lakshmi described to him what it was like growing up in Sri Lanka. What it was like to be an adult and to touch snow for the first time. Or how strange it was to have to listen to weather reports every day in order to know what to wear. When Nimal left, shortly after Aruni's birth, saying that maybe he had married too quickly, she felt he had not just betrayed his family and his culture, but now she felt she had to contend with her own betrayal. She was thirty-four, no country, no marriage, and remnants of a family. Were these losses the price she had to pay for her unwillingness to return?

*   *   *

After Lakshmi pulled into the garage, she sat wondering if she should help the priest out of the car. He made no move, so she got out and walked around to the passenger side, but as she reached for his door, the priest pushed it open quickly and she nearly fell. He was out of the car and almost to the house before she regained her balance.

Lakshmi steered him to the back door. She knew she probably would not be able to keep him from seeing the Christmas tree, but she did not want it to be the first thing he noticed. The priest, however, was more nimble than

17

she expected. He slipped past her and made his way into the living room. He walked straight to the tree as if, somehow, he had known it would be there.

"Your husband is a Christian?"

"No swamin-wahanse. The tree is for my son. He's had a hard time this year, and he really wanted one."

"You're raising him a Buddhist?"

"Yes, but it's hard here. The temple is eight hours away. I try to teach him the prayers, but he's only seven. I saw no harm in letting him have a Christmas tree."

The priest remained silent for a few minutes. He supported one of the silver globes in the palm of his hand and rubbed his fingers across the silver veneer. The ghost of his thumbprint appeared on the shiny surface and slowly shrank away. Still holding the ornament in his hand, the priest said, "But you are the mother, no? You must set him on the right path. Buddhism is like the path on which we journey. We might feel tired and think that there will be no harm in stopping at an inn beside the path. But the inn is warm. The food is good. We may never leave, and then we will not reach our true destiny." A dry shudder shook the tree as the priest released the ornament; the piquant smell of pine needles exuded like a breath.

Lakshmi nodded, "Then swamin-wahanse, you will pray with us tonight? It will be good for my son."

"As you wish, I will pray with you and your family tonight. Your son and husband will be here soon?"

"My children are with a babysitter. She'll drop them off in a little while," she paused, "Swamin-wahanse, I'm no longer married, but my ex-husband is coming here tonight."

"No matter, we will still pray with him."

Lakshmi bowed her head further, "My ex-husband is coming with a friend."

"We will all pray."

"She is not Sinhalese."

The monk turned away from the tree. "This is a very American house, no?"

*   *   *

Lakshmi had come, now, to wonder if she had ever really loved Nimal or if he had simply represented a reason—a very good reason—not to return to Sri Lanka. Still, the divorce had been painful, and she very much wanted to ease the stress of it for Sareth and Aruni. She felt she gained nothing by keeping Nimal and his girlfriend from seeing the children. But, when she

18

opened her front door and saw them—Nimal and Wendy—standing so close to each other, her stomach dropped.

Wendy walked immediately to the tree. "It's beautiful!"

"I helped decorate it," Sareth said.

"Well, you did a good job." Wendy tousled Sareth's hair. He scowled and rubbed his hair flat with his hand.

"I thought you were against having one?" whispered Nimal.

Before she could answer, Sareth asked, "Dad, do you like it?"

"Dad?" asked Lakshmi surprised. "He's your thaththi, Sareth."

Sareth looked up at her, eyes wide. "That's what the kids at school say."

"Your amma is right, " said Nimal. "You should call me thaththi."

Wendy smiled and nodded. "That's okay, honey. In America we call our fathers all kinds of things." She winked at Lakshmi.

Lakshmi invited them to sit on the sofa. As he sat down, Wendy scooped Aruni into her arms and held the squirming girl firmly on her lap. Aruni's tiny hands reached for a silver cross dangling on a chain around Wendy's neck.

"No, no, sweetie," Wendy cooed as she gently separated Aruni's entwined fingers.

"That's pretty," said Sareth.

"Thank you. It's an early Christmas gift from your daddy." She corrected herself, "Your thaththi."

Sareth turned to Nimal. "Mommy got me three presents. They're in the hall closet. We're going to put them under the tree after," Sareth glanced at the bedroom and whispered, "he is gone."

Nimal gave Lakshmi a look. "Amma is giving you three presents? Really?" he said through a gritted smile. "How nice."

Aruni grabbed Wendy's necklace again.

"Let me take her." Lakshmi made a move toward them but Wendy waved her away.

"No, I'll just take it off." Still grasping Aruni with one hand, Wendy unlatched the necklace with the other and quickly caught it as it slipped toward her chest. She placed the necklace on the end table next to the sofa.

When she had first met Wendy, Lakshmi had noticed immediately the physical difference. Lakshmi was so small she bought her shoes in the junior miss section of the department store. Wendy was tall and athletic, with red hair and a round, pretty face. Tiny freckles like pin pricks covered pale, almost translucent skin.

Sareth told Wendy and Nimal about the priest staying in his room. They listened to him nodding as he described saying hello to the priest. Lakshmi was distracted from their conversation by the sound of doors opening and

19

closing in another part of the house. She got up and walked to the kitchen. The priest stood next to the kitchen table. He wore a long, dark cardigan over his saffron-hued robes.

"Swamin-wahanse, can I get you something?"

"It's time to pray," responded the priest. "I will pray with you and your son in the sitting room."

"My son will sit with you now, and I will join you once my guests leave."

Lakshmi returned to the next room and explained to Nimal and Wendy they would have to move to the kitchen.

"We're not planning to stay long," replied Nimal. Wendy touched his arm lightly and he continued, "We have a favor to ask you."

Sareth took Wendy's hand in his and looked up at her. "Can I sit with you in the kitchen?"

"Let's ask your amma," Wendy answered, looking at Lakshmi for approval.

"No putha," Lakshmi pulled Sareth and steered him toward the middle of the living room, "you need to stay here and pray."

"Do I have to?"

"Yes." Lakshmi tried to control her voice aware of Nimal and Wendy watching her. "Sit on the ground in front of the sofa and keep your sister on your lap. Listen to what the priest tells you."

With a loud huff, Sareth slumped on the floor. The priest, who had been listening in the doorway, came and sat with them. He leaned forward and started to speak softly to the children.

*   *   *

In the kitchen, Lakshmi turned to Nimal. "Before I forget. Can you help me put this on top of the tree?" Lakshmi started to show Sareth's star, but it was no longer on the table.

"That's strange. Sareth made an ornament for the top of the tree. Now it's gone."

"Maybe he took it to his room," Nimal suggested. "We'll ask him about it in a minute. But first I have a favor to ask. I'm going to be baptized two weeks from now. That's a Sunday when you have the kids. But I'd like them to be at the baptism."

"You're what?"

"Wendy's family is coming and I would like it if Sareth and Aruni could be there. It's an important day for me."

"You're converting?"

"Amma, Aruni won't sit still." Sareth stood in front of them holding

20

Aruni's hand. Lakshmi pulled Aruni onto her lap.

"Go back and sit with the priest," she told Sareth.

"I don't like him. He's weird."

"Don't talk like that about a priest, putha."

"That's right, Sareth. A priest is a holy man. You should show him respect," explained Nimal.

"Do it for me. Won't you?" Lakshmi asked gently.

Sareth pulled on Nimal's sleeve and pleaded, "But he smells funny."

Lakshmi felt her face grow warm. "If I hear you say anything like that again no television for a week." She grabbed Sareth by his shoulder. "Listen to me! You're never to say bad things about a priest. Now go back and sit down!" Aruni hid her head against Lakshmi and started to fuss. Sareth stood staring at Lakshmi, blinking. He turned to go.

"Sareth," Nimal stopped him. "Your amma said you wanted me to put your star on the tree. Do you have it?"

Sareth bit his bottom lip and pointed to the table. "I put it there." "Putha, please? Just tell the truth."

"It's okay," said Nimal. "Go sit with the priest." Sareth hunched his shoulders and walked slowly away.

As Nimal turned to watch Sareth leave, the light struck the convex surfaces of his glasses, making them white and opaque. Nimal nervously crossed and uncrossed his long, thin legs before turning back to Lakshmi. "I'm sorry, I didn't think this would upset you so much, but this is important to Wendy and me."

"Sareth is confused enough as it is."

"Look it's not like this doesn't happen all the time in Sri Lanka. Think of all the people you know who are raised in mixed families."

"That's different. They live in Sri Lanka. Sareth has to have some grounding, Nimal. You can't just push and pull him at will."

They sat staring at each other, the only sounds the faint electric hum of the refrigerator and the rustle of fabric as Nimal continued to cross and uncross his legs. Wendy leaned over and placed her hand on Nimal's arm, "Okay honey, let's go." To Lakshmi she said, "I'm sorry. This was a lot to put on you. We don't want Aruni or Sareth to become Christian."

"We?"

"I have respect for your culture. I think it's beautiful."

Lakshmi turned to Nimal and said, "You ask too much."

"Wendy is right. We'll go now, but please think about it." Lakshmi buried her face in Aruni's hair without answering.

21

* * *

A light rain began to fall. Lakshmi tried to dodge the chilly drops as she walked to her car. She slipped into the front seat, closing the door so that she could sit in the cold, crisp darkness. While her eyes were still growing accustomed to the dark, she reached for the cigarettes and lighter on the dashboard, but then drew her hand back in surprise. She switched on the car light. The pack of cigarettes was there but the lighter was gone. She felt carefully along the dashboard and checked under the seat. After a few minutes of searching, she decided to wait until morning, when there would be enough light to see. She sat back and closed her eyes.

She thought about Sareth and wondered what he'd done with the Christmas ornament. He held so much inside himself; she could see it in the tightness of his mouth and stiffness of his small shoulders. He had been having trouble at school lately. Some older students had taunted him. Sareth had pushed one of them before the teacher could intervene. The teacher apologized to Lakshmi, assuring her no disciplinary action would be taken against Sareth. She also told Lakshmi she was planning a special class to teach the students about the cultures of India and asked if she would like to make a presentation. We are from Sri Lanka, not India, was all Lakshmi could think to respond. Sareth refused, even when she pressed him, to talk about the incident. And after a while she stopped trying to talk to him about it, afraid to push him too hard and wondering why he would not trust her more.

* * *

The next morning Lakshmi was sitting in the kitchen, cradling a cup of coffee, when she heard the crunch of gravel as a car rolled to a stop on her driveway. She looked out the kitchen window, expecting to see her uncle. Instead, it was Nimal. She opened the kitchen door for him as he walked up to the house. He came in shivering and blowing into gloveless hands. Lakshmi closed the door behind him.

"Look, first I want to apologize for last night," Nimal offered. "I should have come on my own, but Wendy likes the kids and she wanted to see them." Nimal laughed nervously. "Also Wendy left her necklace here last night. I just wanted to pick it up for her."

"I haven't seen it."

"She said she left it on the end table in the living room." Lakshmi led Nimal into the next room.

"It's not here."

Nimal dropped to his hands and knees and looked under the sofa. He stood up shaking his head.

"Maybe Sareth saw it." She called to Sareth, who came running from the back of the house. When he saw Nimal, he ran and hugged him. Nimal picked him up and sat him on the sofa.

"Sareth, Wendy left her necklace here. Have you seen it?" asked Nimal.

Sareth bit his lip and shook his head slowly.

"We won't be angry. Just tell the truth."

"We know you just took it to put it some place safe."

"I didn't take it!"

"Then, putha, who else could have?"

"The priest took it!"

Lakshmi crouched in front of Sareth and looked up at him. "I'm not mad. Just tell the truth."

"I am telling the truth," Sareth whined. "The priest took it. I saw him put it in the pocket of his sweater."

"If you saw the priest take it, why didn't you say something earlier?"

"You said you were going to punish me if I said anything bad about the priest."

Lakshmi sat back, resigned. Sareth was lying now and of all things about a priest.

One more thing to add to the list of all that could go wrong. As if realizing the significance of a detail half noticed from the corner of her eye, she turned and looked at the tree.

There was a bare space among the branches—a space where a silver ornament once hung. Sareth followed her gaze. "He took something from the tree, didn't he?" he asked.

Lakshmi nodded. "Alright. I'm not going to punish you. But go to my room and wait for me. I have to finish talking to your thaththi." Sareth pushed himself from the sofa and ran off.

"What the hell just happened?" Nimal asked.

"My lighter is gone and the priest was the only one in the car. The star is gone and the priest was in the kitchen last night. He was in the living room alone when Sareth came into the kitchen."

"You're kidding me," Nimal groaned. "What am I going to tell Wendy?"

"Wendy? What am I going to tell Sareth?"

"He's just a kid. He'll get over it. But Wendy really liked that necklace."

"Why don't you go confront the priest? Maybe you can wrestle the necklace from him."

Lakshmi stood up and walked back to the kitchen. Nimal followed behind. "Look, I'll figure out something to say to Wendy. But now won't you at least consider letting them come to the baptism?"

23

Lakshmi stood swung around. "What do you mean 'now'? You'll lie to Wendy if I give in to you? Protect our family honor? Protect our cultural honor? Or maybe this proves they should be Christian."

"That's not what I'm saying!" Nimal exclaimed, palms open. "I just want them to be there. They're my family."

"What about them? What about not confusing them?"

"Lakshmi, you don't know what it's like. To get ahead in this country you have to fit in. No one notices everything that's the same about you. Just what's different. My job is closed unless I try to fit in. These guys I work with. They actually make deals at church socials."

"You're converting so you can advance your career?"

"No, I'm converting because that's the world I live in. My friends. My coworkers. Wendy. Wendy is very important to me. I want to share my life with her, and her religion is important to her. I personally don't care what religion I am. Hell, it's more of a sham to pretend I'm a Buddhist just to make a point."

"What are you going to tell Sareth when he asks?"

"I'll tell him the truth. I thought it was the right thing to do."

"For Wendy?"

"Yes, for Wendy."

She leaned against the edge of the kitchen counter to steady herself. "What does this say to our children?" she asked softly. "What does this tell them about who they are?"

"Lakshmi you're not the only one who loves them. You're not the only one who understands them. I do know what they're going through. Has it ever occurred to you I know that better than you?"

"You should go." She opened the kitchen door. Outside, he turned to her and asked, "Seriously, what do I tell Wendy?"

"Tell her what you really think. Tell her you can't trust *those* people." She slammed the door and locked it. She kept her burning forehead against the cold wood long after Nimal's footsteps died away.

*   *   *

Her uncle handed Sareth and Aruni two small packages. Trinkets, he told Lakshmi when she stared at him. "It is only a holiday," he mused as they watched the two children run gleefully into their rooms to unwrap their presents. Her uncle stared at the Christmas tree for a few seconds before sitting down on the sofa.

"Don't say anything, mamma."

Her uncle shrugged. "I've always thought the trees were quite lovely,

24

like the Vesak lanterns. I'd have one if Nalini didn't think they were a major nuisance." He sighed. "One of my friends—a Jewish chap—never had a Christmas tree growing up in Brooklyn. He has a Christmas tree now. You know the reason the bugger gives? He's afraid his patients are going to drive by his house, see he doesn't have a Christmas tree and stop coming to him. It's pointless being afraid of such things. You should do what you want and be happy," laughed the uncle. "The priest gave you no trouble I hope?"

"Well—"

"Very sad life that one. His family gave him to the monastery when he was a boy because they were too poor to feed him."

"That seems sad—to have that choice made for you."

"Still what a hardship his life would have been without the monastery."

"Nimal is converting, mamma."

"Is that so? All that glisters."

"He must love her very much." An emptiness tugged at Lakshmi's chest as she said these words.

"There's nothing you can do about that."

The priest came in followed by Sareth, who was holding Aruni's hand.

Lakshmi's uncle kneeled and bowed his head to the ground at the priest's feet. After her uncle stood up, Lakshmi worshipped the priest as well. As she bowed, she heard her uncle tell Sareth to do the same.

She watched from the corner of her eye as Sareth knelt in front of the priest; he looked, for a moment, just like a little Sri Lankan boy. As Sareth sat up, Lakshmi smiled and winked at him. He smiled bashfully in return.

As her uncle was leaving, he put his arm around her shoulder and kissed her on top of the head. "You're coming to the dana? It will be good for the children to see."

"Of course, Vijay-mamma. I will come."

* * *

By the time they returned from her uncle's home three days later, the tree had begun to turn brown. Lakshmi sent Sareth and Aruni to her room to watch television. She started by taking the ornaments of the tree and placing each one carefully in its original box. After she was done, she took the boxes, the tinsel, and the lights and crammed them deep inside the hall closet. She pulled the tree off the stand. Pine needles pricked at the skin revealed between her coat and gloves as she dragged the tree outside.

When she reached the garbage cans, she caught her breath and stared at the tree at her feet. Despite the bare patches where the needles had fallen away, it was again a simple pine tree, sheared from its roots and resting on its side. She pulled it up and balanced it carefully against one of the cans. With her foot, she arranged the gravel and dirt around the base. After she was finished, it looked, at a cursory glance, as if it had been planted there. Now, she mused, the tree would exist again, for a short time, as it had once meant to be—a reprieve, even if it were only an illusion.

Gettysburg

Kirtan Nautiyal

M ost nights in ninth grade, after the rest of my family was asleep, I snuck into the upstairs game room and turned on the computer, hoping that the loud buzzing and beeping of the dial-up modem wouldn't wake my parents downstairs. As the blue light of the monitor bathed my face, I logged on to Mplayer, where I gathered with a few dozen others in order to delve into the deepest mysteries of the long-ago Battle of Gettysburg. Our medium of study was the 1997 real-time strategy game *Sid Meier's Gettysburg!* which distilled the battle into a dozen or so scenarios that we replayed endlessly in infinite combinations.

We organized into rival groups called clans. The Confederate clans were more popular, but I joined the sole Union clan: the Grand Army of the Republic, or GAR for short. Named after the largest post-war Union veterans' organization, GAR was organized into brigades, divisions, and corps modeled on the actual order of battle at Gettysburg. As a new recruit, I was assigned the persona of one of the junior regimental commanders, Colonel Patrick Kelly of the famed Irish Brigade. When hostilities against the Confederates began, Kelly, who had immigrated to New York City from Ireland following the potato famine in 1846, immediately joined the state militia—then the 88th Volunteer Infantry of the Union Army—and went on to distinguish himself at the battles of Antietam, Chancellorsville, and Fredericksburg. His men knew him as a fine horseman and courageous fighter, and they followed him regardless of the odds against them. When under intense fire at Antietam, bullets whizzing past, he turned to his troops and exaggerated his Irish brogue for humorous effect, smiling and telling them to "lie down, byes [boys], thim little fellows might hurt yez."

As a skinny Indian kid who'd never fired a gun in my life, I inhabited Kelly's role surprisingly well. Using a few simple command buttons arrayed at the bottom of the screen, I maneuvered our forces at the Devil's Den, Little Round Top, and the Wheatfield, sending pixelated men around the map on double-time marches, anticipating opposing flanking actions, and positioning artillery on the high ground. As the sound of rifle fire crackled through the tinny stock speakers stationed on either side of my keyboard, casualties mounted in real time, soldiers falling onscreen, canned sound effects urging us still onward towards victory. Our actions were governed by arcane rules, and the outcomes were graded according to who held the most valuable positions at the end of each scenario. The game would signal a Confederate victory with a series of rebel yells, while a Union triumph would trigger a resonant "Hoo-rah!"

Every time we replayed Pickett's Charge, I moved our regiments a little more quickly, a little more effectively. The apparent simplicity of the game was alluring, containing within it the promise of perfectibility. We cycled through the handful of default scenarios again and again, chatting after each playthrough, pointing out where and how we could do better. We remained online far into the night, and I had a hard time staying awake in my morning classes after only a few hours of sleep. One night, a close relative in India suddenly passed away, and when our family there finally got through to us to deliver the news, they told my parents they'd tried calling for hours only to find the phone lines busy. That got me banned from playing games online after bedtime, but after the furor died down, I quietly rejoined the ranks.

Between battles, talk in our chatroom sometimes turned to the Civil War reenactments that many of the others in GAR went to on weekends. Firing rifles while running around in the mud sounded exciting, and I badly wanted to join them. But aside from the fact that most of these events occurred hundreds of miles away from Oklahoma, where I lived, there was this: I could not figure out what someone of my skin color would have been doing in the 88th Volunteer Infantry, or any other regiment for that matter. Naturally, there weren't any other Indian teenagers in GAR to talk to about it. I briefly entertained the idea of wearing a beaded vest and inhabiting the role of a Native American scout, but my skin tone wasn't right for that, nor were my features. Pretending to be a Native American soldier was just as ridiculous as pretending to be an Irishman; I knew that even then. At the time, I didn't understand that nostalgia could be racialized, that imagining one's self backwards was only safe for a certain kind of American — but even if I had, I wouldn't have known what to make of it.

* * *

My father came to America from India in 1969, and my mother followed him after their marriage in 1983. Two years later, I was born in Ponca City, Oklahoma, where my father worked for Conoco as a geophysicist. They never talked much about their personal histories, their inheritance of place and caste. Time spent listening to stories about their parents and their parents' parents was an unnecessary indulgence, they felt—it was time better spent on the math problems my father assigned to my sister and me. American history interested them even less. Once, on a business trip to Virginia, my father's colleagues brought him along for a visit to the Manassas battlefield. Later, he told us that he couldn't understand what was so interesting to them about a fenced-off field a few hundred feet from a busy road.

History was for school, where I read about Wild West shootouts, the Boston Tea Party, and the Dust Bowl travails of my Oklahoma home. For Cowboy Day in third grade, my mother dressed me up in jeans and a big belt buckle, packing me what she thought a vegetarian Hindu outlaw might have eaten for lunch a century and a half before. A few years later, I checked out a copy of *Oregon Trail II* from the local library and played it for hours, naming my party members, buying supplies, and clicking on buffalo and squirrels to slaughter them with a long-range rifle. In high school, I read about the Founding Fathers, and took it for granted that their ideas about the rights of man were premised on the assumption that one day people like me would exist within the same borders as people like them.

Near the peak of my career in GAR, I caught a re-run of the 1993 film *Gettysburg*, starring Martin Sheen as General Robert E. Lee and Jeff Daniels as the Union hero Colonel Joshua Chamberlain. It was part of that last rank of great epics shot before the advent of computer-generated special effects, and the major set pieces involved thousands of re-enactors charging across the actual battlefield, making real for me what had previously only been a game. Falling artillery shells exploded upwards in showers of dirt and grass, sending bodies flying. Daring officers led the advance with outstretched swords before being shot down by opposing snipers. Most satisfying were the stirring speeches that the colonels and generals on both sides gave before combat, laying out what they believed were this nation's true ideals. I was particularly taken by Chamberlain's words to a group of would-be deserters:

> *This is a different kind of army. If you look back through history you will see men fighting for pay, for women, for some other kind of loot. They fight for land, power, because a king leads them, or just because they like killing. But we are here for something new. This has not happened much, in the history of the world. We are an army out to set other men free. America should be free ground, all of it, not divided by a line between slave states and free—all the way from here to the Pacific Ocean. No man has to bow. No man born to royalty. Here we judge you by what you do, not by who your father was. Here you can be something. Here is the place to build a home. But it's not the land, there's always more land. It's the idea that we all have value—you and me. What we are fighting for, in the end, we're fighting for each other.*

That speech stirred something deep within my teenage heart, articulating better than I ever could what so fascinated me about the war. Chamberlain's words encapsulated what it meant to be an American, I thought. The mortally wounded Confederate officer Lewis Armistead throwing his head to the heavens in a plaintive cry when he learned his friend from before the war, Union general Winfield Hancock, had been shot down in battle as well—that was the price we had to be willing to pay. Every time I caught the movie on

TBS—no matter where it was in its epic run time—I watched to the end in rapt attention. A few years later, when I was earning a little money during college, one of the first things I bought was a DVD copy, which I still have, sitting on a shelf below my television.

America demanded devotion. I'd spent most of my life to that point trying to explain my presence in this country to myself while trying to justify it to everyone else. My father hadn't come here to escape any profound persecution. He'd come to make a little more money than he could have in India, that was all. I wondered if his desire for just a little more was enough to bind me to this land. Our wars offered a compelling stage, a way to imagine proving myself, to ask what I would have been willing to do in the name of this country that I loved. The Civil War was long over, but I still wanted to see myself as willing to sacrifice everything for the ideals Chamberlain glorified in his speech.

Still, Oklahoma was an unlikely place for my Civil War obsessions. We were of the South, but not quite—not even a state at the time of the war. What was then called Indian Territory had been contested by rebels and federals, Confederate-allied Cherokee and Chickasaw armies battling Union forces coming down from Kansas for control of this ground on the western periphery of the war. A strange footnote, really, that the tribes would ally themselves with a nation that codified racism into its Constitution; but so many of the wealthy chiefs owned slaves themselves, and most of the rest felt that the enemy of their enemy could be an uneasy friend.

That the apparent harmonious homogeneity of life in suburban Tulsa obscured a more turbulent history was not something I learned from my parents, nor from my high school history textbooks, which still described the violent destruction of the city's Black community in 1921 as the "Tulsa Race Riot." Jim Crow remained the law in Oklahoma for decades after, just as in Mississippi and Tennessee. But the families of most of my white friends had moved to Oklahoma decades after the South's surrender. Civil War remembrance in Oklahoma, such as it was, didn't take on the brutal sentimentality of the Lost Cause—in Oklahoma, there was no antebellum to falsely idolize. It was more neutral ground, and, already unaccounted for in our racial dichotomy, I felt freer to continue making my own kind of remembrance of an imagined American past.

* * *

In the years after college, the long-running *Antiques Roadshow* became one of my favorite programs on television. Whenever I came across a rerun, I'd sit captivated as elderly white folks in loose khakis and Hawaiian shirts

31

explained the provenance of a dusty piece of furniture or forgotten painting. They'd explain how their great-grandfather brought back an ancient vase from a trip to Shanghai in the 1930s, or how their distant relatives had passed down a Shaker table as a precious family heirloom. A grinning appraiser in a nice suit would look the forgotten object up and down before revealing its secret history. The owner would feign surprise as the real value of their youth was quantified in dollars and cents, then smile at learning some new part of their past. For the span of an hour-long episode, history was knowable, quantifiable, tangible, its mysteries sitting in a closet somewhere waiting to be pieced together. For the price of an entry ticket and a few hours in line, someone would even do it for you.

I began to attend estate sales. I eagerly perused online listings, carefully looking through photos for hidden treasure. At least one Saturday a month, I joined a line outside the best sale of the week, waiting my turn to enter after the doors opened at eight. Jewelry and old porcelain brought the greatest frenzy, but I was drawn to colorful artwork, trinkets from abroad, mid-century barware—I sought ballast.

My parents had come here with nearly nothing and threw out or gave away most of what little they'd accumulated each time we moved to a new rental house. They told me my inheritance was spiritual—accumulated wisdom, not a few useless antiques. Still, I wished for my own heirlooms. Rummaging through dusty attics on hot summer weekends, I was inventing my American roots, collaging together others' belongings and ideas into a story that made sense—what Cathy Park Hong has called "an origin myth of the self."

My father immigrated to the U.S. much earlier than most of my Indian friends' parents, and I took it for granted that he had been among the first of his kind. But as the years passed and my historical scavenging went beyond the confines of estate sales, it became clear that there had been Indians here for decades prior to his arrival. During my fellowship in medical oncology, I learned about the life and work of the biochemist Yellapragada Subbarow, who developed new antibiotics, streamlined methods for synthesizing important vitamins, and discovered the crucial chemotherapy drug methotrexate. My interest in his pioneering work in the 1920s and 30s turned into an obsession: months of research about his life, hunting down obscure articles and an out-of-print biography. As I read on, I learned about the Ghadar Movement, a group of San Francisco-based Indian revolutionaries who advocated for the violent overthrow of British rule in the years before World War I. I read and I read: one book about Bengali peddlers making a life in Black communities from Harlem to New Orleans, another about Punjabi farmers intermarrying with Mexican American women in Depression-era California.

Yet I wanted something deeper, earlier. I wanted brown people in cravats and frock coats. I wanted brown abolitionists, railroad tycoons, and transcontinental explorers. I wanted brown people in uniform firing relentlessly at this nation's enemies, foreign and domestic. I wanted us in every corner of America's history, all the good and the bad, hidden somewhere in the background like we always were. I found a book that contained a drawing from a century and a half old issue of *Harper's* depicting a turbaned "adventurer" from India who'd come to California for the 1848 Gold Rush, but there weren't any more details. Searching through nineteenth century newspaper archives I uncovered the odd "Hindoo" exhibition or traveling speaker, but there was never more than a paragraph or two on these perceived oddities. I thought I'd have to content myself with the imagined outlines of nonexistent ancestors and the echoes of the Gita in Emerson and Thoreau — until, one busy weekday morning, absent-mindedly clicking through the *Washington Post* headlines, I saw a headline about Aaron Burr's "secret family of color."

The article described new research by Sherri Burr, a Black professor of law at the University of New Mexico and herself a descendent of the third vice president of the United States. Professor Burr had found clear evidence that Aaron Burr had two illegitimate children with his Indian servant Mary Emmons, who was born in Calcutta, and that these children—Louisa Charlotte and John Pierre Burr—were his only progeny to survive past the age of thirty. Half-Indian, half-white, both of Burr's children married into Pennsylvania's free Black community and eventually became ardent abolitionists; John Pierre even hid escaped slaves in his barbershop as a conductor on the Underground Railroad. At the outbreak of the Civil War, near the end of a lifetime of political activism, he signed a petition along with Frederick Douglass and others, encouraging free Black men to join the Union army.

His eldest son, John Emery Burr, heeded that call, mustering into the United States Colored Troops. Even though they typically served at the rear, these regiments suffered some of the highest casualties of the war, dying at a thirty-five percent higher rate than their white counterparts. Regardless of their place of residence prior to the war, Confederates deemed them all guilty of "servile insurrection" and often summarily executed them following capture on the battlefield. Still, they served bravely when called upon, most notably at the Battle of the Crater in Virginia and the Battle of Fort Wagner, later dramatized in the 1989 film *Glory*. John Emery, it seemed, was the Union soldier of Indian descent I'd wished for ever since my time in GAR all those years ago.

I wondered whether John Pierre or Louisa Charlotte saw themselves as different from the freedmen among whom they made their lives. I wondered whether Mary had ever furtively given them some nearly forgotten words of Bengali, a verse from the Vedas, or a recipe for one of those delicacies that would have recalled a world now lost to her forever. And, though I know it can't be true, I like to imagine John Emery Burr, at his campfire the night before some tremendous battle, conflicted, thinking about what his grandmother might have taught him about the first scenes of the Bhagavad Gita when Arjuna surveys his own battlefield, unwilling to fight and kill those that shared some part of his blood.

A couple of years ago, my wife and I went to see a production of *Hamilton* in Chicago. We sat in excellent seats, my wife crying through most of the songs, while I marveled at this feat of historical imagination. We could imagine ourselves backwards anywhere, Lin Manuel Miranda seemed to be telling us: a Puerto Rican man could be Alexander Hamilton, a half-Asian woman could be Elizabeth Schuyler, and a Black man could be George Washington. It wasn't until later that I read Miranda had cast the Indian actor Utkarsh Ambudkar as Aaron Burr in his initial workshop productions of Hamilton at Vassar College in 2013. An Indian man could be Aaron Burr, who'd impregnated an Indian woman and had a secret Indian family that turned into a secret Black family that accepted histories had ignored.

Yet many criticized Miranda's sleight of hand as erasing the humble people of color who'd actually existed in the background of the heroic scenes of national self-determination he'd dramatized in his musical — making me wonder if my own backwards imagination should place me with Aaron Burr or with Mary Emmons.

I wanted to be in two places at the same time.

I wanted to be everywhere at once.

*   *   *

In March of 2015, when my wife was still only my girlfriend and we were living in Philadelphia, we went to the hallowed ground of Gettysburg on our drive home from a vacation on the Delaware shore. It had been nearly twenty years since my fascination with the Civil War began, but before that day, I'd never managed to make the trip. We arrived late on that early spring Sunday, the sun already beginning its downward journey over the rolling brown fields. As we made our way through the narrow streets of Gettysburg towards the battlefield, I regretted tacking our visit onto another vacation rather than dedicating all the time it deserved. We rushed through the official museum, spending a few seconds in front of each display, then ran back to the car to drive through the battlefield before the sun set. As we approached, we saw the domes, obelisks, and statues placed by various regiments after the war as memorials to their fallen brethren, gleaming in the chill light. The scene was appropriately somber, the landscape in its eerie emptiness a fitting reminder of all who had once died here. The topography itself seemed muted, the hills less steep than I had imagined when sending my regiments charging up their slopes back in the GAR.

We pulled over at the parking lot for Little Round Top and rushed up the marked path to its summit. The trees were still bare, and fallen leaves crunched under our feet. It was here that Colonel Joshua Chamberlain, holding the far-left flank of the Union line, had made his fateful stand against wave after wave of rebel troops. Looking down the wooded slope. I imagined Jeff Daniels as Col. Chamberlain, delivering his dramatic speech before the battle to the men under his command. Late in the afternoon of July 2, having been told by his superiors that no retreat was possible, his ammunition exhausted, most of his men now dead or wounded, his troops reduced to a single thin line atop the low mountain, he saw the Confederate units massing for yet another assault. Convinced this was the end, he asked his exhausted troops to fix bayonets and countercharge right into the teeth of their advance. The crazed courage of the 20th Maine sent the rebels scattering, averting disaster and perhaps turning the tide of the war itself. Now, so many years later, it was hard to believe that such carnage could have once occurred in this bucolic landscape, but if I closed my eyes, I could almost hear the faint echoes of those long-ago rebel yells.

We moved on to the Wheatfield, where I took a picture of a cannon looking out over the open expanse and posted it to my Instagram. While Chamberlain was repulsing the rebel attacks on his flank, Patrick Kelly and his men were receiving final absolutions from their Catholic chaplain before heading here to play their own role in the proceedings. Gettysburg guide T.L. Murphy writes that Kelly led his Irishmen into the waving wheat that fateful morning holding their regimental flags high, repeating their Gaelic battle cry "Faugh a Ballagh!" Their initial momentum would soon be halted by a hail of bullets, and by the end of the fighting they would be forced backwards to where they'd started, losing nearly half of their men to the battlefield. Still, Kelly's commanding officer would recognize his continued bravery, writing to the president with a recommendation for his promotion to brigadier general. Perhaps due to ongoing discrimination against Irish officers in the ranks, the recommendation never came to fruition, and Kelly would remain a colonel until the end of his war a year later at Petersburg, where he was unceremoniously cut down by a Confederate bullet.

In his famous address, Abraham Lincoln spoke of how the dead had given their "last full measure of devotion" to the ideal that this "government of the people, by the people, and for the people" would not "perish from

35

this Earth." I looked out over the empty landscape where over fifty thousand soldiers had been killed or wounded, most of them now forgotten. The armies quickly moved on following the decisive battle, leaving the few residents of the town of Gettysburg to struggle with the thousands of bodies left behind. Already decomposing in the searing summer heat, the bodies were buried in shallow trenches only to be uncovered by the next rain, after which wild animals tore the limbs free. The carcasses of the thousands of horses killed in the fighting were burned in a giant bonfire near town, the fumes of which violently sickened town residents for days afterwards.

I wondered if the American identity I'd spent decades crafting could stand up to what this battlefield seemed to silently demand. In 1923, after fighting in the American army during World War I, Bhagat Singh Thind was denied citizenship because he "would not be considered white in the understanding of the common man." Nearly a century later, Captain Humayun Khan was killed while fighting in Iraq, and when his father spoke of his sacrifice at the Democratic National Convention in 2016, the eventual winner of that year's election spoke of him flippantly, denigrating his mother's silence. I hadn't risked everything like Thind or lost everything like Khan, but despite what they and their families had endured, the ideals for which they had fought still meant something to me. As the sun continued its descent at Gettysburg that day, the line between those ideals and the lives we lived by them continued to blur. All Patrick Kelly had wanted when he had emigrated from Ireland was a wife and a small store that he could call his own. Instead, he'd found himself drawn into a war, fighting for a country that never fully accepted him. He'd died for that country. Our country.

In his 1961 book *The Legacy of the Civil War*, Robert Penn Warren wrote, "a high proportion of our population was not even in this country when the War was being fought. Not that this disqualifies the grandson from experiencing to the full the imaginative appeal of the Civil War. To experience this appeal may be, in fact, the very ritual of being American." What was a nation but a collective conjuring born of such ritual? The mysterious attraction of that war had once seemed comprehensible to me, written in the subtle movements of pixels on a screen. Yet in the years since my first and only visit to Gettysburg, its truth had become more elusive, muddied by all that had come into our nation's politics. Still, I searched on in my own way, finding my imagination returning again and again to those bloodlands, as if I hoped to find in the sacrifice there some means to renew my belief in the myths that had once sustained me, some way back to the collective history I still held dear.

Fresh Off the Plane

Jaya Wagle

I

One week after your arranged marriage, on your maiden intercontinental flight from Ahmedabad International Airport to Dallas-Fort Worth, you will sit next to your husband for more than twenty-four hours, half of which the two of you will spend sleeping, exhausted from your four-day-long wedding celebration, a hurried trip to Bombay to get your visa, and a small rooftop reception at his house. The devastating aftermath of the 2001 Gujrat earthquake, two days before your wedding, is still being felt in the aftershocks of the land and people's consciousness, and though you are not superstitious, you can't help but wonder what it portends for your arranged-marriage-wedded life to come.

II

On that same flight, somewhere over Cairo, Egypt, when you both finally wake up, he will head to the bathroom to brush his teeth and gargle with the small bottle of mouthwash kept in the cabinet above the tiny basin.

Six months later, after the two of you have settled into your domestic life, you will scoff at each other's dental hygiene routine—he brushes his teeth first thing in the morning, you like to do it after drinking a tall glass of water and a cup of strong *adrakwali* chai, made the way you have always liked, one-fourth cup of milk, three-fourths cup of water, two teaspoons of sugar, one teaspoon Brook Bond Red Label loose tea leaves, freshly grated ginger root, boiled till the chai is terracotta brown.

He will tell you he grew up drinking tea made with Vagh Bakari (lion and goat) tea leaves, a brand whose television ad you had watched with derision for how it turned a dominating mother-in-law into a docile, motherly figure after drinking the tea her daughter-in-law made. As if tea could solve differences and strengthen marital ties.

A month after settling in your one-bedroom apartment, you will start buying both brands and mixing the tea leaves in a big container, so the flavor of Vagh Bakari and the color of Brook Bond can be enjoyed with the morning cuppa.

He will start making the morning tea, because you can never wake up early enough to make it for the both of you. He'll tell you he is thankful you didn't choose to be a doctor, or your patients would've died waiting for you to get up and make your morning cup of chai.

38

III

The only chai that is offered on the Lufthansa plane is a paper cup of warm water with a tea bag seeping in it. You don't care for the tepid flavored water, so you switch to coffee with milk and two sugars. He drinks black coffee, a habit he picked up after living in America for the last two years. In time, you will grow to appreciate the dark roasts at local coffee shops but will always add a generous splash of milk, two sugars, and a sprinkling of nutmeg that will remind you of Ma's instant Nescafe with a dash of nutmeg.

It is morning somewhere over the American continent when you realize that all the coffee you drank is pushing against your bladder. In the tiny bathroom of the Lufthansa plane, you will hitch up your kameez, and struggle to untie the strings on your salwar so you can squat on the cold steel toilet to pee, wash your hands and straighten your clothes and swirl the mint green liquid that stings your tongue, spray perfume under your armpits and behind your ears because you want your husband of one week to think you can smell of peaches and roses and minty fresh breath 38,000 feet above the earth.

A few weeks later, you will hear his discourse on why stereotypes about Indians are not that far off in his circle of acquaintances—body odor (they don't wash their clothes often), bad breath (smell of spicy food lingers), bad posture (hunched shoulders). In time, you will start noticing these things too, and then adding your own anecdotal observations to his list—horizontal stripe T-shirts, oily hair, mustachioed men mumbling out last syllables.

IV

When the mustachioed friend of your husband picks up the two of you from the airport, you will sit in the heated cocoon of his Honda Civic (*desis* drive Hondas and Toyotas, reliable, dependable cars with a good resale value) and listen to the two men from the back seat of the car talk about green cards, parking garages, weather, a big garbage bag full of his mail, friends who cleaned his apartment during his three-week India vacation to get married. The mustachioed man will drop the two of you at the 750 sq. ft. first-floor apartment with one bedroom, living room, galley kitchen. He will help bring in the luggage, four big suitcases and two carry-ons.

You will walk in the apartment, over the rose petals strewn on the beige carpet, past the entrance, balloons and buntings on the speckled white walls, the living room with two brown leather couches and a big screen TV, a grey plastic patio dining table in one corner, to the small bedroom with a queen-sized bed, wood and wrought iron bedframe, a particle board office desk, a desktop and keyboard.

The fact that you are in a foreign land where the ritual of stepping over your husband's threshold will not involve a container of rice that you will topple with your toes will hit you with a force that you are not prepared for.

Over the years, you will miss out on many more rituals and festivals and celebrations, but for now, you circle back to the living room just as the heater kicks in. You sink on the leather sofa, that's called a couch, and look around the apartment that'll be your home for the next five years.

V

It takes five seconds for a 911 call to go through but you don't know that when on your first day you decide to call home and let your parents know you've reached America and not to worry, it's very cold here but the apartment is warm and cozy and you feel fine, just a bit tired and yes, you will call later, you need to hang-up because by then you are tearing up and realizing how far away from home you are, but this is your home now and you will have to make the best of it with your husband who is talking you through the steps of making the international call, dial 91, then city code, then area code, then phone number.

You will dial 911, realize your mistake and hang up.

Him: "Did you call 911?"

You: "No." It couldn't have possibly gone through.

A second later, the phone will ring. He will answer it.

911 Operator: "Sir, we received a call from this number."

Him: "Yes, my wife dialed by mistake. She was trying to call India."

911 Operator: "Sir, get off the speaker phone and get her on the line."

He will hand the phone to you, his face turning shades of red at the implicit accusation in the operator's voice.

You: "Hello?"

911 Operator: "Ma'am, did you call 911?"

You: "Yes. I'm sorry. It was a mistake. I was trying to call India."

911 Operator: "Ma'am, are you sure you are not in any danger? I can send an officer over."

You: "No, I'm fine. Really."

911 Operator: "Okay Ma'am. Have a good night."

The silence in the 750 sq. ft. apartment as you unpack your suitcases will be as loud as the hum of the heater so the knock on the door ten minutes later will be heard immediately. Standing outside the door will be a tall policeman, asking your husband who called 911. He will be blond and blue-eyed, just like the cops you've seen on TV. Your husband will point to you, standing a little bit behind him, and explain, once again, that his wife was trying to make an international call. He'll be asked to go in the other room, so the policeman can talk to the lady of the house. You will again repeat your story, tell him this is your first day in America and you are tired, and jet lagged, and it was just a mistake, really.

The six-foot-tall policeman with his piercing blue eyes and thick Texan accent will look at the rose petals on the carpet, at the balloons and bunting on the walls, the open suitcases in the middle of the living room, and then he will tip his hat with a slight smile, mumble something into a walkie-talkie and wish you both a good night as he leaves.

The poise and confidence you thought you were projecting so far to impress your husband will be shattered by the debacle of the 911 call and though the two of you can't laugh about it now, in the future, you will be able to tell your friends about this with self-deprecating humor as he shakes his head at your frivolity.

This will end your first night in America, sleeping on your marital bed with your husband who seems to have calmed down from the humiliation of being obliquely accused of domestic battery. That night, you will also find out that your husband snores, that he needs the fan on every day of the year, that the bed you are sleeping on has a mattresses on top of a box spring (in India, you have slept on firm mattresses re-stuffed every year with cotton batting), a fitted sheet (only in America), and a comforter that does not warm your feet as quickly as the *razai* you left back home.

VI

Before you lie down and wrap your cold feet in the warmth of the comforter, before you call 911 by mistake, you will go out to dinner with his friends, two men and a woman, to a neighborhood Italian restaurant. They are the ones who cleaned and decorated the apartment with rose petals, buntings and balloons, to welcome you to the country. He will see you shivering in your *salwar kameez* and leather jacket and turn on the car heater full blast and the passenger-side seat warmer. The ten-minute ride to the restaurant will feature dark, empty streets, twinkling lights in the surrounding apartment buildings, a strip mall with a gas station, a dry cleaner and a laundromat next to the Italian restaurant and a Great Clips.

You have never eaten Italian food except for pizza, so you will let the only other woman in your group order something for you. She says eggplant parmesan is a safe bet, and your husband will ask if that's ok and you will say yes even though you don't like eggplant. It is not like you to eat foods you don't like but you are tired. On the flight you've already listened to his rant about how he hates that his brothers and parents are so fussy about food. He has lived by himself for seven years and doesn't care how the food tastes if it fills him up. So, you will swallow the eggplant parmesan with sips of water and listen to his friends talk about work and green cards and parking garages and how much mail your husband will have to sort through.

In the coming weeks, you will start a losing battle with junk mail because your husband is paranoid about identity theft. He will not want you to throw anything away with his name and address on it. Instead, he'll take it to work every few months and shred it there. In the meantime, it will pile up on the plastic patio/dining table and you will sort it as bills, junk mail, catalogues, coupons. In a couple of months, you will give up the sorting, because you are a realist who knows creating order out of chaos is futile.

VII

There is an order to international travel that you won't appreciate when you are jet-lagged and weary, standing in line at the airport gate clutching your carry-on luggage. The stewardess scanning your ticket and passport won't care about the pronunciation of your name. All she will care about is if the spellings in the two documents match. You won't know it when the customs official at Dallas-Fort Worth International scans your passport and stamps, but from here on, you will forever spell your name like a code being transmitted over the police scanner: "First name Jaya, spelled Juliet, Alpha, Yankee, Alpha. Last name, Wagle, spelled Whisky, Alpha, Gerald, Larry, Elephant."

Even though you can speak and write proper English, you will have to relearn words, pronunciation and different meanings of American English: Lift is not an elevator but a ride; ladyfinger is a dessert, not the vegetable okra; coriander is cilantro; brinjal is eggplant; "good for you" can be used to patronize or compliment, same with "bless you"; your name, in Spanish, is pronounced Haya, in English Jaaya. You will learn to spell in American English, substituting 'z' for 's' and 'o' for 'ou' or else red squiggly lines will appear under "colour" and "realise".

These realizations will come slowly but nobody will make you more aware of your Indian accent and British English than a high schooler working behind the front desk at the local natatorium where you will take adult swimming lessons because it is Texas and everyone swims in the summer and you have always wanted to learn to swim. When you approach him to ask for a schedule of practice hours, he will say, "What? What is it you want?" You can hear him and his buddies sniggering, but you won't know why so you will repeat the question. "I want the schedule for practice hours."

High Schooler: "The what for practice hours?"

You: "You know, a list of times I can come and practice my swimming."

More sniggering.

High Schooler: "Oh, you mean a *schedule*. Here you go."

As you walk away you will hear laughter behind your back. Later, your husband will tell you "schedule" is pronounced with a "sk" sound and not the "sh" sound you had grown up with. You will never speak schedule with a sh sound ever again, and no matter how much you try to modulate your 'a,' 'e' 'g' and 'j' sounds, there will always be high schoolers of all ages laughing at your pronunciation and your accent.

The exception to the rule will be old women in your library writing group who will wonder how you manage to not only speak but write in English so well.

"How long did you take to learn English?" they will ask.

"I learnt it growing up."

"In India? That is amazing!"

And you will smile and nod and accept the compliment because they remind you of your grandmother and you don't want to explain to them how English is taught in schools and you went to a convent school, one of many established during the British Raj to raise a class of bureaucrats and clerical staff conversant in the Queen's English, where you not only spoke and learnt English language skills, all your courses were also taught in English. It is easy for you to relinquish rhetorical control when faced with the elderly.

VIII

How do you take control of your life after an arranged marriage, in a foreign country, confined to a 750 sq. ft. apartment while an icy rain falls outside?

You will watch a lot of TV (*Friends* and *Seinfeld* reruns, *Frasier* and *Saturday Night Live*), familiarize yourself with the local mall, shop at the Gap, get a haircut at ULTA, visit Sam's Club and Walmart every weekend, buy ginger and tea leaves and a stainless steel pot with a lip and a strainer to make your chai, eat Pringles and Ferrero Rocher for lunch, read *The Bridges of Madison County* and *The Bluest Eye*, and a few months later, you will start going to the apartment gym because your clothes are tighter than they should be on the waist.

IX

You will quickly realize that there is a lot of choice in America when it comes to clothing, so much in fact that on your first trip to the mall you will gawk at all the glass-fronted stores of brand names you have heard of (Tommy Hilfiger, Calvin Klein, Ray Ban) and the ones you haven't (Chanel, Louis Vuitton, Balenciaga). You will buy blue jeans from the Gap, and a shift dress from The Limited, and you will look at the price tags and quickly convert them to Indian rupees. Over time, you will unlearn the subconscious habit of converting dollars to rupees, but in that first year, you will be conscious of how much of your husband's money you are spending at the Gap, Pier 1 Imports, Target, and Old Navy. You will revel in the joy of fuss-free-returns until one day your husband gets exasperated, driving you from store to store over the weekend to return or exchange merchandise because you don't have a driver's license or a car.

X

His exasperation will make you reconsider your daily routine and you will enroll in the nearby community college for a weekly fiction writing class. Every Wednesday evening, he will drive you six miles to the college and wait for you in the empty cafeteria while you sit with seven other students and a silver-haired teacher named Bette Wisapape around an oval table, discussing the difference between show and tell and importance of sensory details in storytelling.

In that class, you will hear for the first time an old lady who seemed to be justifying slavery, stating, "Didn't the black people capture other black people and sell them into slavery?" This will be your first brush with racism that is not directed at you—but it will not be your last.

In that same class, you will also make friends with a blonde-haired, green-eyed girl, an insurance claims adjustor, who will write a story based on her experience as a prison guard in a Wyoming jail. She will become one of your best friends in your adopted country, eventually holding one of your legs in the hospital room as you give birth to your six-pound son. Your husband will be holding the other leg, an incident that will cause shock and awe in your family since Indian husbands typically pace outside the birthing room instead of assisting in the birth of their children.

XI

Before your son is born, before you join the community college and make a friend, you will rearrange the apartment, because you have time on your hands. You will realign the couches and the TV in the living room and stack all the books in the apartment in the middle of the living room to simulate a coffee table. You will drag out the big, pressed wood computer desk out of the bedroom, and put it in the living room where it will sit at a right angle to the TV. The bedroom will look bigger without the computer desk. You will replace it with a $10 particle board side table from K-Mart and use it for your books, creams, and earrings.

During one of the cleaning sprees of the small walk-in closet in the bedroom, you will come across a sheaf of papers with an English translation of Kamasutra. You will sit on the carpeted closet floor, reading the descriptions of the acrobatic, erotic poses and wonder why your husband printed them. You will call your husband at work and read some of the text to him and ask him about his intentions. He will start laughing and so will you because read out loud over the phone, they sound ridiculously impossible to perform without spraining an ankle or wrist. Soon, the two of you will start going to the apartment gym because you are both getting out of shape, lying on the couch together, watching Food Network and exploring the hitherto unknown joys of first, second, third, and fourth base.

XII

At the apartment gym you'll watch BET and run on the treadmill and the elliptical and watch sculpted bodies gyrate to Jay-Z, J Lo, Mary J. Blige, Alicia Keys, Usher, Ginuwine, Outkast. The songs and videos are such a contrast to your own mellow tastes in Hindustani classical music with its emphasis on lyrics and melody based on raagas, taal, and sur. But you enjoy listening to the fast-paced music while walking to nowhere on the treadmill.

You'll make friends in this gym with a girl from India. She and her husband will become close friends with the two of you. You'll all go on vacation to New Mexico, stay at KOA camps overnight (your first camping experience that will remind you of sleeping under the stars on the flat rooftops of your home in the summer), drive through the long, flat stretch of I-20 and US 380 between New Mexico and Texas, marvel at the double rainbows in the expansive blue sky, eat at the flying saucer McDonalds in Roswell, shiver in the caverns of Carlsbad, explore the ruins of Chaco Canyon in New Mexico.

Over the years, you'll lose touch with her after they move to another city.

You will later find out she cheated on her doting husband with another man and the two got divorced. They will become a footnote in your memories of your first days in your adopted country.

XIII

In your adopted country, you will start your driving lessons with your husband, because Sears is the only place that offers driving school for adults but it's $80 a lesson.

Every weekend, you will practice driving on the empty streets of his office park, learning the rules of four way stops, yield signs, changing lanes and blind spots. He will hold on for dear life and yell "Brake, brake, brake!" a quarter mile from the stop sign. You'll come to a screeching halt and get offended at his theatrics. He will say he fears for his life. You will not get the concept of a "blind spot" until you almost sideswipe a car in the left lane during one of your failed driving tests. On your third driving test, you'll get your driver's license. For the first two years you'll drive up and down McArthur Boulevard and never venture out on the highway because the community college, the mall, the grocery shops, Sam's Club, are all equidistant from your apartment. There is no need to venture out on highways with cars driving seventy miles an hour.

XIV

Before you start driving your own car, before you take contentious driving lessons over the weekend with your husband, you will need a driver's license. It will not be easy because you will be on the H-4 dependent visa, which makes you eligible to be in the country but doesn't give you a Social Security number or permission to work.

The Department of Transportation will ask you for your SSN. You will show them your passport. They will ask you to get a note from Social Security office stating you can't have an SSN. The SS office will tell you they don't issue such letters unless they get an official request from the DOT. You will go back to the DOT for the letter and they will tell you to get a letter from the SS office requesting a letter to that intent. The SS office will finally give you a letter asking the DOT why they need a letter that says you can't have an SSN. The DOT will give you another letter. The SS office issues you another, based on the DOT's. Five years later, it will be easier to give birth to your son than it was to get the driver's license.

XV

As soon as you get your driver's license, you will enroll in some more classes at the local community college. In your fiction writing class at the community college, you will write a story about a new bride and her first time in America. The story will start with her first international flight from India to America (a long flight spent sleeping, waking up and talking), her impressions of the streets (antiseptic streets filled with silent cars), the apartment she shares with her husband, her mishap with the 911 operator, her restaurant experience on her first day. The story, titled "Coming to America" will end with the lines: "She dreamt of gargling with a mint green liquid in a tiny bathroom aboard a Lufthansa airplane."

You will write this story over and over for nineteen years.

Nafisa Ali's Life, Love, and Friendships, Before and After the Travel Ban

Aruni Kashyap

Nafisa:

It would be unkind to say that Nafisa's life is boring. "Staid" would be more appropriate. Nafisa lives alone in a rented apartment. She goes to work at her lab, where she is a scientist. She is new in town. Though she has seen brown people at the grocery stores, she isn't able to guess if they are Bangladeshis or Pakistanis or Sri Lankans. So she doesn't smile at them. When she gets done with work, her husband Adil is asleep since it is dawn in India. She doesn't call him but leaves a text saying "Hey I am home" so that he doesn't wonder after waking up if she has reached home safely. Adil worries because she doesn't have a car, and mostly walks to her lab. To take the bus, she has to walk almost a mile to the stop. He worries about her a lot, and his irrational worry is the most exciting thing in Nafisa's life. That's why sometimes she doesn't text him after reaching home. He wakes up and makes a panicked call, asks her in a hoarse morning-voice if she is all right. She likes it. She finds his groggy, broken voice sexy, and though she is okay, she lies and says that she is sad. He talks to her for a while to make her feel better. She often complains to Adil that it is dull here. She wishes aloud on the phone for something interesting to happen. Nafisa's wishes would soon come true. There would soon be some unnecessary drama in her life, and she would regret complaining that a few weeks ago, she was bored with her regular, everyday life.

Nafisa doesn't have the courage to drive in America. She has failed the learner's permit test twice, and the women at the local DMV are so rude and so loud and they ask so many questions and want so many documents that she doesn't want to ever go there again. Despite the problems with boredom or her commute, Nafisa doesn't want to leave this town. She wants to work hard, increasingly hold senior positions at the lab and get fancy grants from wealthy corporations to conduct research about gene editing, which will cure cancer. She is on a work visa and when students who are on a student visa meet her they give her both admiring and envious looks. They always ask, "My God, how did you get a work visa?" Because I am brilliant, she says in her mind but aloud, she says, "Oh, I was just lucky."

She doesn't tell anyone but she has decided to apply for a green card and eventually become an American citizen. When Adil enters the country, they will make a baby. The baby will go to India with an American passport because he will be born here. The baby will be a boy. She is sure about that. She is confident about her plans, too. She knows they are foolproof plans. She will do everything by the book. She will follow all laws. She will never get a DUI because she doesn't drink, has never been to a bar even to dance with friends. In fact, she has never broken any laws in her life; not even home curfews or love laws that tell us who should date or marry whom. When it was time to date, she found a good Muslim boy, also an Assamese speaker. Born and brought up in Bangalore, he had taken a keen interest in her when they met for the first time in college. She was the only Assamese speaker in the entire college, and through her, he was able to connect to his roots.

Sometimes, she doesn't text Adil after reaching home. He panics and calls her repeatedly. She watches her phone's screen and realizes that his panicked calls are the most exciting part of her life. She perversely enjoys his fear.

As days go by, she creates different kinds of fictitious situations: "Adil, stay with me please till the bus arrives, I guess I am going to faint; the bus will directly take me home." Adil says endearing things to her and she sniffs his fear, which makes her feel safe. After reaching home, one day she lies to him that she has a fever. He asks her to take a Tylenol. "I just don't have the energy to get up; you just talk to me." He is watching a movie with his friends. She likes it when he comes out of the theatre for fifteen minutes, encouraging her to go to the kitchen to take a tablet. That night, she sleeps better because she feels secure. The loneliness of the city doesn't bother her. This continues— the only drama in her life, until the real drama happens. We will come to that in a bit.

Nafisa and Annie:

The second most exciting thing about Nafisa's life is the conversations with her neighbor Annie. She actually doesn't like Annie or talking to her. But she likes that someone notices her, accosts her, and talks to her. It is a reconfirmation of the fact that Nafisa is a human being, made of flesh and blood, and is visible to others. Otherwise, after stepping out of her white lab coat for the day, she doesn't know anyone or have anyone to talk to. Annie has black hair and wears pretty, printed shorts that Nafisa wants to steal. She wants to wear such shorts one day and sit on Adil's lap at a park and run her finger through the back of his neck. She knows she would feel him growing.

Annie quarrels a lot with her boyfriend, who lives with her. Max calls her a "bitch" and shouts, "oh, fuck you." She also screams, "Fuck you, bastard." They also have a lot of noisy sex. One night, when she hears a woman's moans, Nafisa worries and wonders if she should call 911 because the characters in *Law & Order* do that. She peeps out from her second-floor apartment. She finds Annie grabbing the pillar of the first-floor apartment's portico, Max

51

behind her. He is clutching her stomach, and his chin digging into her hair. Nafisa stretches her neck and finds them having sex in the dark, with little light from the street lamp falling on them. Nafisa is aroused and ashamed for being excited. Her cheeks grow hot. She could never imagine herself having sex in public.

Annie talks nonstop when she accosts Nafisa. She doesn't have a job, and Nafisa wonders how she can live without responsibilities. Sometimes, when she finds her in the morning on the way to the bus stop, Nafisa misses the bus because Annie doesn't stop talking about her cat that died six months ago, Max who is a veteran, their damaged car that Max rammed into a tree, what their health insurance would cover and not cover because Max has PTSD since serving in Iran, and she has some chronic back pain after a car accident in Chicago that also partly injured Max because he was driving. Max was already on a disability cheque; after the crash, even she filed for disability. Now they both live on these cheques and his military pension. Nafisa doesn't want to know any of that, but she is patient and polite and listens quietly. Annie often forgets what she told her a few days ago so most often, Annie repeats her stories: the cat that died six months ago, disability cheques, cars ramming into trees, military pension, etc.

Annie likes Indian food. She says that Nafisa's food, when she cooks, smells good. Nafisa isn't sure if she would invite them to her house because she isn't sure if she would be able to stand Annie talking for several hours. The longest she has spent with her is forty-five minutes when Annie perhaps said 400,000 words and Nafisa literally said these four words: "Oh," "really?" "That" and "Okay."

But Nafisa feels sorry for Annie; and especially sorry for Max. She has seen him on his manic days. He goes under the car with a toolbox and comes out after many hours. He is usually bare-bodied while doing this. Occasionally, he crawls out of the car and walks around the parking lot. Nafisa can see that from her dining table or if she stands near the fridge. Max wears boxers when he works on the car. When he bends forward, she can see part of his buttocks—they are really tiny shorts, like the ones that are trendy among undergraduate freshman girls. Nafisa can't ever imagine wearing those even to bed. Actually, she watches him because she waits for a glimpse of his ass. This is something Nafisa wouldn't acknowledge even to herself. So often, after getting a glimpse of what she has been waiting for, she walks away from the window and murmurs, "Ya Allah, why did I waste all my time watching Max?" Then she does some housework or cooks.

52

Nafisa and Adil:

On the days she doesn't want Adil's attention, she types that she is fine, and keeps aside her phone. She doesn't even watch an episode of *Law & Order*. Instead, she sits at the dining table with a cup of tea and observes the parking lot through the window on her right. She doesn't buy tea leaves here. She buys tea leaves from India because that is where you get the best Assam-tea. Assam-tea is stronger and brisker. She prefers tea to coffee. With the electric coffee maker, coffee making is so much more convenient that she ends up drinking coffee in the morning. That's why she makes tea after work. The milk is boiled with cardamom and tea leaves over a low flame while she is changing and wiping off her makeup with a wet tissue. She likes her teatime. She finds that time relaxing and luxurious. But at this point in the day, despite finding it relaxing, she also feels a little sad. She feels lonely. She wants Adil to be with her. She wishes he didn't have to postpone his arrival for another six months to be present for his mother's hysterectomy; Adil is her only son. She reminds herself that she is here, as a researcher and immigration authorities will issue him a dependent visa. He will look for a job once he is here, and when he gets a job, he will get a new visa. They will have a baby boy. They will have a house with a large green lawn. They will live happily ever after.

When she thinks about Adil's arrival, her mood changes, and the evening becomes slightly bearable, but her sadness doesn't end. Though everyone in this small town is out on the streets running, she feels as if the whole world is asleep and she is the only one who is awake, watching the world, like a jobless night owl, without anything exciting in her life.

That's going to change soon.

Nafisa and her mother:

Adil thinks Nafisa has a lot of drama in her life already because of her mother. Nafisa left home for higher studies in 2002, and since then, she has owned a cell phone to remain in constant touch with her mother. In 2002, it was costly to call between Indian cities, so she would send a "Missed call." One missed call meant "I have reached home safely" and two missed calls meant "Please call me back."

These days, after coming home from her lab, Nafisa sends a text to her mother, too. When she is cooking dinner, she posts photos to her mother via WhatsApp and rings her before sleeping. Her mother never keeps her phone

53

on silent. Nafisa is her only child. After her retirement, her life revolves around Nafisa. In fact, she suspects that her mother lives in US time. They have two clocks in their bedroom: a blue clock set to Atlanta time, another black clock set to Indian Standard Time. She suspects her mother only follows the blue clock. The black clock is made of granite. It is more expensive. The blue clock is cheap, bought online. On certain nights in India, Nafisa's mother wakes up and starts calling her if she hasn't texted "I am home." If she is with colleagues, especially during late nights, her mother will call her every two hours to check. It has started to become embarrassing, but she hasn't been able to convey that to her mother.

It is Friday. Late night here, and late morning in India. Nafisa is standing in front of a restaurant on the east side of the town. Though it is just ten pm, it feels as if it is one at night since she lives in a small city. She isn't able to find a ride after her dinner with her lab mates. Her friends have left. They offered her rides, but she was sure she would find an Uber. She hasn't found an Uber. They are all forty minutes away. Uber is also on surge so they are charging her sixty dollars for a ride that should cost her only fifteen. Eventually, when Nafisa reaches home in a local cab booked by the waiter, her phone comes back to life. It screams with a ton of notifications both from Adil and her mother. Her father receives her call. Nafisa learns that while she was still waiting for a ride, her mother had a panic attack after Nafisa's phone died. Her mother threw up, and then sat under the water tap, letting the cold-water drench her whole body. When her mother hears the voice, she regains normalcy.

Adil complains that she had called him around fifty times during that hour when Nafisa's phone wasn't reachable. She wanted Adil to call his friend in Michigan and ask if he could reach Nafisa.

"It doesn't make sense, so dramatic."

Nafisa understands why Adil is irritated. But doesn't take it well when he calls her mother dramatic. Her mother has always been like that, since childhood. "Adil, you don't know what it means to grow up during an insurgency," she says in a cold, steely voice. Adil doesn't argue, but Nafisa feels terrible about her mother. She vows to keep her phone on and orders a power bank.

Nafisa and Max:

After talking to her parents and Adil, she is exhausted. She pours herself some peppermint tea, adds a few drops of honey, turns off the light, and sits on a chair. The fridge is behind her. On her right, there is the window with the blinds pulled up. It is shut, but the sound of cars moving on the road is loud. Because of the streetlamps, she can see an occasional lone person—mostly students—hurrying home.

She thinks how her life would have been different if rebels in her state hadn't demanded to form a separate country by seceding from India. If her childhood wasn't mottled with news of bomb blasts and skirmishes and rapes and gun battles between the security forces and rebels. She thinks about her mother and forgives her because sitting here, watching the cars in the parking lot and staring at the damaged bonnet of Annie and Max's car, she isn't able to imagine what it must have meant for her mother to send her to school at the other end of the city every day, and tell herself that her child may not return home if violence erupted. The fear of death was so normal, but it didn't mean that the experience was bearable. Ironically, that's why she had forced Nafisa to leave the state and carve a life for herself. And now she has, far away from home in a small, predominantly white town where the cab drivers are more than surprised to know that she is a scientist, "Wow, you must be a brilliant lady if they hired you all the way from India." She knows that it is not a compliment.

She stands up and looks at the road and slides the window open. The sound of cars becomes louder. A gust of cold wind. The smell of crushed leaves. She realizes she is bored. Nothing happens in her life. Standing there, she imagines herself at fifty. She is now an old woman who has done nothing adventurous, who has done everything by the book, every expected thing, and never something surprising. Does she want to get into trouble? No, she doesn't want to get into trouble, but she wants to do something exciting. Suddenly, she recalls the forty-minute car ride from the restaurant to her house when her phone was dead. Those blissful forty minutes! Watching the quiet night outside, she had felt free in a very long time. She felt single! Yes, Nafisa gasps, stamping one of her legs—she felt single and free and liberated. And now, with the phone in her hand again, after making those calls, telling her mother she is okay, talking to Adil and promising him that she would take the power bank next time, she feels trapped. I wish I were single—not unanswerable to anyone's worries; she gasps and is surprised she feels that way.

It is twelve a.m., and that's why when she hears Max, she is startled. "Hey, how are you?" She is almost scared to death. "What a lovely day! So bright!"

Bright? She wonders if he is drunk. What is he doing here this late, in his shorts, in this cold? The streetlight bathes him. She notices that his body is glistening. He is sweating.

"Yes," she says, but is crept out.

55

"What a lovely day!" he repeats and crawls under the car. She notices beams of a flashlight under it.

This is a car that will never be repaired.

That night she dreams that Max is roaming around the parking lot with a machine gun. The lot is mottled with drops of blood. She wakes up, startled, and sweaty. She turns off the heating. This was a bad decision; she should have never moved to a new country without Adil. What was she thinking? She had never lived alone. Never had to shop alone. Never even went to a conference alone—the two of them used to pitch joint-abstracts and be on the same panel. She should have waited for other opportunities. What is she doing in this small town in Georgia all by herself? She wants to weep. There is a lump in her throat. Everything is quiet and slow. So quiet that she can hear the wind. So quiet and windy that she feels as if she is walking on a country road, alone, for miles, lost.

The phone beeps.

She looks at her phone screen and finds a message from Adil, "Received the documents from your university we need for the visa. *Bhal lagise.*"

Suddenly, she hears the sound of leaves rustling. She is calm. She isn't walking on a lonely country road anymore. She is home. With her cup of tea, her leg on the ottoman. She is reclined on a comfortable wooden chair that has a lovely cushion. Everything will be okay on nights when she would wake up startled to find him lying next to her. She will ask him to switch off the air cooler, or the ceiling fan. She will not step out of the bed when Adil is here. There will be someone to take care of her.

Annie and Max are fighting, and she can hear bits and pieces.

"Fuck you"—Annie's voice.

"Oh fuck you—you are responsible for all my misery." Max's voice is louder.

"Ya right, just blame it on me. I am the one who....right?" Annie's voice is louder now.

"All you do is complain...just fucking complain...leave me alone!"

"You fucking leave me alone."

"*You* leave me alone."

Nafisa and Annie:

The next day, Adil schedules his visa interview and books his tickets to join Nafisa in two months. Perhaps that is why she accepts Annie's suggestion to go to the Indian restaurant in town.

On the way, Nafisa wonders if she should tell her about Max repairing the car at 2 am, but she restrains herself not because she wants to be polite but because she has a strange feeling about it; as if talking about it would ruin Annie's mood. She is often upset about her dead cat. She often cribs about her insurance. Today, she is cribbing less. But Nafisa is surprised that there are no signs of last night's fight on Annie's face.

They walk downtown because it is just one and a half-miles. The weather is good. Annie asks if Nafisa would mind if she smoked and she says she wouldn't though she would. She talks about her love for Indian food, the better options available in Chicago, where she was born. Nafisa nods her head quietly: partly because Annie talks so much that she can't contribute at all, and partly because she just wants Annie to speak; she is also tired by the walk. This is a hilly city. So she just wants to think about Adil's arrival, his smooth visa process, his mother's well-being. When they reach the restaurant, she doesn't tell Annie that like most Indian restaurants in America even this place is named "The Taj Mahal Restaurant," that the spice levels in the buffet are really low to cater to an American taste, and that it is run by a family from Pakistan's Punjab. She thinks it would burst Annie's bubble because she wants to have "authentic" Indian food but Nafisa wants to tell her that India is such a large country that there is nothing authentic; everything is authentic because if you say something about India, stress it as authentic, the absolute opposite is also true in some corner of the country.

They pick a table near the large window. They can see the university buildings from here. In India, Nafisa studied in a private university that never made it to national rankings. It was a small campus of just three acres. Now, the size of this campus, the massive lawns, the beautiful gothic buildings just amaze her. She still has so many things to explore: the huge botanical gardens that have many themed trails such as the white trail, purple trail, yellow trail, blue trail. She wants to walk with Adil in the purple trail wearing purple printed shorts like Annie. She will find a lonely spot. She will sit on his lap, slowly hardening him. She will rub his neck with her thumb and flick his earlobes with her tongue when no one is looking. Will she be able to do that? She wants to; but in public? The thought makes her tense. Her cheeks are warming up.

Annie and Nafisa sit down to eat after serving themselves from the buffet. Annie says that she is sorry if the noise her boyfriend makes is bothering her at night.

"Oou..." It takes a while for it to sink in. Nafisa wonders what it is about then realizes that Annie means the late-night quarrels. As if calling them "noise" makes them less disconcerting. Nafisa lies, "No, I have heard no noise."

"That old man who lives alone, he complained about us to the cops—you know."

"The one who drives a black SUV?"

"Yes, that's right," Annie says, chewing the chicken tandoori. "Asshole. He is horrible. I mean—if you have a problem with us, why don't you fucking talk to us?"

Then she bitches about that neighbor for the next fifteen minutes: how he called the cops on them twice, and how it is true that they fight a lot, how people should come and tell them to keep it down instead of calling the cops. Nafisa thinks it doesn't take much common sense to understand that you shouldn't fight late into the night when your neighbors are sleeping. She just says, "That's terrible."

Annie is agitated now. Her face is red. She says the food is spicy though there is just a hint of chilli powder. She bitches about the neighbor more.

Nafisa says, "Yeah, it is spicy." She doesn't find it spicy; she finds the food here quite bland. She wants to add chili flakes, but this is not Italian or Mexican food. The chilly has to be nicely fried and mixed with the dish; not sprinkled on the top at the end. She also doesn't want Annie to find out that she lied.

"But I still like it," Annie continues. "I get it, you know, I get it that we fight a lot. This isn't the first time neighbors have complained about us. That used to happen a lot in Chicago, too, when we were together. But we fight a lot less now. We are working hard on our relationship. Our therapist says we should get a dog, but I don't like pit bulls, and Max wants nothing but a pit bull. We were just fighting about that, and he started blaming me for everything terrible in our life. Did you hear us fight? This was last night. That old fart complained, and the sheriff sent a cop to our house. Max was so wound up, he left the house and started to repair the car. He does that when he is stressed and during this manic phase. Did I tell you he is bipolar?"

"Oh, I see. I am sorry. I didn't hear you guys fighting—I returned very late."

"It is okay. At least things are taken care of. Do you want something sweet?"

"No, I am good. How about you?"

"I would love that mango pudding."

When Annie leaves to get the pudding, Nafisa reclines on the chair and wonders what she is doing spending time with her. She doesn't like Annie, but she is happy that someone notices her, asks her if she would like to get out during the weekend for lunch. She wants to tell Annie that they are really noisy, that Max should start wearing longer shorts and they shouldn't fuck outdoors, but Nafisa decides otherwise. She dislikes herself for clinging onto this semblance of a friendship with a person she would never be caught dead with if she were in India. She is confused for finding their dysfunctional, scattered and morbid life strangely fascinating. Like a harmful, addictive family soap opera, she wants to continue watching them. Breaking the friendship with Annie meant switching the TV off. She wanted it to continue—this train wreck of a soap opera. Besides, everything will be okay when Adil is here. She won't be hanging out with weird people, people she doesn't like.

When Annie returns, she isn't holding a bowl of mango pudding. She is in tears. She asks Nafisa if she is done. "We have to go, don't worry. I paid already."

Nafisa follows her. Words such as "wait," "what," "What happened?" and several other incoherent sentences tumble out of her mouth as she tries to catch up with Annie. She has eaten a bit too much. She feels bloated. On the sidewalk, she is not able to walk as fast as Annie. The speeding cars make her nervous. The sun feels hotter.

"You go ahead, I will take a cab."

But Annie just turns to her, and weeps, "I am sorry, I am sorry. I have to be fast, but no, I won't leave you here. Actually, we should take a cab; I forgot that we didn't bring the car."

"What happened? Tell me what happened? Can I help?"

"No, you can't. I have feared this. You know—he has, Max—Max has these manic phases when he goes out in his car. Oh god, I should have never left the car home. Today, when I wanted to bring the car, he said we could just take the bus. I didn't know he was planning to go out. And it is a bit embarrassing also to drive around in this car with a broken bonnet. It is such an old car."

Nafisa is breathing fast now. "Is he okay, just tell me what happened."

"He's been arrested because he hit another car and this is the second time he has done this. We don't have the money if we have to pay a fine or higher insurance."

She begs her to calm down, "Annie, I got this. You just wait. I will take you home."

The cab driver tries to chat with them but when he hears monosyllabic replies, he keeps quiet. The car smells of lavender, and it is really cool inside. Annie looks out of the window. She has calmed down now but with her forlorn, lost look, her pursed lips, looks resigned.

She whispers, "Nafisa, I am really sorry I panicked. But you know, with so many men getting killed by cops, you can't always be calm when Max gets into trouble. He is not a danger to society, but he drives very badly when he is in his manic phase, and now, this is his second time. I don't know how many hundred more dollars we will have to pay now in insurance."

Before they are about to reach their apartment complex, before they see the cops, before Annie starts looking for their lawyer's number, she reclines on the backseat and murmurs, "You know, I love him, but I am not his therapist. I feel I am his therapist, and he dumps his shit on me. Sometimes, I just wish I was single."

Nafisa feels a weight on her heart. As if someone has pressed her chest gently—that's the kind of pressure: of reassurance, of companionship. *Sometimes, I just wish I was single.*

She wants to ask why she won't get out of this relationship and seek out her independence, but she isn't sure if that would be a good question. So, Nafisa doesn't say a word. She enjoys the reassuring weight on her chest, puts one of her hands on Annie's shoulder and pats it. It means, she understands.

The parking lot has three police cars. Their blue lights blink, and since the sky is cloudy, it feels like evening though it is just 2 p.m. Nafisa hurries inside and watches. Max is sitting inside one of the cars. He is bowing his head. His hands are cuffed. She feels scared. Scenes from Law & Order come to her mind. She has read reports of men killed by cops, especially black men. She is worried about Max, though he is not black. Her heart starts to beat hard. He will be fine, she tells herself, patting her chest. He will be okay, he is a veteran, and she presses her chest with her hand and pulls down the blind. Later that night, Annie texts her that he is now released. The judge ordered his release.

She texts back, "You take care of yourself." She pauses for a few minutes after that.

"Thanks, babe. Hugs," Annie writes back, but Nafisa pauses more, staring at her phone before writing,

"Sometimes, even I wish I was just single."

"I fucking get it!!" Annie writes back.

Nafisa and Adil:

Nafisa wakes up late the morning after the department conference, but even at 10:30, she is still sleepy because she attended the dinner party where she talked to other scientists till late. Some of her colleagues danced and asked her to join, but Nafisa isn't comfortable dancing, and she has never danced with another man but Adil.

However, unlike other occasions, she stayed till late, enjoying the party. Now, she decides to go to the lab later than the usual time. The day before was a good day but busy and exhausting. To meet so many people who cared about the same things as she did was reassuring and now she feels she isn't the only person spending days overwhelmed and excited by the sound of test tubes tinkling; she isn't the only one awake when the world is sleeping.

But she is shocked when she finds several missed call notifications from Adil. What happened? Is his mother okay? Did her mother call him again because she was unable to reach Nafisa? Missed calls from India are bearers of anxiety. Her heart sinks, and instead of calling Adil, she calls her mother. After all these years, that is her biggest nightmare: that she will be sleeping through one of her parents' death and by the time she reaches, it will be too late; a garlanded photo waiting for her with a candle burning in front of it.

And that's why, when she finds those notifications from Adil, she calls her mother's cell instead. Her mother sounds normal. She is watching her daily soap, and her father is reading the paper and commenting on the increasingly terrible world, "We are all going to die due to climate change. Imagine, what will happen when two-hundred million Bangladeshis will move to India in search of living spaces?"

"Let's talk about it later," she says, Adil had called her for something specific. It must have been important—he called several times.

When she rings Adil, he is sad, "I don't have good news. I should have traveled with you, Nafi. Now, I don't know for how long I will be stuck here."

"What are you saying? Is your mother okay?"

He tells her that his mother is okay. She is recovering well, and after he leaves, one of his cousins will arrive to stay with her. That cousin is responsible. She will cook and clean and talk to his mother and go shopping together; nothing to worry about. She couldn't come before because she was writing her exams. Now, she is free for three months before the results are out. She will be with his mother. "I am surprised you don't know what is happening. Don't you read the news?"

She is still groggy, "I had a late night, and I woke up just now. What happened? You know I don't like cable, and that's why I don't have it."

Adil sighs, "I may have to cancel my tickets."

"What?"

"I don't know if I will get enough back now that I am canceling just a month before my travels. I don't even have so much money to waste if I have to cancel my tickets."

"But why?" she screams and sits up on the bed, his sentence working like a shot of caffeine. The mattress bounces under her body. "Why do you have to cancel your tickets?"

Adil pauses.

"Why do you care?" he asks. "You were sleeping till late. You were at a party, must be dancing with someone random. You are having fun and here

61

I am, roaming around in Delhi, hiring a cab, haggling with auto rickshaw drivers, standing in line in front of the American embassy. Do you know how long the queue is?"

"Adil—have you gone mad? Why don't you tell me what is wrong?"

"Do you really care? You are having fun. You just don't care."

This has never happened before—Adil has thrown tantrums before, to get her attention, but he has never been this unreasonable and it is not that he accuses her of having fun while he is toiling away in India to get all the paperwork done, taking care of his mother, worrying about her. It is his accusation that she danced at a party. It is so unexpected, so out of the blue that she loses her mind. She wants to scream, "Fuck you" like Max or Annie but she bites her tongue. "Adil, you are getting me panicked now. You need to tell me what has happened."

She walks to her dining table, where she rarely dines. It is her workstation. It is the same place from where she watches people running or hurrying towards their destinations, the parking lot, Max getting arrested and just the road lying there like a black snake's back when the world is asleep, and she is the only person awake.

"It is Trump. You know my flight is via Saudi Arabia. I mean, I am not the citizen of a Muslim country, we are Indians, but you never know, you never know with this government—we can't forget our names, our religion, can we? He has banned travelers from some Muslim countries. I don't know what to do. Maybe divert the flight via Frankfurt?"

Nafisa tries to sound calm and reads the headlines on Google news. "We don't even go to the masjid, Adil. I mean—we are both atheists. I inject chemo to fat rats in the laboratory and don't believe that God has created us." She tries to sound funny, but he isn't reassured. "You still have forty days, Adil. You are going to Delhi next week for your visa interview." She tells him, but at the same time she realizes she doesn't believe her own words. For the first time in her life, she feels very Muslim. She wishes her name were Katy or Catherine or Bipasha.

"Well, what if they reject my visa at the interview?"

She ignores the fears. She decides not to let it affect her. "By then, something will happen. All these countries that run these luxury airlines are not going to just sit and take this when people start to cancel their bookings, you know?"

Though Nafisa says he will be fine, that she will book him a ticket via Frankfurt or Amsterdam or a direct flight from Bombay to New York, she disconnects the phone as soon as possible. Her laptop is covered with drops of tears. She feels alone again. That feeling of being awake when the world is sleeping wraps her like a dark shawl over her face because she knows that even if she books him a new flight, it would be such a dent on her little savings she has made since coming here that it would take both of them to shop from cheap stores and eat lousy food. She has never lived like that before—from paycheck to paycheck.

Nafisa and Ian:

"Come to the house party," Annie asks her that afternoon. "We have sausages, sandwiches, pulled pork."

"I am not sure, Nafisa replies. "I will let you know."

She is sure she will not go to the party. She doesn't want to meet Annie and Max and their friends. She is worried they are noisy and crazy and public-fuckers, just like Annie and Max.

But in the evening, though she is at home, there is no peace. She sits with a glass of water on the loveseat and tries to clear her mind because Adil's messages and calls are driving her crazy. She can hear the music from the party. Come anytime, if you change your mind, Annie had told her. She is still upset with Adil. How could he accuse her of dancing with "someone random?" Of course, he meant "some random man," not "someone random." He has a dirty mind. Something has changed in a single night between them. She wants to shout at him but she hasn't because he is going through a hard time now.

Adil has been sending her every news item he can find about the Muslim Ban. She wants to think something else other than the Muslim Ban. She wants him to stop, but she knows that if she says, he would be hurt. She doesn't want to respond to his political commentary, which is now veering towards alarmism. Back in India, he hasn't slept all night, which means, she hasn't been able to sleep after her lunch, or watch *Law & Order* and relax, have some me-time.

"Adil, what would be the worst?" she asked him an hour ago. "I would just go back. Find a job at the Indian Institute of Sciences. Don't panic. Go to sleep."

But he doesn't go to sleep. After about half an hour, he starts sending her conspiracy theories: they are now going to eject people with green cards from the country, people with green cards wouldn't be allowed to enter, new Muslim citizens would be disenfranchised, Chinese Americans would be sent to internment camps, and naturalized Indians would be losing their citizenship. This is followed by a barrage of misinformed advice: take your passport every day, keep copies, don't go outside the city without your passport, reach out to your department head, and ask for help.

She starts to get a headache. She tells him, I am going to take a nap now—you also get some sleep. She turns her phone on silent mode. She sits on the chair, sips some water and makes a decision.

Annie had told her that she had invited a lot of people to the party. But there are only three other faces excluding Nafisa: a handsome man who says this is his last month in this city and a red haired woman who has a younger boyfriend with a long beard reaching his chest. They look happy together. He gets her beer after beer, as she talks to Annie, but he spends most of the time with Max, while occasionally checking if the red haired woman needs more beer. They are smoking outside on the portico full of trash and dried leaves and pots that perhaps had herbs in them once upon a time. They are getting quite drunk. Max is tipsy, and when Annie asks him to be careful, he screams at her, "Shut up, you don't get to tell me…"

"Hahaha, he always shouts at me when he gets drunk," Annie laughs loudly, cutting his sentence. He leaves, in search of more beer.

But Nafisa notices that Annie's eyes are misty. She forces a smile and asks everyone to eat more before adding, "I get so anxious when he drinks. My anxiety …"

Annie is taking out mugs and plates from the dishwasher. Nafisa walks up to her and asks, "Do you need any help?"

"No, babe," she says. The word "babe" makes her uncomfortable, and she doesn't understand it if lovers use it for lovers or friends also use it for each other in America. "I am fine, are you having fun?"

"Yes, it is great. I am so happy to be here," she says though she doesn't mean it. She wants to get out as soon as possible. She wonders if she made a mistake by not bringing her phone. What if Adil is having a panic attack? Should she run and get her phone? But she told her that she would be napping. She is worried if he finds out she is attending a party, he may get offended: *I am frightened to death here, and you are dancing at a party?* He is very capable of saying horrible things when he is stressed.

No, no, she can't share the news with Adil that she is at a party.

Okay, I will stay here for a while, be a good neighbor—she tells herself and thinks that her presence is also perhaps perfunctory; neighborly duties, and she wants some distractions.

"I hope things have settled down now—I mean, with Max." She hesitates as she says that, but she has been thinking about the arrest, so she has to check.

"Oh, thank you for asking." Annie shuts the dishwashing machine and heaves a sigh of relief. "It is just a matter of time, you know. We will get our settlement and then move out of this place. This city is too small actually, and it stresses him out. He needs a lawn to work on, a tree's shade, some space to plant stuff — get busy, you know? We will be fine after that. We don't have to live from cheque to cheque."

"I didn't know about this settlement, but it sounds good." Nafisa isn't sure if she should ask anything further, but she has already pressed the button. Annie loves talking about her life and the problems in her life. "I told you that we had an accident in Chicago, remember? It was a drunk, teenage girl who just rammed her large SUV into our car. I have severe cervical pain because of that. It is unbearable, and I can't work for long hours at a desk. I can't accept any job or go to school. I do hope I will complete my coursework someday, but I am not sure if I will be able to meet all the challenges. So we are really looking forward to this settlement."

"I am so sorry. This sounds like a lot of tension." Nafisa gasps. "So when will this settlement reach you?"

"Oh, in a couple years." She shrugs. "Maybe more. But our lawyer is trying his best to get it done soon. I mean, he will also get a cut, so it is also in his best interests. So, if we get this settlement, we will put in part of the money for a house here. The houses are cheap here, not so expensive like Atlanta. You have to come to the housewarming."

"That would be so nice." Nafisa is genuinely excited for the two of them. "There is much to look forward to."

There is loud music. The people are talking. The little apartment is noisy and stuffed and she feels warm. Annie lowers her voice when she says this to Nafisa, "And until the settlement money reaches us, I have to live with him in this house. I can't even break up with him. It is one of the terms—because we filed the lawsuit together, as one party, as a couple."

Nafisa scans the table for food. Annie has now laid the plates and cutlery. There is only meat: chicken burgers, sausages, pork chops, and some mac and cheese. She doesn't like any of this. She grabs more corn chips and salsa, sits in a corner and debates if she should eat the chicken burger. She likes pork, but only when it is cooked with garam masala.

Ian, the handsome guy, says it is a pity they didn't get to speak to each other despite living in the same building. She agrees, but honestly, she doesn't care. He says that he has been busy mending a relationship. He has found an excellent job in Oklahoma, and his boyfriend works as a waiter in a local restaurant but is not willing to move. It is such a good job that his boyfriend will not have to work, perhaps go back to school, and concentrate on writing more poetry; he always wanted to be a poet. But his boyfriend doesn't want to live in Oklahoma. Nafisa asks why, and Ian pauses at her question. He is surprised. He says, he doesn't want to go; there is no reason. There is no reason—Nafisa is astonished. It rubs it the wrong way, perhaps.

65

He doesn't want to, I mean, he just doesn't want to go, he repeats. Then he gets defensive that his boyfriend—who is now his ex-boyfriend—does not have to have the right reason to not want to go.

"So you guys just broke up?" Nafisa asks, sipping more pink lemonade. She can't believe she is drinking pink lemonade—she used to make fun of it.

"Yeah, he was just not listening and wouldn't do long-distance. It was horrible—the last few months were horrible."

She is quiet. She feels sad for him, and then she realizes it would be rude in this country to not explicitly say that she is sorry. "I am sorry," she says and finds it funny that there is a tinge of nasal sound in her sentence. She is becoming American, or as Adil would joke in Hindi: Umrican. Umrican indeed; nasal sounds, pink lemonade that tastes just like regular greenish lemonade, drinking coffee in the morning and watching *Law & Order*.

"Thank you, I really appreciate it," Ian says.

At home, she thinks about the word "mend." Ian used that word "mending a relationship." She sits with her cup of tea, watches the world outside, and thinks, what an apt word: mending. Everyone is mending something. Max is mending his car, Annie is mending their relationship until the money comes, Oklahoma-bound Ian spent the last few months mending his relationship only to fail, Trump ensuring that a lot of mending would be required once he steps down from the throne; the throne itself would need mending.

And Nafisa? Would Adil turn up? How would his visa interview go? What if his visa is rejected? Would he come here and mend the boring life that forces her to have strange friends who are reeling under a broken relationship and a broken car and are yet together because there is something promised ahead? What if that money never reaches them or takes too long to reach them? Would they go on living together? What kind of living is this—to sail a ship with holes, and continually drain out excess water with a mug to stop it from sinking?

She thinks about the Muslim travel ban again. She doesn't want to read the news. It is stressing her out. Her iMessage and Whatsapp are full of updates from Adil – all about the travel ban. She is annoyed with him for not sleeping and unburdening his stress on her. She is the one who is alone here. She is the one who has failed her learner's permit test. She is the one who is stranded after dinner, making friends with people she has nothing in common with. She is going to become an old lady who has done nothing out of the ordinary, adventurous in her life. She sees herself with Adil when she is fifty: with grown-up kids and lots of test tubes. Gosh, what an experience. She is fifty. She tries to remember how many parties she has attended and can't.

It is late.

She paces her balcony and thinks about Ian. She admires how quickly he can move from mending to moving on. She wants to be like him, but she also knows that she would immediately fail and the thought makes her laugh. Ian is so handsome. Great thighs, amazing shiny, taut neck, broad chest. She feels sad that he is gay as if she would have given it a thought if he were straight.

First, she is surprised that she finds it so funny—I didn't even drink at Annie's house, why am I laughing like this—she wonders, and then she says aloud, "I didn't even drink at Annie's home, why am I laughing like this?" There is some peppy music coming from Annie's. Perhaps, everyone is dancing. Annie had asked her to stay. "Stay, we will have some girl time, it will be fun. The boys are going to be so sloshed," a slightly drunk Annie had told her, holding her hand firmly, prodding her to stay.

Nafisa steps out of her house and pushes Annie and Max's main door. It is unlocked, and she is really having her girl time with the elderly lady—though Ian was dancing with them, too. Max has taken off his shirt and is shaking his ass. He is wearing those shorts that reveal his butt when he bends. He is bending a lot. Annie repeatedly slaps his ass and shouts shake-that, and he shakes it harder, aiming it at Annie like a dog wiggling its butt to get attention. His upper jaw is digging into his lower lips.

"OMG is the music too loud?" Annie asks, slightly worried. She is slurring. The lady with a younger boyfriend with long beard continues to dance. Max is completely oblivious.

"No, I like the music so much that I thought I should come back. Am I weird?" Nafisa screamed at the top of her voice, giggling.

"You are being fab, babe!"

"Come on, woohoo," Ian says.

Annie slaps Max's ass. He shakes it harder.

"I thought you planned some girl time!" Nafisa steps in, a bit hesitant. Annie drags her to the middle of the room—the dance floor for that night. Max follows them, shaking.

"You don't like me here?" Ian is screaming, "Don't worry, I am a straight woman. Who said I am a man?"

"I love it that you are here! You are my new best friend!"

Max comes in between the group of two women and the man who claimed to be a straight woman and continues his dance. He bends a lot. Nafisa takes tequila and starts laughing. "Shake it, Max," she screams. "Shake it."

"Max," Ian screams. Max goes near Ian and starts to twerk, rubbing himself against Ian's crotch.

"Are you getting aroused or something?" Annie asks. "My boyfriend is hot."

"You are so sloshed," Ian says, placing his hands on his crotch, laughing. "Max is naughty today."

Nafisa starts to shake her body a little and click her fingers—like she used to in her college days when she had just begun dating Adil in Bangalore and they used to go to a lot of slam poetry events. She looks at Annie and laughs. She throws a flying kiss to Ian, and she walks towards Max and slaps his ass. Annie encourages her.

"The world is asleep, and we are dancing," Nafisa screams, shrugs, before bursting out laughing. She had always wanted to have fun like this but after meeting Adil, that opportunity never came because Adil is serious; he doesn't like such debauchery.

"We are fucking dancing," Annie says, shaking her body vigorously and suddenly, Nafisa likes her. She feels an ache in her heart and wants to be her good friend. She holds Ian by the waist, faces him, still dancing, brings her mouth closer to his face and screams: DO NOT GO TO FUCKING OKLAHOMA.

Mail and More

Anuja Ghimire

Niva's accident was mundane. It wasn't the winter weekend of ice and twenty-car pileup on the bridge over Highway 75. Just a misjudgment of the speed of the black sedan turning left when she slowed down and turned right. Although the sound of metal crashing into metal was loud for a low-speed collision, it was a small impact. Nevertheless, if only she'd braked sooner. If only her hands on the steering wheel had turned clockwise quicker.

The crash was already a blur. Did she slow down first? Did the other car slow down in anticipation of a minor accident in which she would have to take the blame?

Her apartment was just two traffic lights ahead, and her boss's store was five minutes behind. If she hadn't caught sight of the caution tape across the gas station from yesterday's nightly news, she wouldn't have slid the car on the turn. The QT sign, the icy patch, and the black sedan appeared at once when Niva had forgotten that the car she was driving wasn't her own.

The black car slowed down, and a hand motioned Niva to follow to the empty parking lot on the right. The driver, a woman, got out of the car first and then her passenger, a man. They were both several inches taller than Niva, now even smaller with trepidation. She got out of the car, phone at hand. Several cars slowed down and moved on. In the church parking lot, the steeple too was watching. The passenger and driver circled around their car first and approached Niva. Though she had a better view of the gas station, Niva's own problem was real—not the boy from the news, not his family waiting for his body in Kathmandu.

"You got insurance?" the driver asked.

"My boss does," Niva said. The flip phone was hot in her sweating palm. "I should call him first."

"Wait a minute. You got a license?" the passenger asked. He smiled. The effort's effect was misplaced. His hands were in his jacket pockets.

Niva stiffened, worried if he would pull a weapon— a knife or anything sharp from it— as soon as he was near her. But the hands stayed in the pockets. The smile also stayed. "Yeah. Yeah," she answered. "Should I call the police first?"

"Didn't you say you're gonna call the boss?" the driver asked. She played with her hair the entire time and did not appear as if she had just been in an accident. "What does he do? I mean—where did you say you worked?"

"A store. Yes. Yes. Do I ask him to come here? He's only five minutes away." Niva wanted the blame, the punishment and the pain right away. "Wait a minute. I can't. There's nobody else at the store."

"Can you drive? We can follow you to the store. We'll take care of the business there," the driver proposed. She was now applying lip balm with a pocket mirror and smacking her lips. "We can wait until you feel ready to drive, if you want."

"Sure. Yeah. We don't have to wait. Follow me," Niva lied and turned to face the car again. One big dent on the driver side. That was all. The headlights were intact. The paint wasn't scratched. But the screech and the thud played in her mind in an endless loop. The beige Toyota rattled like a prong when Niva started the engine. Life was supposed to work out after the college degree. Working under the table for one Indian store owner after another was not in her American dream.

The couple had switched positions when Niva checked to see if they were following her in the streets of South Arlington. The man was behind the wheel with plenty of space between his car and Niva's. In the five-minute drive, Niva wanted to practice breaking the news to Tej, but her mind wasn't ready to add that task. If Swetha was working today, Niva wouldn't have crashed Tej's car. Swetha wouldn't have stuffed the trunk and the back seat of the car like Tej did. The plastic bags filled with packing peanuts wouldn't have blocked the rear view. Niva had left for the post office in full bladder because of the broken toilet door at the store. Swetha would have called the building maintenance man. She would have let Niva stop by her apartment, use the bathroom, and grab a snack.

The parking spot in front of the entrance was empty. Niva parked under the oak tree, next to the black sedan that was already parked.

"I'll call him first," Niva said from the rolled down window. Tej was in the passenger seat before she heard the dial tone. She didn't know where to look when his face was too close to hers in the car. Tej was always chewing a clove, and this time, she could smell it on him, too. She found his hair parted in the middle, always rolled up sleeves, and restless hands more unsettling than ever.

"What did you do? Who are they? Why didn't you go to the post office?"

"I'm so sorry. I had an accident. I hit their car," Niva explained.

"Always call me first. Always. Never bring anyone near the store. Never. They'll think I'm rich. They'll claim they're injured. They look perfectly fine. Look. They're already stretching their necks and wincing," Tej whispered his anger in Hindi. "Take the day off. Go. Call your friend. Go home. I'll deal with these thugs."

Swetha would have asked Niva to sit with her inside. She would have given her a Parle-G biscuit and water. She would have held her hand. She would have told her a story about how she had once hit a tree or a shopping cart with her car and how she was driving again and how the fear leaves and how the body moves on. Swetha would have known Niva didn't need to call her friend who'd moved out last week and left nothing but the 1989 Camry which she drove to work that morning. Swetha would have gone to the post

71

office herself because she knew Niva's car was unreliable on winter mornings. Swetha would have asked her if the news about a boy her age dying just like that had shaken her. She would have offered Niva a phone card to talk to her mother one more time.

"Watch the store while you wait," Tej ordered in English.

"I need to go to the Subway first," Niva said. It was the only store in the strip mall with a fully functioning toilet and without a salivating owner.

Neither the couple nor Tej noticed Niva had returned to the store. Through the glass door, she could see the pair leaning on the black sedan and Tej cracking his knuckles. Tej didn't waste any time and was in and out of the store with a cash-filled envelope. The exchange lasted half an hour. The parties settled without calling the police. Niva wondered how much her weekly pay would be cut.

"Next time, be careful. Thank God, it was just a dent. You can go now," Tej said. "Never mind. Did you call your friend already? I'll go to the post office. Watch the store. Please."

Tej didn't leave. He paced back and forth, unbuttoned the top of his shirt to let his gold chain breathe, twirled the gold rings in his fingers and rushed to the backroom. He lit one more incense stick in the storage for Ganesha and, Niva assumed, broke the news to Swetha in Gujarati over the phone. If Swetha were at work that day, she would not call Tej on the phone from the backroom.

The backroom was the corner for anything the customers shouldn't witness—Swetha's tears, Tej's harsh words, the phone calls Tej didn't know about. Niva wondered if Tej and Swetha also faced the wall with racks and boxes while making phone calls—Tej while insulting Swetha, Swetha while venting to the man she actually loved. If she turned her back, Niva could pretend, the life-size poster of Ganesha wouldn't hear or see her secrets.

If it were any other Wednesday, Swetha would smile when she came to the desk from the backroom. She would talk to Niva but only to ask her to watch the glass door. A silver truck would park in front of the store at ten, and a bearded man with a ghost stricken face would come in with a parcel—always a book for a daughter back East. The media mail was the easiest and the swiftest transaction but he would always tip Niva, who would try to pretend to go to the backroom. Swetha always stopped her by grabbing her wrist under the counter. Wednesdays were slow days. Sometimes, the bearded man was the only customer. Niva had work hours on that day only because of Swetha. Niva doubted there was anything more than the phone calls and the bearded man's weekly appearance at the store.

"I knew his wife. We were both his students in college. She was my best friend. She died. Cancer. His daughter lives in New York. She was also my friend. She cut him off after his second marriage. She won't visit, even after her stepmother's slow death," Swetha once said about the bearded man. "I feel sorry. For him."

"Is Swetha-ji feeling better?" Niva knew the worried look on Tej's face. Without Swetha, the business was impossible. People paid for the overpriced stamps, envelopes, and packaging for Swetha. She took care of anyone who stepped inside. A sticker for a child, a pen for the writer, a mint for the truck driver, or just a squeeze on the hands with liver spots.

"No. What a rotten day. I have to take her to the hospital. Again. Do you know that they bill us before they check her? Looters! And when I ask what is wrong with her? Nothing. Why am I telling you all this? Well, can you stay till four?" Tej didn't wait for Niva's answer. He didn't hear when Niva asked about the baby. This was the third pregnancy in a year for Swetha with no baby to show. He didn't ask her if she needed to buy lunch, and left with the dented Toyota.

Niva knew it was ten when the silver truck parked in front of the store. The bearded man stayed in his spot for a half hour and left. She wanted to tell Swetha that he was probably looking for her and that he didn't come in. She wanted to call Swetha, but they were only friends inside the store and without Tej around. She wanted to tell her about the accident, and the man switching the seats when they drove to the store, and the boy from QT. She wanted to ask if this time the baby would keep after three months. But she didn't. She knew Swetha would be back before the doctor clears her for work. She would be bending, sealing boxes with packing tape, loading packages for the UPS, FedEx guys, and transporting the rest to the post office. She would be back before another young student would make the headline for dying in a store.

"Mail and More, how may I help you?" Niva answered the phone, thankful for the distraction.

"The police will call you," Tej alarmed her and instructed her on the exact narrative of the accident and hung up before Niva could ask questions. At least, he didn't call on her cell and spared some charge.

The toilet door was tricky. If wedged right, it would stay open. Sometimes, the door could only open if someone yanked it from outside. Two boxes would have to keep it open, and she would have to finish her business in less than two minutes. Niva hadn't emptied her bladder when the door started sliding and pushing the boxes in. One foot jammed between the boxes and the door frame, Niva dressed herself, flushed the stench and got out. She kicked the bathroom door because she had to hit something and washed her hands with bottled water in the backroom. Ganesha was watching her again. The grime under her boots marked her pilgrimage to the silent poster. Niva prayed for the boy from QT. She knew her hunger, headache, and wait to go

73

home were all better than being lifeless on the floor of a gas station. There was another college kid, a Bangladeshi, in the QT bathroom when the Nepali boy was at the register. When the Bangladeshi heard the gunshot, he stayed in the bathroom and called the police. The officer had to drag him out by the jacket sleeve and rouse him with cold bottled water on his face to identify the dead body of his friend. Niva knew better than to watch the nightly news, the series of crime, the announcements of different dead bodies like a musical chair of crime scenes in the Dallas-Ft. Worth Metroplex, but *Law & Order* was only a weekly show.

Niva had lied to her mother that she never worked in any store that had a cash register. "Arlington is the safest part of Texas, Aama." Only the kiosk in the mall where she sold perfume had a cash register but also a guard nearby and a buffering crowd. Another lie—she was never alone in any of her jobs. Who would pay her for her company? "Yes, I had seen him once in a concert. My old roommate went to the same community college," Niva said when her mother informed her that the boy's mother was her maternal uncle's neighbor in Kathmandu. The mother was unconscious in the hospital. "Yes, Aama. I am perfectly fine." In every phone call that wasn't in the weekly routine, Niva had to convince her mother that she was far from the disaster in her worry— the hurricane in Louisiana, the ice storm in New York, the shooting in Dallas.

When the store phone rang again, Niva decided she would tell Tej she had quit. "Tej?" she asked instead of the business greeting.

"Are you a vegetarian?" he asked. "Listen, I am at the Kebab place picking up dinner. I wanted to ask you. Don't worry; my treat."

"No, but I like their vegetable biryani. Thank you," Niva said. Swetha must have reminded him that she had been in store all day without lunch.

"I'm sorry you had to stay all day. I will be there in ten minutes," Tej said.

It was as if Swetha was speaking through him. *Was she hospitalized? Why would she not cook otherwise!* Niva turned on the light in the backroom and inspected the bathroom door for any sign of her kick. The wooden door showed no evidence. She wiped her footprint from the bathroom to the backroom with a paper towel under her boots. Although she wasn't sure if she was allowed to, she lit an incense stick for the evening for Ganesha and prayed for Swetha, the QT boy's mother, and her own mother.

Tej was already at the counter with the takeout Styrofoam box and a plastic spoon when Niva returned. "You can eat before you go." He handed her a bottle of water, slumped on the chair, and closed his eyes.

"Thank you," Niva said.

The biryani was still warm. Niva swallowed each morsel of half the biryani like a lump was breaking through her throat, food pipe, and back. She would save the other half for dinner tomorrow. "Can I leave now?"

"Yes. Thank you. Swetha is in the car, but she's sleeping. Can you come on Thursday and Friday? Do you have classes?"

"I have classes on Tuesdays and Thursdays. Tomorrow, I can't come until noon." Swetha would have known her schedule. Niva didn't want to skip her classes just because Tej bought her biryani. She had promised her father she would get all As. She had missed his funeral because of her exams, and her student visa that would have to be renewed again if she went back. She was not going to miss her classes. She was not going to mess up her chances of graduating with honors. Her mother was hanging on a thin thread of hope of her bright future.

"Oh. Swetha is on bed rest," Tej bargained. "The accident—it's all taken care of."

"Can't you please open after noon? Or stay for a couple of hours. Please?" Niva didn't want to explain that her classes were more important. She wished Tej would look into her eyes and see her face, fifteen years younger than his, and see in her a child he so desperately wanted. She wished Swetha were standing behind the counter. She wished for an end to the bargain.

Tej pretended to check the cash register when both knew that the day was without transactions. He took out the account book to fake a tally.

"I have to go finish my assignments. See you at noon," Niva mumbled and fished for the car key in her purse. Through the glass, she could see the evening had little life left. Swetha's gold *mangal sutra* and cubic zirconia studs sent back light to Niva. Swetha's curls were loose and sticky with sweat. Inside the steel frame, she almost seemed at peace. Niva couldn't see the dent on the Toyota, but she knew it existed.

Niva wanted to tell Tej that she couldn't work in the two room and a quarter bathroom store forever. She only realized when she walked that her toes stung from the kick to the bathroom door. But Swetha's hands were on the hollow belly. Niva wanted to tell Tej that perhaps just this once she could ask a friend to take notes for her and miss just two classes. Just once. "You know what," she began speaking, but Tej didn't answer. "Tej-ji?"

Tej's head was on the counter. A sliver of drool formed in the corner of his open mouth. Niva pulled a chair near the door and placed her purse on her lap and the plastic bag of biryani on top of it. Her hands held the bag in place and measured the heat that slowly left the rice. She heard hiccupped snores and took turns to watch which one of her bosses would wake up first and let her go.

75

Drinking Chai to Savannah

Anjali Enjeti

Drinking Chai to Savannah

I am sitting in the middle seat of the third row of a minivan. A heap of purses crowd my feet. Elbows and knees jab my sides. We are gridlocked on I-285 during Atlanta evening rush hour in a crawl-pause rhythm, our progress as tedious as arranging the frames of a stop motion animation film. The nose of our van points southeast to Savannah, the historic coastal town Union Army General Sherman spared during the Civil War. When raindrops the size of nickels smack our windshield, the hazard lights on surrounding vehicles blink on like garlands of bulbs on a Christmas tree.

"Hey," my friend in the second-row calls, craning her neck to make eye contact. "Do you want chai?"

I lean forward. The seatbelt catches my breastbone. "You want to make a stop already? We'll never get there at this rate."

"No, no," says the driver, my neighbor from up the street. "We brought a thermos. And cups."

I am incredulous, not only because my friends thought to pack chai on a four-hour road trip, but because, judging by the way the rest of my friends continue their chatter, I am the only person who finds it odd.

It's no wonder. Among our seven passengers, six have immigrated to the U.S. from South Asia. They sip chai from morning to night. Percolating pots of fresh ginger, full fat milk, and cardamom serve as background music in their homes.

I am the only one of us born and raised in the States, the only one who considers bagged tea to be actual tea, the one who stubbornly refuses to wear saris to celebrate South Asian holidays, the clueless audience for conversations rattled off in Hindi, a language I don't understand.

I am the interpreter of academic monograms like S.A.T. and A.P., the friend who suggests they not worry so much about their kids' grades or test scores, the beloved Aunty who sticks up for their children whenever a parental rule interferes with their enjoyment of authentically American childhoods.

Steam from the chai forms a layer of film on my face. I inhale its aroma, hopeful it will ease the dull ache in my gut, the sinking feeling my friends probably can't decipher because they grew up in countries where their brown skin and names did not summarily mark them as outsiders. Not even these ladies, my closest friends, know that I harbor a deep-seated fear of small American cities and towns.

Like the one we're headed to.

* * *

It is the winter of 1990, just after the U.S. begins bombing a Saddam Hussein-led Iraq for invading Kuwait in Operation Desert Storm. I am seventeen years old. Famished, I pull into a Wendy's parking lot after a long day of school and play rehearsal. I jump out of the car, throw open the glass door to the restaurant.

A long line snakes through chain rails. The stench of oil-drenched French fries wafts through the air. I take my place at the end, extract a five-dollar-bill from my pocket.

Two men get in line behind, contemplate their orders. One has a voice that's raspy and thick. A smoker with a cold. His friend chuckles lightly between phrases. They settle on cheeseburgers. Chili. Two large fries.

The dozen people ahead of me page through magazines, run fingers through beards, adjust baseball caps. A woman with long hair cradles a bald baby. A stream of drool leaks from her pouty lips.

I tap the face of my gold-tinted Timex. I'm running late. I could ditch the dining room for the drive-through, but the last time I tried that tactic it backfired.

"Hey, you been watching the news? Crazy shit, huh?"

It's one of the men behind me, addressing his companion. The one who wants the chili.

His buddy cackles. A response pours out of him, as if he's had it bottled up all day and now that it's been uncapped, he can release it into the ether. "Hope those bastards in Eh-RACK get what they deserve, blow SAD-um away, take out the whole damn country. God damned Ragheads are taking over the world."

My back rounds with an audible sigh. I think to myself, Suh-DAHM Hussein is the president of Ir-RAHK, not Eh-RACK. He doesn't wear a turban. Not everyone east of the Mediterranean Sea does.

One of the men, the raspy one, has apparently read my mind. He moves closer. His shadow eclipses mine. His hot, tobacco-tinged breath seeps over the collar of my dress. "We need to drive the sand n*ggers out of this country, too."

His voice is low, quiet. Each syllable erupts with spittle. I imagine it sticking to the back of my hair like discarded chewing gum.

"They don't belong here. They should go back to where they came from."

I shut my eyes. The force of my held breath presses against my ribs. My mind floods with everything I ever learned about self-defense, and two years' worth of expensive tae kwon do lessons: Stab their eyeballs out with your keys kick them in the groin smack their ears with your flattened palms yell "Fire" "Don't touch me!" round-house kick to the neck piss your underwear vomit in his face.

I try to figure out what might work here, in this public space, when these men have yet to lay a hand on me.

79

My saddle oxfords inch forward. The shoes behind me echo in tandem. "Muslims... Arabs... illegal alien bastards..."

The thumping in my eardrums drowns out the prepositions and verbs.

All I have to do is leave. All I have to do is lift my leaden feet, place one in front of the other, dart toward the exit. But if they follow me out, I will be alone with them in the parking lot. No one will hear my screams over the music flowing from the dining room's speakers, the calling out of order numbers, the tantrumming toddler in the booth.

A young woman with a blond bob smacks her gum, flips open a compact to check her lipstick. She's waiting at the counter to pick up her meal. I stare hard at her profile, will her to look at me, to engage me in a conversation about the weather. Anything. She's oblivious. Or maybe she knows exactly what's happening, but just doesn't give a damn.

"Can I help you?"

It's the visored woman behind the register, addressing me, the first person in line. She keeps her eyes on the buttons, bobs her head to a silent rhythm. I scan the overhead menu, a menu I probably have memorized. Suddenly I don't know why I'm here, what I want to eat.

My mind has become a string of ellipses, a blinking cursor on a blank screen.

Impatience settles between her eyebrows. Her long, fuchsia nails tap the side of the register. I want to signal her about the two men terrorizing me. I think of bank tellers held up by robbers, how in the movies they slide their fingers ever so slightly under the lip of the counter to push a panic button. I wish I had one of those.

My order comes to me. "One baked potato, to go, please."

I want a frosty, too. I always get a frosty. But I'm too afraid to tack it onto my order. The machine's slow expulsion of thick chocolate will take too much time. The baked potatoes sit under warming lights, like baby chicks in an incubator. In mere seconds a gloved hand can caress the oval-shaped aluminum pod like a silver football and hurl it into a bag.

I thrust money in the cashier's direction. She takes her time counting out bills in my palm. Coins shoot out the side of the register like pinballs. I slide further down the counter. My fingers run along its edge, as if it's base in a game of tag.

The two men step up to place their orders. I catch a glimpse of them in my periphery. One has light-brown hair, too-thick sideburns. The other strokes his sculpted goatee. They have soft, clean faces, pressed clothes. They are young. Nothing like the caricatures I'd imagined.

I would never have pegged them as racists in a line-up.

At the counter, their demeanors transform. Their voices assume a

80

relaxed, friendly, tone. They've turned their hatred off like a faucet.

"Yes, Ma'am," one of them responds, when the cashier reads back the order.

Did I imagine their cruelty? If I am the only witness, did it really happen?

My aggressors begin their perp walk alongside the counter, rattle off stats for their favorite basketball team.

A woman wearing a headset calls my number, hands me a paper bag. It crinkles loudly in my grasp. I bolt past the condiments, the soda dispenser, around the trashcans, throw open the glass door.

I don't look back.

My hand shakes so badly I can't slide my key into the keyhole. When it finally complies, I dive into the driver's seat, slam the door shut, turn the ignition, hit the stick shift into reverse. I speed around the drive-through line until the parking lot spits me back onto the main road. My hands grip the steering wheel so tightly it indents my palms.

I glance in the rearview mirror.

I think of all the things I should have said to those men: I was born in Michigan, have lived in Tennessee for seven years. I'm not Iraqi or Arab or Muslim but even if I were, I don't deserve your hatred. I'm a harmless teenager who loves Def Leppard and Coca Cola and John Hughes films.

A few miles away, I pull into a gas station, open the paper bag, tear into the spoon's plastic sheath. My stomach growls. But when I unwrap the foil, the brown, leathery skin and white buttered flesh initiate my gag reflex. I stuff everything back inside the bag, jump out of the car, hurl it into the nearest trashcan. It hits the bottom with a hollow thud, like a stone.

* * *

When you are brown in America, there's no such thing as exculpatory evidence. You are an aberration, a foreigner from a foreign land, no matter your American citizenship, no matter if every home you've ever lived in was built on American soil. Every disparaging comment about terrorism is directed to you. Every illegal border crossing implicates you.

Your great American privilege comes with severe limitations.

As I grew older, I would remember to keep my hands visible at all times in chic department stores in the elite suburbs of St. Louis, to stifle the flow of tears post-9/11, in the Philadelphia International Airport during security checks so humiliating and exhaustive I'd miss flights, to remain calm while waiting to cast a vote in a presidential election amid racist remarks fired off like a round of bullets, to shrink myself in overwhelmingly white spaces, to be both present and disappear, like dust in the wind.

81

Despite my American birth, I am not any more tied to this land than my foreign-born father is. I have inherited his immigrant status, like a dominant gene. It will underlie my identity narrative, no matter how many legal documents verify my nationality, no matter how many times I testify that I belong.

No matter who stands behind me in line.

* * *

The weather in Savannah refuses to cooperate. Sheets of rain soak through our jackets, smudge the lenses of our glasses, drench our shoes. We seek refuge in a red touring trolley reminiscent of the one in Mr. Rogers' Neighborhood. As we step into its belly, I survey the tourists poring over guidebooks, tapping their phones. I worry one of them will mutter something derogatory about this group of seven brown women whose mere presence seems to have doubled the minority population of this historic district.

They ignore us.

Relieved, I settle into a bench seat, rest my forehead against a misty window, shift my attention to the landscape, the elegance of the low country, in the way Spanish moss swathes live oak branches like a much-beloved quilt.

* * *

The rain trickles to echoes in gutters. The sun elbows its way through the last gray clouds. Our silhouettes weave between Corinthian columns of grand estate homes, traverse through Savannah's famous squares. The soles of our shoes meet colonial cobblestones laid well before any of our family trees branched into America.

We convene for lunch at Clary's, the infamous diner featured as a gossip hub in John Berendt's book *Midnight in the Garden of Good and Evil*. At the table, our hands cradle mugs of coffee to warm damp bones. We slurp down French onion soup, sink teeth into buttermilk biscuits as fluffy as clouds. When we've licked our plates clean, we ask the server to take our photo, gather to one side of the table, and squeeze together to fit in the frame.

The pose triggers the memory: I am standing in line at Wendy's, hot breath at my neck, stress crushing my chest. Twenty years later, not even the shelter of dear friends, the festive tone of a cocktail-infused weekend, can protect me from this trauma. It has imbedded itself in my psyche, has reared its ugly head without warning or apology, even in moments, like this one, of levity.

This is its legacy.

82

I have wondered over the years about those men, where they are today. I wonder if they understand what they stole from me, how their slurs vibrate in the tympanic membrane of my eardrum in perpetuity. I wonder, in the intervening years, if they have changed. And then I read an article about the current state of racial hatred in the U.S., in the world, and I feel certain they have not.

Outside of Clary's, evidence of the weekend's storms linger in shallow puddles and tree branches thick with beads of saturation. My phone's storage space diminishes as photos supplant bytes. Here we are, clinking wine glasses over dinner, there we are, posing in front of The Cathedral of Saint John the Baptist, perusing t-shirts at River Street Market, feigning fear on a ghost tour.

When it's time to leave, to resume our lives, reunite with our families, I crawl back into the third row, middle seat, rest my weary head on the shoulder of another. Our van, due northwest on I-16, departs the city, bisects the low lands of the coastal plain, toward Atlanta, through the state we all call home.

Necessary Failure

Tarfia Faizullah

NECESSARY FAILURE

"I just have to ask," says the woman in the box office of the Alabama Shakespeare Festival Theater in Montgomery, where I've been working for a handful of months, "What are you?"

*　*　*

I grew up in Midland, Texas, as the child of Muslim parents who immigrated to the U.S. from Bangladesh in the 1970s. I spoke Bangla with my parents, English at school. At the cafeteria lunch, I sawed through chicken fried steak smothered in cream gravy, then ate rice and lentils with my fingers for dinner. I went to an Episcopalian private school where we attended chapel daily. In the evenings, I knelt with my parents on prayer mats while the sun descended down into the branches of the oak trees overlooking the golf course in the suburbs where we lived.

*　*　*

"Homo Sapiens," I retort, irritated.
"Oh my gosh," she exclaims. "You're gay?"

*　*　*

In Midland, my young, beautiful mother and I shopped at the local Dillard's to visit the glittery, perfume-laden makeup counters. I would watch blond-bouffanted women ignore her until it was clear she was willing to spend some serious bank on fancy powders and lipsticks. "Where are you from, honey?" they'd ask, sliding the receipt across the glass counter with a smile. "Your English is so good!"

*　*　*

"And your English is great!" she continues. "But really, where are you from?"

I won't do it, I tell myself. I refuse to tell her my ethnicity unless she asks. "I was born in Brooklyn," I say patiently, when "Texas" apparently isn't the correct response.

*　*　*

In my early twenties I moved to Alabama because I fell in love with an economist who was a seventh-generation Texan with kind eyes and silky hair.

He lived in Troy, a tiny town about forty minutes outside of Montgomery and a few hours from the coast of Florida. I was trying to escape the confusion that comes with being told what not to be. He waited tables at a steakhouse, and I worked at the theater and at a shoe store. I wrote poems, and he considered the radical nature of numbers. We became Waffle House regulars. I befriended a Moroccan girl. During Ramadan, we fasted together in solidarity.

*   *   *

She tries a few more no-but-where-are-you-REALLY-froms, then asks, "What's your cultural heritage?" "Bangladeshi," I say, relieved. She chortles, as though we have been playing a game of charades and she has just correctly interpreted my gestures. She exclaims: "I knew you were Middle Eastern!"

*   *   *

The Muslim Association of West Texas used to be in an office building on the south side of Midland beside a strip mall housing a 7-11 and what was once a Mrs. Baird's Bakery. Every Sunday, I would dutifully but begrudgingly pull a scarf over my head and make my way to the entrance where I slipped off my sandals and added them to the growing mosaic of shoes in the front hall. After prayer, my friends Nadia, Layla, and I would bend our heads over Sunday School lessons at fold-out tables made of fake woodgrain. Nadia and Layla's mom, Auntie Najja, was my mom's best friend. Iraqi, she wore gorgeous, ornate rings on slender fingers and pronounced my name "Thorfia." We recited Arabic passages from the Qur'an until the break, at which time we were given Southern Maid Doughnuts. We would eat them greedily, licking the glaze off our fingers.

*   *   *

It's a slow day in the box office, so I decide I want to make a deeper connection, to learn to walk away from an interaction like this without rage. I swivel the computer screen around to show her where the Middle East is and, then, where Bangladesh is. I point to the corner of the state of Texas, to where Midland is. I tell her it's flat and smells of petroleum. She nods, and I trace the borders of my different homelands, trying to show her the new shining thing I might be—informed by many places, beholden to none of them.

*   *   *

87

We eventually married, he and I, and returned to Texas before we moved to Richmond, Virginia, so I could go to graduate school at Virginia Commonwealth University. There, I would drive down Monument Avenue and take note of the still and silent statues of Confederate soldiers, immortalized with their swords outstretched, their horses' hooves lifted. There, I would write poems about women raped in Bangladesh during the 1971 war. There, I would walk past Jefferson Davis's grave, upon which there were always fresh flowers.

* * *

The next morning, on my drive from Troy to Montgomery, I stop at my regular gas station to buy my first 32-ounce Diet Coke of the day before I head to work. I'm still rubbing the sleep from my eyes when I hear the familiar voice. It's the woman from the box office the day before. "Ohmygosh, Clyde!" she exclaims to her husband. "Look! It's the gay Middle Eastern girl from yesterday!"

* * *

James Baldwin, a son of the Great Migration, wrote that "An identity is only questioned when it is menaced."

The Poet Ai, born Florence Anthony in Texas, wrote, "People whose concept of themselves is largely dependent on their racial identity and superiority feel threatened by a multiracial person. The insistence that one must align oneself with this or that race is basically racist. And the notion that without a racial identity a person can't have any identity perpetuates racism ..."

* * *

Eventually, he and I ended our marriage, and I moved to Detroit. Contained within me, these even newer geographies. I live in a neighborhood with a strong Polish and Bangladeshi population. I eat chili cheese fries and write poems about the young Bangladeshi girls I teach. This, then, is what it means to me to be a poet of the New South: to wrestle with whether identity is a word to defend against or embrace, whether there is any language that allows me to locate myself within these borders, then cross them. To be informed by place, but not beholden. To fail, but with beauty, in my crossing. To be unafraid as I carry the newness of myself forward with its distinct histories—to honor the shine of each of the selves which make me, to honor the seams between.

Nature Exchange

Sindya Bhanoo

NATURE EXCHANGE

NATURE EXCHANGE

Behind the tennis courts, Veena finds the grassy clearing that has been fruitful for her. Since her move to the area a week and a half ago, she has found a dead monarch with its wings intact, and half a mouse skull.

Today, she has less luck. She picks up a handful of green-capped acorns and two pine cones. Then she spots something shiny in the grass. An iridescent abalone shell, surely dropped by a child who brought it back from a beach vacation in Florida or California.

"Hi."

She turns to find a boy, hardly four years in age, standing behind her. He has bright eyes. Brown eyes.

"What are you doing?" he asks. A sweatband made of blue terry cloth keeps his long blond hair out of his eyes.

A woman, her figure flat as a pancake, stands at his side.

"Sorry," she says to Veena. The woman raises her eyebrows and offers Veena a knowing smile, at once both apologetic and proud. "He likes to talk."

"I dropped something," Veena says to the boy.

"I can help you find it," the boy says. "I'm good at finding things."

She thinks about giving him the shell. It is in her right fist, its edges pressed against her palm. With her other hand she massages her side. She has an ache in her hip that she notices only when she stops moving.

Finders, keepers, a voice in her head says.

"No, you can't," she says out loud. She massages her hip again. The boy watches her do this.

His mother takes hold of his hand.

"We should go," she says. "Finish our walk and let this nice lady finish hers."

The boy persists even after Veena turns to leave. "What did you lose?"

* * *

Veena puts the morning's haul into the tote hanging from the doorknob of her bedroom, a room she has all to herself. The tote contains a portion of her son Neel's collection. The rest is still in her moving boxes. Before she and Mitchell separated, it had hung from their bedroom door and he frequently complained that it was too heavy, that the knob would fall off. But he never made her move it.

The last time they took Neel to the nature center was on a Sunday, two weeks before he died. Two years ago now. He was seven. The exchange is a single large room near the nature center's entrance, a place where children can bring in found natural objects and trade them in for points towards prizes, all from nature. The shelves have bins and drawers and everything is

90

neatly categorized. There are lotus pods, sand dollars, barnacles, sea beans, devil's claws. Bark, pine cones, paper wasp nests. Dead, dried-up insects: butterflies, beetles, grasshoppers, earwigs, houseflies. Tiny pins with slips of paper pierce insect bodies, identifying them by sci- entific name. *Dermaptera. Musca domestica. Caelifera.* Some items are local, others are most certainly ordered in bulk from a wholesaler.

Everything has a price in points.

Small, standard shells such as scallops, clams, and cockles cost twenty points. Shark-eye shells are twenty-five. Big or unusual shells cost up to two hundred apiece. A large conch, of which there is only one on display at a time, is one thousand. Little polished stones, fifty. Small geodes, five hundred. Mid-sized geodes, two thousand. Big geodes, four thousand. And the elk antlers, up on the highest shelf in the back corner of the room, unreachable by any human under seven feet tall without aid of a step stool, are ten thousand points. They are gleaming and polished, each side with four spiky branches. A donation from a hunting family that loves nature.

"The young man with his eye on the antlers," the white-haired woman behind the desk said when Neel walked in on that final Sunday. The woman's name was Rosemary.

She looked at Veena and Mitchell. "I love him," she mouthed, her lips, colored raspberry, moving deliberately. She wore a seashell-patterned blouse. She was typical of the center's employees: patient, older, a lover of nature, eager to share that love with the next generation. She was always there on Sundays, and Veena knew her blouses well—the one with planets, the one with dinosaurs, the one with microscopic organisms, the one with mammals of the savanna.

Neel surveyed all the objects in the room, moving from shelf to shelf. He opened drawers, ran his small fingers across the edge of a prickly pine cone, peered through the mouth of a sand dollar with one eye. He blew air up towards the strands of hair that fell across his eyes. He needed a haircut.

Then, abruptly, wordlessly, the moment marked, as always, by a satisfied sigh, he was done. He took his canvas bag to Rosemary, and carefully placed his three rocks for trade on the desk, leaving a gap between each one. Up to three items could be traded in per day.

He watched as Rosemary picked up the rock with lustrous flakes.

"Tell me about it," she said.

Neel took a small notebook out of his bag and flipped through it until he found what he was looking for. The notebook itself had little written in it, just a drawing and a word or two, but his oral report was thorough.

"A gift from Toby, found in his grandmother's backyard. Likely to be igneous with mica."

91

Rosemary nodded. "I believe you're right."

When she set it down in a different spot, Neel moved it back to where he had first set it.

"Sorry," Rosemary said. Veena could hear the kindness in her voice. She understood Neel. So many people did not.

Rosemary picked up another rock. "And this?"

"Discovered last Friday at four p.m. in my backyard. Fossil seashell. Cretaceous."

"A mold, isn't it?"

"Of course," Neel said. "Not a cast."

Rosemary leaned in.

Still holding the fossil mold, she pointed to the third rock.

"Parking lot of Publix, while Mommy was putting groceries in the car. Ordinary gravel, but shaped like a blue whale."

"Wonder can be as ordinary as a piece of gravel," Rosemary said.

For Rosemary, the questions were protocol. The mission of the exchange was to help children observe the natural world around them, to be curious and respectful, and also have fun. Asking questions was also a way for her to confirm that they did not disrupt anything alive in their pursuit.

"All nonliving today, Neel?"

A simple question, but Neel had a long answer. He explained the scientific definition of nonliving: things that cannot grow, move or breathe. And of the living: anything that has ever needed food and water and produced waste.

Rosemary's eyes did not glaze over when Neel spoke. There was no smirk. Instead, she looked at Veena and seemed to silently acknowledge Neel's brilliance.

"So, a dead thing is living," Neel concluded. "Because it was once alive."

"That's right. Let's add it up, shall we?" she said.

Neel moved close to Rosemary as she input his points, as if supervising her work. He did not understand the concept of personal space, according to the school counselor who was trying to help him with it.

"Move back," Veena said. He was so close that Rosemary could probably feel his warm breath on her neck.

"He's fine," Rosemary said.

Neel spent a few of his points on an extra-large sand dollar, a polished tiger's eye with silky shades of yellow and brown, and a white wolf tooth shaped like a crescent moon. He was always careful not to spend too much.

"What's my current total?" he asked.

"After today's purchases, you're at three thousand, four hundred and ninety-eight," Rosemary said.

"Still a lot left to go," he said.

After the visit to the exchange, Veena, Mitchell, and Neel had plans to visit Veena's parents, who lived farther north, in Roswell. But first, they went to Taco Planet, for a late breakfast, the three of them each ordering the same migas tacos.

"Do we have to go to Ammamma and Thatha's house today?" Neel asked. "I wanted to play with Toby."

"You can play with Toby tomorrow," Veena said. "You know, I only met my grandparents a few times. We didn't go to India often."

"I know," Neel said. Mitchell patted his back.

"You're lucky we live so close to them," Veena said.

"So lucky," Neel said. He rolled his eyes. He had just started doing that.

* * *

In the shower, hot water streams over Veena's body and she turns the handle to make it hotter, allowing the jets to scald her back.

She wanted to make time for the nature center today. The daily three-item limit meant it was important that she went frequently. If Mitchell helped, if he added points to Neel's account too, it would be so much easier. But he would not help.

"Veena," he said, when she told him the address of the house she was moving into, how close it was to the center. "You need to stop."

For the first two months after Neel died, Veena and Mitchell had sex every night, starting from the night Neel's body was taken to the morgue at Emory University Hospital. It was she who sought him out under the cool sheets, wrapping her arms around his shoulders, tearless but full of sorrow, hopeful that she could lose herself in his hair and scent. Everything else was impossible—walking, smiling, opening mail, eating—but the sex was addictive, a temporary relief, as dismal as it was necessary.

Then, after those two months, it stopped—the relief, the need, the desire. She jumped when Mitchell touched her, pulled away if he tried to kiss her. His proximity was intolerable.

* * *

Veena works in supply chain. She has for years. She quit at twenty-nine when Neel was born, and then returned to the same job five years later, when he started kindergarten. Her company's software follows the life of a product, from its birth to its death. The orange: from the tree, to the truck, to Publix, to the brown bag. A bottle of shampoo: from the supplier, to warehouses, to salons around the country.

93

Her job is to make sure that the company's clients are happy, that the software is properly tracking their oranges and shampoo and books and purses and battery-operated puppies that somersault. If there are any problems, she is there to help.

At the client site today, the corporate offices of a major retail chain, she does what the in-house analysts should be able to do themselves. Inwardly rolling her eyes, she adjusts the system so that it sends a remote-control car to a warehouse in Tucson instead of Omaha. She doubles the shipments of a face cream to Kansas City and cuts in half what is being sent to Dayton, realizing by the end of the process that it is her company's software that is faulty, not the in-house analysts.

She finishes by noon and phones her office to say she is sick, unable to attend her afternoon meeting. Then she drives home and crawls into bed, choosing to skip lunch altogether, though her stomach is hollow with hunger. She skips lunch often. She will be thirty-eight in a month and her metabolism is waning.

When she wakes up from her nap she has a headache, and takes an ibuprofen. If she hurries, she might make it to the nature center before it closes. She pulls on a pair of jeans, a T-shirt, and her Tulane hoodie, and heads to the car.

* * *

At the exchange, Rosemary greets her.

"I've missed you. It's been months," she says. Her thick, long white hair is loose around her shoulders. Her blouse is covered with marsupials of all sorts, some that Veena recognizes, some that she does not, all with babies in their pouches.

"I just moved to the neighborhood," Veena says. "I'll be coming more often." She says nothing about Mitchell or the separation. She takes the items out of the bag and sets them on Rosemary's desk. Veena looks up and checks, as she always does, for the antlers. There they are. Still gleaming.

"Don't worry, they're still available," Rosemary says. She looks down at what Veena has brought. The abalone shell, the mouse skull, the dead butterfly.

Rosemary does not ask questions about the objects. She enters points into Neel's account that Veena knows are too high. It is a silent transaction, a compassionate one, and one that breaks the rules. Only children are supposed to trade.

Veena does not thank Rosemary, though her gratitude is immense. She must leave as little room as possible for either of them to be implicated.

94

* * *

It was a school shooting. Neel was the only one who died. Two shots went into his body. One in his abdomen, one in his leg. Only one other person—the art teacher—was shot, but she escaped with minor injuries. An officer from the scene called them with the news. Neel was rushed to the hospital. Veena cannot remember the officer's name, only that he had lied. "He didn't tell us how bad it was," Veena later said to Mitchell. "He just said to come to the hospital."

"Would that have been the right thing to do?" Mitchell replied. "To tell us on the phone?"

Within ten minutes of the call, Veena and Mitchell were at Neel's side, his eyes closed, unconscious, his broken leg in a brace. He yawned a few times, his mouth in an O like an infant's, his lungs hungry for air. Then there was a terrible, soft gurgling sound. That was it.

His backpack had made it to the hospital somehow. In it was his lunchbox, and a brownie, half-eaten, that Veena had packed that morning. Before the staff wheeled him away, Veena sat and ate the rest of the brownie, turning the mushy bits in her mouth as she looked at Neel's shut eyes, the hair that would never be cut. She didn't offer any to Mitchell.

The man who killed Neel was forty-two years old, father to a five-year-old boy himself. Six months later, he was sentenced to life in prison. The night of the sentencing, neither Veena nor Mitchell could sleep. Mitchell because he thought it was not enough, Veena because she knew that nothing ever would be.

* * *

Days, weeks, and months go by. Spring turns to summer. Veena's parents go to India, to visit her sick grandmother in Coimbatore.

"Can you take care of the plants while we're away?" her mother asks.

"I don't know," Veena says. It is an honest answer.

"Veena," her mother says. "Ammamma is dying, and the plants need water."

"Okay," Veena says.

"Veena?"

"Yes?"

"Please take care of yourself while we are gone."

Fall approaches. Veena runs, collects objects, goes to the nature center, eats takeout and prepared items she buys at Whole Foods. Her hip pain is persistent, but she gets used to it. Rosemary gets her up to 7,438 points.

95

Veena begins to order objects online to take into the nature center. Shells, coyote claws, and, for $24.99, a racoon skull. One day, unable to control the impulse, she orders three mid-sized geodes from Arizona for $150.

Every other Sunday, she goes to her childhood home to water her mother's plants, pinching off dead leaves, as her mother instructed her to. "The way to promote new growth is to get rid of the old," her mother said.

Her mother had wanted Neel to be cremated, as per Hindu tradition, but Veena and Mitchell buried him in Mitchell's family cemetery in Dallas.

"We only bury children who still have their milk teeth," her mother said. "Children of Neel's age should be cremated. We do not preserve the body, Veena. He will not be able to rest peacefully."

That was what she and her mother had fought about, that two years later they still had not fully recovered from. *Baby teeth*. What would Neel say about baby teeth? *Living*.

*   *   *

One day in late September, Veena goes to the nature exchange and finds a college student behind the desk instead of Rosemary. The girl is toying with a scallop shell, carelessly bending it at its edge as she chews her gum.

"So your son isn't here? Is he sick?" the girl asks. Her jaw moves vigorously as she chews.

"Yes," Veena says.

"What happened?"

"Broken leg."

"He's sick and he broke his foot? Poor kid."

Veena nods. She takes out the objects she has brought: a flat, polished rock; an unusually large pine cone, and three inches of snake skin.

The girl writes a number down on a piece of paper and hands it to Veena.

"I'll enter it later," she says. "Computer's down, but give me your son's name."

"That's it?" Veena says. "Twenty-five points for all this?"

The girl blows a bubble and pops it with her tongue. "This is how we do it," she says. "I went by the books."

Veena writes Neel's name down on the piece of paper and slides it towards the girl.

"Here's the account holder's name."

"You mean your son?" the girl says. "So you wanna pick something out? Poor kid might want something."

"He wants the antlers."

"Ten thousand points."

"I know. We're saving up."

"That's nice. He'll have to come in and get them himself though. That's the rule when it's a big prize like that," the girl says, an air of authority about her.

"He might not be better for months," Veena says.

"It might take months to get the points anyway."

"I don't know if he can come in."

"I mean, we can hold it for him if y'all decide on it," the girl says, her eyebrows furrowed.

"He's dead," Veena says. "He's been dead for two years."

The girl stops chewing her gum.

"But he did break his leg," Veena says, wishing she had left it at this in the first place. "He died with a broken leg."

The girl goes to a bin full of shells, sticks her hand in and fills Veena's paper bag.

"Take them," she says. "I won't tell my manager."

If Neel were alive, he would be nine, almost ten. Maybe reading *Harry Potter*, or having sleepovers. He would be moving towards adolescence, but he would still be sweet. Still collecting his treasures and playing Lego with his best friend, Toby.

In the initial months after Neel's death, Veena tried many things. She took up yoga. She let an artist paint grief on her naked body. The artist had lost a child too, years ago. The artist wore loose, flowing skirts, and big hoop earrings. Her coppery hair was long and wild.

"I don't understand those mothers who don't want their babies to get bigger. The ones who want to freeze them in time," the artist said, as she painted a green line from Veena's belly button down to the top of her pelvis, just above the mound of hair.

"You hardly have scars," she said to Veena.

"I used stretch mark cream every day," Veena said. "I wish I hadn't."

Afterwards, Veena looked at herself in the full-length mirror mounted to the wall. It was a cheap mirror, and it made her look thinner than she was. She studied the art and ran her fingers over the dry paint. It would be photographed for her memory and then washed away in the shower the following day. Grief was an elongated lavender foxglove, its small bulbs alive but drooping. It was a cluster of rocks. Igneous, Neel would say. Red tulips. A small fountain of water. There were two brown lines on the rocks. Two squirrels in abstraction, maybe? And three streaks in the air. Butterflies?

"Why so many flowers?" Veena asked.

"Grief is alive," the artist said. "It's everywhere." Her eyes were anxious. "You don't like it?"

97

"It's beautiful," Veena said. "I wish I could see the beauty without the pain. Just for a moment."

When she showed Mitchell the art that evening, he looked away from her naked body, as if she were blinding him.

"Do what you need to do," he said.

"Isn't this hard for you?" she asked.

When he looked back at her his eyes were full and glistening. "You're making it harder."

Neither of them had any interest in activism, in fighting publicly against gun violence or school shootings. Time did nothing to change this. People called now and then: a father from Sandy Hook, a brother from Red Lake, a mother from Columbine, inviting them to join the cause, to campaign.

Instead, they sent generous checks. "This is all we can do right now," Mitchell said, speaking for both of them.

Six months after Neel died, right after the sentencing, Veena had a bench installed at his elementary school, with an ocean scene painted on it, a beach, waves, birds above. They shared a love for nature, mother and son. She had once worked at the aquarium, right after college.

Neel's class was there for the unveiling. There were still twenty-three children in the class, Neel's spot replaced by a brown-haired girl who moved from Michigan just weeks after the shooting.

The children planted an oak sapling next to the bench. Neel's teacher, Ms. Hackbarth, started the digging, and each child in the class took a turn. Two children placed the sapling in the ground and all the children took turns patting dirt around it, their small hands frantic and eager. Mitchell was out of town for a business trip. Veena had offered to reschedule the event.

"I'll see it soon enough," he promised.

After the planting was done, Ms. Hackbarth gave Veena a hug and sent each child in the class up to Veena to do the same. When Toby hugged her, Veena held him extra-long, sniffing him for any essence of her son that he might have retained. Then, single file, the children and their teacher went back into the school. Veena stayed in the playground alone, sitting on the bench.

Once a month, she still goes to the school and sits on the bench. She invited the artist who painted her body to join, but she never came. Mitchell came once or twice, but not after that.

"There are people who let their wounds heal and there are those who pick at them and pick at them," he said. "I can't be picking."

This month, she spends some time cleaning the bench, using wet wipes on the legs and on the seat. Then she sits and waits. Nobody comes.

98

*   *   *

The gum-chewing girl is there the next time Veena goes to the nature center, in early October.

"Hey," the girl says.

"I've got some good stuff," Veena says enthusiastically. She opens her brown paper bag and takes out the three geodes she ordered from Arizona.

"Look, I'm really sorry about this," the girl says. "But your son's account has been deactivated."

"What do you mean?"

"The points belonged to him. Since he's gone, the account had to be deactivated."

Veena can't tell whether the girl is lying. She hears the words as if she, Veena, is reading them to herself, as if they were typed out and handed to her.

"Where's Rosemary?"

The girl sighs. She is not chewing gum today. "I feel really bad about this, but I don't make the rules."

"Where's Rosemary?"

"She's on vacation, visiting her grandchildren. This has nothing to do with her."

This girl was too young to understand. Veena had renewed her nature center membership on the phone for two years, keeping it at the family level, never taking Neel off.

"If you have other children, I could transfer the points," the girl offers.

"I don't have other children," Veena says.

*   *   *

At home, Veena feels sick. She takes a box of day-old cucumber sushi out of the fridge. She eats with her fingers, lifting each piece to her mouth, eating it dry, letting the rice and sesame scrape against her tongue, not bothering to open the soy sauce packet. It's a sign, she tells herself. She must not go back. Mitchell was right. She had to move on.

But the next day, she skips work and drives to the nature center. She bypasses the exchange and walks into the presentation hall, where she sits in the front row. A few families are there with young children, though the room is mostly empty. She has seen this same turtle presentation many times, with Neel.

The captive turtle's name is Felix. A woman named Barbara with a polo shirt and khakis and a white plastic name tag pinned to her chest takes Felix out of a deep wooden crate. The turtle inches forward.

99

Barbara explains that Felix has a friend, another captive turtle, named Felicia. They've been together for ten years.

A kid around nine or so raises a hand. "Do they have babies?" he asks.

Barbara shakes her head. "Good question." She reaches forward to pull Felix back. He's getting away.

"Even though we take care of them really well, in captivity they are under stress," Barbara says. Veena feels like Barbara is looking at her. "It is very hard to reproduce under stress."

The kid's hand shoots up into the air again. "Are they happy?" he asks.

"Well," Barbara says, "They are comfortable."

* * *

After Neel's death, Veena and Mitchell became like other childless adults who had no reason to be home early in the evenings, whose post-work hours were leisurely, a time to relax and read a book, to go for a quick run, or to even sneak in a short nap. Mitchell found some peace in all this, Veena did not.

Some times of the year were harder than others. Neither she nor Mitchell grew up celebrating Christmas—he was Jewish—and they never made a fuss over Santa or presents. It was actually Halloween, not Christmas, that was difficult for Veena now. What a cruel holiday it was, to make light of death and caskets, of bloody wounds, to bring packs of eager children to her doorstep.

Perhaps that is why, this year, Mitchell calls her on Halloween morning. It is the first call from him since she moved into the new house. She invites him to come over in the evening. When he says yes, she is surprised.

They drink cream soda mixed with Kahlúa in tall glasses and sit on the living room couch waiting for kids to come. It is cool and breezy, the windows are open, the air brittle and fragrant with burning hickory from a neighbor's fire, a perfect night for trick-or-treating. At first, no one knocks, and Veena is anxious, but then dozens come, little ones with their parents, older ones in groups of five or six. Goldilocks. Annie. A decapitated ant holding its own head. A gaggle of geese. A pencil. Storm troopers.

When Veena runs out of candy and the doorbell rings again, she panics. Then she tells Mitchell to open the door and keep the kids waiting. She goes upstairs and comes back with Neel's tote.

At the door, she opens the tote for the costumed children: a spooky potato growing sprouts, a zombie rockstar, Harry Potter with a scar on the wrong side. They reach into the bag and retrieve a rock, a shell, a pine cone. "Cool!" the potato says. "Accio!" Harry Potter says.

After 8 p.m., the younger children stop coming and high schoolers show up. The big kids have put little effort into their costumes: a hobo, a girl in yellow sweats holding a sign that says "banana," a boy wearing a T-shirt that says "Too Cool for a Costume."

"They're too old to be here," Veena whispers to Mitchell, who is standing behind her with his glass. "I don't have anything for you," she says to them. She tries to shut the door, but Mitchell stops her, and presents Neel's tote to them.

"Take something," he orders.

The teenagers reach in and pull objects out, a piece of sea glass, an arrowhead, a lotus seed pod, dry and hard, the color of rust.

The banana girl throws the pod to the ground and crushes it with the tip of her yellow sneakers.

"Let's go," she says. "There's nothing for us here."

One of the boys throws the arrowhead into the bushes. "Weirdos," the other one says.

"Give them back if you don't want them," Veena shouts as they walk away.

A rock comes flying towards her and hits the side of her bad hip.

"Hey!" she shouts, but the kids run off, and Mitchell leads her inside, to the couch.

She does not protest.

He pulls back the edge of her jeans and inspects her. There's a small red bruise. He touches it and she winces.

Her head on his chest, she tells him about the canceled nature exchange account. How she feels like she cannot go on without the antlers. There is nothing she wants more. She sobs.

"I'll get you antlers," he says. He kisses her, first on each of her eyes, and then on her lips. Now he is crying too. "I'll buy some. I'll order some."

"I want *those* antlers," she says. "Neel's antlers."

"Okay, I'll get them for you," he says.

They are careless, his words, but they give her hope.

She licks the salt of her own tears and then, her voice a heavy hush, says, "Come upstairs."

*　*　*

She goes to the nature center one final time, with Mitchell. It is a Sunday. The plan is his: walk in, make a large donation, ask for the antlers.

"Whatever they want," he says, "I'll give it to them."

A sense of adventure fills her as they drive, a sense of pursuit. But when they get to the center, there are no antlers, just the gum-chewing girl at the desk whose name Veena still cannot remember. Since they last met, the girl has pierced her earlobes, Veena notices.

"Someone claimed them," the girl says. "Just this week."

"You have them in the back!" Veena says accusingly. "I know you do."

"No," the girl says.

Veena strides past the girl's desk, opening a door that says "Staff Only," shouting, "I'll find them. You're keeping them away from me."

How could she come so close and have it end like this? She feels that she is two Veenas now, one version of her unable to control the other.

"Hey, what are you doing?" the girl says. "Hey." She looks at Mitchell. "You need to stop her."

"Veena, honey," Mitchell says, following her in.

"Help me," Veena says. "Or stay away."

The girl is on her phone, calling for help.

The backroom is full of shelves, like a warehouse. Veena walks up and down the four aisles, opening the largest of the plastic bins she can reach in search of the antlers. She moves quickly. Mitchell catches up. He puts his arms around her, his grasp tight. She fights it.

"Stop, Veena. Stop."

"I need to find them."

The girl is in the back room now too. And Rosemary is there. Veena stops trying to escape Mitchell's grasp, and studies Rosemary's blouse. It is covered with acorns. Neel hated acorns. He hated them because they were so plentiful, so easy to find. So boring.

Veena wriggles out of Mitchell's arms and starts opening bins again, throwing things to the ground in fury, surprised by her own recklessness.

"Tell me where they are," she shouts at the girl, who has stopped chewing her gum. "Tell me!"

Rosemary walks up to Veena, coming closer until they are nose to nose. Veena has never been this close to her, close enough to smell her. Lavender perfume, and under that, a trace of staleness, something musty. Raspberry-colored lip- stick, breath like oranges. And one long white hair sprouting from her chin. *Living*, Veena can't help but think.

"The antlers exist," Rosemary says. "Just because they aren't here anymore, it doesn't mean they don't exist."

Veena cannot stand any longer. She collapses to the floor, draws her knees to her chest, and rocks back and forth. The rocks, the shells, the pine cones, the antlers, everything belonged to those who were alive. That's what Rosemary was saying, wasn't it?

She feels light-headed, a little dizzy. She looks up and knows how it seems to them. Their faces, all their faces, are twisted with pity. The older woman understands her pain, the younger one is alarmed. Mitchell is alive and present, but too long in her company and he would decay.

For now, she has no choice but to stay where she is. In order to exist, she cannot choose life, just as she did not choose death.

"Why?" Veena says. "Why does someone else get to have them?"

If one of them answers her, she does not hear it. Instead, it is her own voice that speaks to her. In her hands, the antlers had no future. They belonged in the home of the boy from the park, or Toby's, in the hands of the active, curious, living child who had carefully collected points, and proudly claimed it for his bookshelf.

Mitchell offers her his hand. "Come," he says, his voice gentle, and patient. They walk to the parking lot hand in hand. She knows that when they get home, he will not come inside.

Encased

Ali Eteraz

ENCASED

At her seventeenth birthday party at the Bandu Khan restaurant on Airport Road in Mobile, Alabama, Saba Muhammad went up to some of the ladies in attendance and casually said, "I have more than one mother."

This statement, before it got twisted by the ladies in the community and before it caused her mother Misra and her aunt Mehvish to suffer a nervous breakdown, had been made with the best of intentions. Saba had simply wanted to tell the world that her younger aunt Mehvish, who was unmarried, nearly blind, and who had played a large role in raising Saba, deserved recognition for her assistance in raising her. Secretly, Saba hoped that on the strength of the compliment maybe one of the aunties would find Mehvish, who was now approaching forty, a suitable and traditional Pakistani husband.

However, the community did not interpret Saba's statement in a generous manner. The predominant reading given by the aunties was that Dr. Murtaza Muhammad, Saba's father, who nearly twenty years ago had gone to Pakistan and brought Mehvish over to come stay with his family, had actually impregnated Mehvish on the trip and then the whole family—husband, wife and blind aunt-mistress—had conspired to cover up the affair.

The aunties believed this to be the most likely scenario for two reasons. One, because they thought that it was against the nature of the Punjabi man to feel empathy for anyone in his wife's family and therefore any act of concern had to have been driven by "ulterior motivation"; and two, because many of the women in the community had themselves engaged in affairs with Dr. Muhammad and so could only presume that when he was alone with his wife's far younger sister he must have slept with her as well.

At the time of the Bandu Khan comment Saba had not been aware of the turbulence it would cause. She had just graduated from Baker High School and was on her way to Oglethorpe University in Atlanta where she planned on studying medicine. For her, the throwaway statement was merely a final chance to publicize the unnamed and unrecognized sacrifices that were made inside her house. Instead, the whole thing became an unwanted lesson in learning the degenerate nature of her community, as well as a shocking insight into her father's character.

The latter discovery, far more than her mother's and aunt's deteriorated health, was what shook Saba the most. Her whole life she had looked at her father, Dr. Murtaza Muhammad, near legendary pediatric cardiologist and head of the local Friends of Pakistan chapter, as if he was something vintage, from among a special collection of self-made men that Allah no longer put in America, these kind of contemporary Crusaders, who had risen from the feudal lands far in the distance, answering the call of the God of Capitalism, and ridden out to the American frontier and made it their home, their domain. The suddenness of her changed perception, a change which had to take place inside of her without a singular opportunity to verbalize or accuse or chastise, caused her a great deal of anguish. She could no longer see him as the saint of success, but something far more powerful and sinister, like an Emperor, whose purview is always built upon some kind of violence. Within three weeks of being in Atlanta she stopped attending classes, and spent most weeknights going out to Trip-Hop clubs and popping E, while using the weekends to go off with various "friends with bene's" to Miami, Montreal, and Paris.

The partying came to an end in the spring semester of Saba's freshman year when her periods suddenly stopped and she found out about her ectopic pregnancy. In a state of desperation and panic, it was Dr. Muhammad to whom Saba turned for the painful and complicated abortion. Because he was a pro at discretion he kept his daughter's secret from both Misra and Mehvish, as well as the medical charts. He set her up at a clinic in Pensacola, paid for a private nurse and made nightly trips on I-10 to check up on her. Then when she wailed and moaned from the medication he held her hand and asked her what he could do to make her feel better.

"Tell me about the women, daddy," was what the daughter whispered. "Just tell me all about them."

Confession was not something Dr. Muhammad had ever contemplated; but pity got the better of him. Partly to help Saba pull through the pain and partly because of the desperation in his daughter's voice Dr. Muhammad started his story at age fifteen, with Sadia the maid at the bungalow in Lahore, and confessed his way to Mrs. Siddiq from Houston whom he was currently seeing at hotels at various medical conferences. He told Saba everything. Why he went for the married ones ("they are more ashamed to reveal"). Why he operated inside the community instead of the white women ("because I need the smell of Islam"). Why he didn't think he would ever be able to stop ("I am a lover at heart"). In between hallucinations featuring dub-step DJs and conversations with Islamic angels Saba listened to her father, accepting it all, passing judgment upon nothing. Most of the time she pretended to be asleep to keep him talking.

It was all a set-up on her part. Her patience was designed to lead up to one singular moment many days later. It came when her father drove her up the winding single-lane road that led to their house, the warm sunlight piercing through the shortleaf pine branches only to die futilely upon the tinted Benz, the late September sky a hazy purple. "What about Mehvish khala," she asked in a near inaudible whisper. "Did something happen there?"

Dr. Muhammad brought his left hand to his mouth and coughed, then straightened his arm to lower the window and let in the warm breeze until the air conditioned car became humid.

107

* * *

Saba only spent three days at the house—a mere three days in the house in which she was raised, the beloved two story house located in a subdivision called Enchantment Lakes; its front lawn bejeweled with her mother's jasmines, her aunt's gardenias and Saba's own pink roses; the house that under the influence of Lollywood films during her childhood she had referred to simply as "*jahan*" or universe.

Every time Saba came down for a meal, finding her mother and aunt in their faded floral *shalwar kameezes* and gauzy *dupattas* fidgeting over pots of steaming basmati, hips bumping into each other's as they drank *chai* on the veranda, their fingers inadvertently touching over trays of chilled fruit in the living room, their paths intersecting across the sunroom, the clinking of their bangles in constant competition, she felt a hot flush develop at the pit of her stomach, pass through her body and then creep up the back of her neck and into her head. She couldn't speak to either of them anymore and the method she used each time she was spoken to was to switch from Urdu to rapid fire English and the conversation quickly died down.

Her first attempt to quiet her thoughts was by way of the Quran. She retreated to her room, wrapped herself in a black *chador* with white crochet flowers and then on folded feet sat upon the prayer rug with a copy of the book. Reading the Arabic in a muted singsong murmur did nothing for her. The inability to melt away the cobwebs by way of hypnotic recitation made her begin reading the translation of the verses—which was an even worse idea because she started seeing things she didn't like: punishments that seemed anachronistic, wars against infidels that had no meaning in today's world, and mentions of polygamy. The last reference, in particular, made her shut the covers with a harsh snap. She wondered if her father had ever conceived of having more than one wife. She wondered if the world would have reacted less harshly towards him if he had hidden his weakness for women by way of religion. She wondered if it was even allowed in Islam for a man to be married to sisters simultaneously. At the end she concluded that none of it mattered. The issue before her wasn't one of religion, or morality, or even the dictates of society.

The issue was about love—and that was something that God and all the Prophets had left to poets to speak about. Within moments she was rummaging through the old ghazals in her father's study that she had picked up on her last trip to Lahore. The CD she withdrew from the stack was Iqbal Bano, the one in which the old crooneress sang the poetry of Pakistan's greatest poet, Faiz Ahmed Faiz. Gripping the CD case to her chest as if she was a child clenching a schoolbook, Saba ran upstairs and let the stereo play. Within moments

108

she was lying on her stomach, awash in tears, through blurry eyes writing verses in Urdu onto tiny little pieces of paper and throwing them around her body to make a protective encasing. Eventually she settled on one particular line as her motto: "We, for whom there is no idol, no god, besides the way of love." She folded the yellow sticky note seven times until it became an oblong square. Then she stuck it inside the leather casing of a *taweez* and wore it around her neck.

Back in Pakistan most people put Quranic verses in a *taweez*—but the blatant blasphemy of her act somehow improved her mood.

That night, as her mother and aunt slept in their respective rooms, Saba packed her bags and walked to the Greyhound stop on Government Boulevard. It was a four mile walk and she was breathless and sweaty by the time she reached.

"I am never coming back home," she texted her father after she had bought her ticket.

The reply—"Ok"—came but a few second later, but Saba didn't see it. Since the phone was in his name she had tossed it in a ditch.

* * *

Saba could've gone back to Oglethorpe and borrowed her way through, but she figured getting in debt without a safety net was probably not a good idea, so instead of going up to Atlanta she took a bus ride to Birmingham and tried to enroll at the University of Alabama, where she could get in-state tuition. The registrars were aghast at her attempt to skip the year-long application process, so Saba parked herself in the Dean's parking spot until he showed up. The Dean was so impressed by her grades in high school, and by the prospect of gaining a gifted minority student, that he let her in after an interview and then awarded her a scholarship that was enough to cover tuition and board.

When it came time to pick her major Saba chose chemical engineering because it seemed a good way to secure her financial future. The other reason she liked it was because as a child she had wanted to be an alchemist and this seemed like the closest thing to that the world had to offer. Chemical engineers could turn one thing into another.

During college Saba applied that same principle to her persona, engaging in a series of alterations to herself.

The first substantive change was to declare herself a Shia. It was the idea of Hussainiyat—to be sacrificed at the hands of heartless monstrosity—that drew her in. She liked that the principles of martyrdom and mourning were so intrinsic to the faith. She wasn't pious or conservative about it, nor

109

did she attend the mosque; but she became well-educated on the theology. She particularly liked how so many Pakistani poets invoked Shia imagery. It seemed to her a good religion for a victim.

The second thing she did was to change her last name. She went to the probate court and changed from Saba Muhammad to Saba Fatima. She liked the name Fatima because it was central to the Shia faith and because the original Fatima was a woman that, despite having an immense father, had managed to leave her own legacy in the world through the men she loved in life, particularly Ali, Hasan, and Hussain. As Saba settled into the name she often imagined that like her namesake she too would overcome the shadow of her father.

What Saba Fatima quickly realized—being the only girl and only American amidst a bunch of Chinese and Indian guys in the engineering department— was that her studies would take over her life. She designed and invented processes, constructed instruments and facilities, planned and operated networks. She worked in atomic science, with paper, dyes, drugs, plastics, fertilizers, foods, and petrochemicals. She worked with raw material, with environmentally friendly polymers, and most excitingly, she brewed beer. What she was surprised to learn was that it was a socially portable degree: there was always a frat guy or young desi bloke trying to talk her into cutting him and his crew some form of mind-altering substance from household chemicals—and sometimes if she was in the mood she would go along with the request.

While she had many male acquaintances Saba did not make an effort to keep a boyfriend. There was a time when she let a date grope her in the parking lot out of pity for him but getting molested made her feel so disgusted that she became concerned that if she continued with such behavior she might end up turning celibate for life. Another issue was that nearly all of the engineers were non-Americans and though many were quite intelligent, even geniuses, they socialized with her in an inanely submissive manner just because she spoke English better.

The basic problem, though, was that many times the mere thought of sex sent Saba spinning back into reflections about the triangle that she had grown up with without ever knowing about it. Many nights Saba would lie in bed and try to figure out how her mother and aunt must have sat together and worked out the minute details of sharing a man. Many nights Saba would lie in bed and try to understand whether it was pity on the part of her mother or power on the part of her father or perhaps even manipulation on the part of her aunt that had ever allowed for such an arrangement to occur. There were so many questions that she had, so many times when she wanted to go back home and just demand that all the cabinets of memory be strewn open to her so she could...*know*. Yet each time she was assailed by the temptation she fought it off. She turned it into something else—mostly self-portraits.

The act of taking her own picture was an elaborate ritual that took place every few weeks. First she came up with the look she wanted to adopt, usually while she was in the shower, or in the middle of a workout. The evening of the act she decorated her hair—sometimes leaving the curly black tresses messy and at other times chopping off some length. Then came the part she liked the most, wardrobe, makeup and jewelry. The clothes she wore ranged from what the Pakistanis she once knew would have considered "extreme obscene"—skirts, halter-tops and booty-shorts—to extremely traditional *shalwar kameezes, chadors* and *saris* that were obtained from a budding Indian fashion designer named Sita. She then put on, depending on her mood, rose colored lipsticks, fiery green eyeshadow, and skin darkening foundations. Finally there was the jewelry. Big desi chokers with brass teardrops, golden kundan necklaces with red and green gems, and big chandelier earrings. In addition she sometimes wore studs and challas in her nose, toe rings, heavy anklets, thick bangles and even the bridal teekas on the forehead. She once saved up enough money to buy a jewelry collection called "Devdas" which were the identical pieces worn in the remake of the classic film. Eventually, all of these self-portraits, which were taken with a timed Nikon, lay strewn about her room or ended up on a secretive website where she could browse through them when she was taking a break from work.

The portrait taken during junior year finals, right after she cut her hair short, was her favorite. In it she wore a brown halter-top with a gold-plated choker, a matching clasp on her arm and dream catcher earrings; her head was turned slightly to the right with one hand delicately rustling her hair; her brown lips were in a slight part and a look of supercilious venom swam in her eyes. Every time she looked at the picture she noted with delight how she could carry the contradiction of showing so much bare skin all while bearing so much traditional jewelry. It gave her confidence. It affirmed to her that while she could appreciate the good things of her family's past, she was not, like her mother and aunt, and even her father, beholden to it entirely.

Saba wanted to be certain that not every one of the portraits be done in outright retaliation to her family. So there were many where she was in grungy clothing, torn-up shorts, wearing big glasses; some where she was standing and looking at herself in a dirty bathroom mirror; some in which she had a zit or was caught in the act of blinking. These portraits, though, she stopped doing, because the spontaneity and simplicity of them had started reminding her of the house in Mobile, of her mother embracing her from the back in the middle of the kitchen, of her aunt humming a ghazal by Nayyara

Noor, of her father smelling of cigar and pickled mangoes.

She missed all of them.

* * *

It was Budweiser that helped him find her.

After Saba graduated she decided that she liked the idea of making beer so much that she became senior chemical analyst with Annheiser Busch in St. Louis. Her new employer was so excited by the prospect of getting a pretty "ethnic" girl on the team—their first woman—that they plastered her picture and biography all over their website. Apparently the tech guy at Budweiser had used Saba's name as it appeared on her University of Alabama transcript instead of how it appeared on her current resume. Dr. Muhammad, who did not drink beer, ended up seeing the bio because four years earlier he had set up an automated Google search for the name "Saba Muhammad" and it sent daily deliveries to his email inbox that he checked before sleeping.

On her first day of work, Dr. Muhammad, wearing a charcoal three-piece suit, showed up at her office. She saw him before he made his way into the common area and retreated behind a wall to look at him. He appeared gaunt even as his paunch was more prominent. He had grown a beard and it was mostly gray with speckles of black. There was a weariness in his eyes that was less physical exhaustion and more panic. In that moment she tried to ask herself what it was about him, from a purely physical perspective, that women found alluring. The answer Saba settled upon was—nothing. Dr. Muhammad was below average.

Initially, this answer gave her a great deal of comfort, because it assured to her that in terms of taste she was different than her mother and aunt and all the other mistresses. But then she wondered that if it wasn't his looks then it had to be something *else*—and that deviant turn in her thoughts caused her to close her eyes and force out a big long breath.

"Daddy!" Saba came out suddenly from behind the counter and without looking at his face pressed herself against his arm. "You found me!"

Then as he put his thin arms around her she closed her eyes and let herself cry. Secretly, ever since she had left, she had held out hope that he would seek her out. The act of looking for her would prove that he loved her more than he loved his weakness.

* * *

Saba took her father back to her spacious apartment overlooking the Mississippi and heated for him a plate of *kadu gosht*. As she moved around the kitchen he, refusing to sit on the dinner table, sat with legs dangling

112

on the stool at the bar, his heels occasionally hitting against the bar. He kept commenting how he could see the Gateway Arch, to which she simply nodded and smiled. She put the steaming squash and meat in front of him and apologized for not having any bread.

"How can you eat this without bread?" he said with unexpectedly severe dejection. "You get my stomach all excited then tell me you are giving me soup? That's all our food is without bread. Soup! We don't eat soup at home."

She was sitting with a spoon in her hand, hoping to eat from the same plate as him, to share oil and vegetable and meat with him, but his comment caused all the softness in her spirit to dissipate. In an insurrection of rage she began hitting the countertop with the utensil. She hit the Venetian gold granite over and over and over, increasing in tempo and rage, until he was forced to reach forward and grab her wrist.

"What is the matter with you?" he said angrily, trying to restrain her.

"Let me go," she shouted, struggling against him. "Let me go. You don't deserve bread. You don't deserve anything."

Her flurry only caused him to try and control her further. He stood up behind her and tried to give her a pacifying embrace. But in the struggle her elbow jutted into his stomach and caused a wheeze of breath to escape out of his larynx—and then he stumbled.

She turned to him, suddenly, trying to reach out a steadying hand.

Much to her surprise, he actually reached for her, but instead of her hand or her arm he caught a hold of the *taweez* dangling from her neck. His fist closed around the black leather casing and as he fell to the floor the chain snapped and the square *taweez* ended up in his hand.

"I didn't realize I raised a daughter who believed in this Sufi irrationality," he said, now on the floor, splitting the *taweez* with the nails of his thumb, reading the verse she had scribbled long ago.

"Just let me have it back," she demanded. "And please get up."

"I am fine here," he said. "I belong on the floor."

She hovered over him, uncertain whether out of deference to sit down next to him; to simply walk away and out of spite let him wallow; or to sit down on one stool still standing and thereby be above him.

As Saba wondered about what to do, her father began humming the *ghazal* to himself.

* * *

When she was seven years old Saba and Mehvish *khala* had gone to the public library on Government Boulevard and rented a copy of *2001: A Space Odyssey*. Saba had become smitten with the massive black obelisk. It was so quiet yet so amazing, capable of starting mysterious chain reactions, cause pacifist monkeys to engage in war, create electrical storms across the solar system. What she couldn't understand, however, was what to call the object.

"What is its naaame?" she had repeatedly asked Mehvish *khala*, who, on account of her weak English could only shrug her shoulders.

"You should give it a name," she had eventually said to her niece in Urdu.

"I can't think of a good one," Saba had complained.

Mehvish had bitten her lower lip for a while, looking at the screen until her eyes turned watery and then lifted Saba into her lap. "Let's just call it Murtaza," she had said.

"Like Dad!" Saba had smiled.

Now, as Saba watched her father cry on the floor of her apartment she kept thinking of that evening. Murtaza Muhammad was supposed to be the obelisk. He was dark and severe and secretly in control of everything. Weakness seemed so antithetical to his character. Thinking about the way Mehvish *khala* associated her father with power Saba felt that it was her duty to make her father stop crying, to restore his mana to him, if for no other reason than to send back to Mehvish *khala* the man that had given her protection when no one else would.

This burgeoning sentiment was interrupted, however, by the sudden appearance of another childhood incident. This time Saba was eleven years old, on the same couch in the living room where she had watched the obelisk, except she was sitting with her mother. Misra was wearing a warm tan colored *chador* which framed her round face and matched her light brown eyes. She had just finished praying *esha*, the night prayer, and was now reading stories about the prophets to her daughter, specifically the one about Yusuf, to whom Allah had given ninety-nine parts of the beauty of the world.

"A woman named Zuleikha tried to seduce Yusuf when he lived at her house but he told her that since she was already married he couldn't be with her. It was this act of Yusuf that was most pleasing to Allah. Do you know what that is supposed to teach us, Saba?"

"No."

"It teaches us that even if you have everything—like Yusuf had beauty— God values morality more."

Saba now understood that her mother had been speaking about her husband who presumably had everything in the world but didn't have restraint.

Thinking of those two episodes in tandem Saba felt she finally understood everything that had happened in her house.

Becoming aware didn't turn into a moment of sublimation. Nor did it make her feel vindictive towards her aunt or feel pity towards her mother. It

114

simply made her curious about her father.

"Why were the two of them not enough for you?" she said loud enough for him to hear. "They gave you everything."

Her father looked up for a second and then, putting his face back in his palms, hid himself.

*   *   *

In the morning she let him drive her back to Mobile. It took two days and they drove mostly in silence, stopping at rest stops and gas stations to switch driving duties.

For the night they stopped at a Howard Johnson at the I-10 in Baton Rouge. The attendant recognized the doctor and looking towards Saba asked him if "you will take the usual room." She whimpered in response and immediately ran out of the lobby.

"Saba stop!" Dr. Muhammad begged. "Please!"

"I don't know what I was thinking!"

"We can stay somewhere else!"

"Aren't all the hotels infested with your whores?"

She reached her father's Benz and began kicking the passenger side door. Denting the black steel was the only form of abuse she was in a position to inflict. He stood back and let her kick. After five minutes, when she could neither see through the blackness in her head and her toes were thoroughly jammed and numbed from pain, she walked over to a bench underneath the hotel's awning and let her black hair fall over her face. The noise in her head, the soft voice of her mother reading the Quran, the whisper of her aunt humming songs, the imagined moans of faceless women in Howard Johnson, prevented her from hearing the roar of a door opening and shutting, of a car coming to life, of tires screeching away. All she wanted to do was to have her hands turn into claws so she could grasp his heart and ask the palpitating mass if Dr. Muhammad respected anything, if anything was sacred to him.

When Saba opened her eyes she was all alone. Sitting next to her on the bench was the black *taweez* with the leather casing. Sticking out from one corner was the verse—"We, for whom there is no idol, no god, besides the way of love"—that belonged to the leading poet of her father's homeland.

Rinse, Repeat

Sayantani Dasgupta

RINSE, REPEAT

It's the email from my apartment-leasing company that alerts me to the severity of the situation. For days now, I have been watching the slow build of Hurricane Florence, a dense, white clot over the Atlantic Ocean, a menacing eye, much like the eye of Sauron. Satellite images show landfall will be in four days' time, in Wilmington, North Carolina, my home since the last month, a touristy beach city of about 100,000 residents. Thus far, several long-time residents have assured me this isn't that out of the norm during our annual "hurricane season." That we have something called Hurricane Season, in effect from June 1 to November 30, is in and of itself deeply alarming.

But I am here now. What's the point in scaring myself any more than necessary? I have heard it said over and over again that most hurricanes are fairly anticlimactic. Almost boring. All they cause is lots of rain, punctuated by power cuts.

However, the email, with the subject line, "Get Ready for Hurricane Florence," and divided into three sections, with twenty-five points in all, is something else. It is a manifesto. A call and plan for action.

I reread the instructions, and although many do not apply to me—I don't have to bring in my plants or patio furniture because I don't own any—the visual heft of them tightens something inside me.

Right then, a Facebook notification pops up. It's a message from James, one of my former students from Idaho, where I used to teach before, and who now lives in Greenville, North Carolina, two or so hours away from the coast. He is a middle-school English teacher these days, and shortly after my arrival, he had driven down to eat lunch with me. Inside an Irish-themed restaurant, we had relived our memories of Idaho, and listening to him talk passionately about teaching and his students had easily been one of the best welcome-to-Wilmington experiences.

"Come to Greenville," James's message says, "we are sufficiently inland. This one looks big."

I turn off my laptop, and step out into the balcony. For the thousandth time, I wish I wasn't dealing with this on my own. I wish my husband was here. He was, for the first two weeks, helping me settle into my new life and apartment, the latter selected sight unseen, based purely on its location. A twelve-minute walk to my department on campus, a short drive to the ocean in one direction, and about the same in the opposite direction, if instead of the beach, you wanted to hang out in Wilmington's historic downtown.

But now he has returned to our home and his job in Idaho. He will join me in three months, by which time he'd have wrapped up things at work, and packed the remainder of our belongings. That was the plan, until, Florence came calling. Now, I don't know.

I lean against the railing, and it occurs to me that for the first time since

118

my arrival, I am not covered in a thin film of sweat. Miraculously, there is a breeze. My husband joked nearly every day that he was here, "Breathing in Wilmington is like being inside a whale's mouth. Sticky, smelling, unforgiving."

Neither he nor I are used to this level of humidity. We are products of drier cities. He is from Los Angeles, I am from New Delhi, and together we made our life in Moscow, Idaho—green and lush with wildflowers in spring, dry and arid in summer, cold and rainy in fall with leaves turning orange, red, and fire; and snowy and icy from November to March. Wilmington, North Carolina, is our first experience of the South. Wilmingtonians have warned us that it is humid here year-round, and that we will want the air conditioner on for at least six of those months.

I lean back and breathe in deeply. Beyond the line of trees and apartments, some fifteen minutes away, there is the Atlantic Ocean, and hovering over it, Hurricane Florence. But you wouldn't think that looking at the gently swaying, skinny branches of the longleaf pines, or today's clear blue sky, the kind of blue you long for on the best day of your life.

* * *

My first time walking along Wrightsville Beach, I called my mother on WhatsApp. I wanted her help in choosing my new desk. I was split between two options, both refurbished and from the 1950s, both housed at a local consignment store. The first desk was grey and brown, the second, olive green. Ma helped me choose (the olive green), and we continued to chat for almost an hour, her from landlocked Delhi, and I with the Atlantic in my background.

During his time here, for three mornings in a row, my husband and I went to the beach to watch the sun rise. We stuffed our pockets with gifts— shells, sea glass, smooth stones, gnarled bits that looked like the fossilized bones and teeth of prehistoric, unknowable animals. All through our move, my husband had said that his first task upon seeing the Atlantic in person would be to heckle it. Having lived in Los Angeles nearly all his life, "his" ocean was the Pacific. There was no way the Atlantic was going to match its magnitude.

But its first sight, its sheer enormity made him forget his previous resolve. He whispered, "This is my favorite moment."

I couldn't bring myself to say anything. I just nodded. We had arrived in Wilmington, exhausted and broken from the packing, angry and impatient with the moving. For the last several weeks, we had survived on Domino's, our lives dominated by bubble wrap, tape, brown paper rolls, movers who

119

didn't always answer their phones, and employers that didn't pay for moving expenses, not even for this cross country move from Idaho to North Carolina.

But the ocean took it all away. It absorbed our exhaustion, and healed the fractures. Each morning we left the beach holding hands, ready for the day in our new home.

I've wanted this all my life, this proximity to the ocean, ever since reading *Twenty Thousand Leagues Under the Sea* at age nine. Ever since dragging my husband to Point Arena, California, for a holiday, where we paid through our teeth to stay at the former lighthouse keeper's quarters.

* * *

But it's one thing to love lighthouses, and quite another to face up to hurricanes. And Florence is supposed to be a big one. Experts have predicted it will be a Category 4 hurricane with the potential of turning into a 5. Hurricane Katrina was a 5. It killed nearly 2,000 people, and kept New Orleans inundated for weeks.

What does Category 5 mean for Wilmington? Wide-spread flooding, sandwiched as it is by the Atlantic Ocean on one side and the less-than-cheerful sounding Cape Fear River on the other. Massive power outages. Fierce winds uprooting hundreds of trees, toppling and ripping apart homes and other properties, not to mention the potential loss of lives.

And what does it mean for my two-bedroom, third-floor apartment? According to the simulation video shared by the admin of the local hurricane watch group I have joined on Facebook, my apartment could lose its roof to high winds; I could lose access to water, electricity, and the internet; any of the neighboring pine trees could crash onto my building or sail in through a window, unleashing rain and other debris onto my just purchased furniture, pots and pans, and all the accoutrements that go into turning an apartment into a home. This move, from Moscow, Idaho, to Wilmington, North Carolina, has covered a distance of 2,776 miles and all my savings. In the whirlpool that's been cross-country travel, the week-long orientation program, and the slew of classes I have never taught before, I have forgotten to buy renter's insurance. If this apartment goes, it will take with it everything I own.

* * *

Sure, I know nothing about hurricanes, but may I interest you in a class on how to write? That's the job that's brought me here. I am an assistant professor of creative writing at the local, public university. I can teach you all you need to know about different kinds of essays —flash, memoir, narrative,

120

segmented, collage. I can recommend books you should read to strengthen your authorial voice, or, tighten your narrative arc. I will share with you all my strategies for writing strong dialogue, and I will tell you passionately why you must read a lot of fiction and poetry even if you are committed to writing nonfiction every day of your life.

In my time here, I have settled into a semi-routine: on weekends, I shop and cook, I watch movies, and I share a meal or two with some of my new colleagues. On weekdays, once I am done teaching my undergrads, I walk the five or so minutes from my office to the campus library. I am immediately at home here, anchored with one book or more at the coffee shop conveniently located inside. Here, I grade, I meet with students for conferences, I read, research, and write.

I am constantly homesick for the home I have left behind, for the cafes where I wrote and met up with friends, the bookstores where the sales staff knew my name, the incredible restaurants that were steps away from my door, and those friendly strangers who made up life in Moscow.

Here, in Wilmington, I am years away from recreating the robust community of friends my husband and I had gotten used to. Here, most of my evenings are mine alone. Once I am done on campus, I walk home, while my husband stays on the phone with me. I try not to tell him about my loneliness, so I tell him about my students instead, about how energized I feel by their questions, and by the depth of their commitment to becoming better writers and readers.

But then there are other days, usually after I teach my three-hour-long, graduate-level workshop, that I return home feeling overwhelmed, drained, and completely out of depth. I have not taught at this level before, and given my students are not that much younger, I am convinced they know as much as me. So, I imagine their derision. I wonder if they have nicknames for me. I worry they will speak to the Chair, and tell him I am not needed here.

On those evenings, I sit in front of the TV for hours, seeing-not-seeing reruns of *The Office*, scrolling, scrolling, scrolling on my phone, leaping from one social media app to another, here, a birthday wish, there, a cat video, unwilling, unable, to even get up and wash my face, forget about fixing dinner, or sleeping on time so as to be ready for my early morning class next day, all the while, playing in my mind everything I should have said and done but didn't, the ways in which I should have exerted my authority and scholarship but didn't.

When I share my doubts with a senior colleague, she smiles. She assures me I am doing okay. But my doubts remain. If anything, they burrow deeper. They ask nonstop, "Are you really okay? Do you think this is fine? Is this all one can expect from you?"

121

*　*　*

Like every other place on earth, Wilmington is complicated.

It's the site of the only coup d'état in US history. On November 10, 1898, two days after a democratically-elected government came to power, it was overthrown and replaced by white supremacists, at least sixty people killed, and *The Daily Record*, a Black-owned and run newspaper torched. Today, the site of the state's only African-American newspaper and possibly the country's only Black-owned newspaper is an ordinary parking lot.

Downtown Wilmington, where many events of the Massacre of 1898 unfolded, still carries bronze statues commemorating Confederate soldiers and politicians such as George Davis, whose speech in 1861 recommended that North Carolina secede from the country so as to preserve its right to slavery.

Not that I am surprised by this. I know how history functions. I understand the role of erasure and remembrance, both as a student of history and literature, and because I am from Delhi, one of the oldest cities in the world, built, extended, and rebuilt on whims of current rulers and the ruins of former dynasties. I also know that attitudes and prejudices don't die just because they should. Often, they linger, and raise their heads in the most unexpected ways.

Perhaps that explains why at a campus event during my first week, two white women, both staff members, introduced themselves, shook hands with me, and by way of making conversation, said, "All good jobs go to black and brown women these days." I stared at them, thinking they were joking, and that the punch line was just around the corner. But they kept discussing this amongst themselves, and to my face, without any trace of irony or humor.

It also explains why in my one month here, I have heard so many horror stories from my Black students. "I don't go downtown if my date is white," one of them has said. "They look at you weird. You could be inside one of those nice restaurants, you know, with twinkling lights and all, or you could walk down the river, grand, and old and historic, and they will still look at you funny."

Physical ramifications of the hurricane aside, I, a brown woman, do not want to be by myself in a stretched-thin-for-resources, predominantly-white city, desperate to recover from a natural disaster. When Hurricane Katrina lashed Florida, Mississippi, and Louisiana in 2004, I was still in India. I remember seeing the many images of looting and rioting in the news. I remember my then boyfriend's smirks. "Americans should stop calling themselves a first-world nation. It's easy to imagine such crimes in developing countries like India, especially after a natural disaster. Look at them now. They are just as uncivilized as the rest of us."

Though I have now lived in the US for over a decade, there are several times in any given day when I feel out of place, when I wonder if I am being too familiar or inappropriate, if I am crossing a line of American etiquette or social norm that I, as a foreign woman, should not. *Did I smile enough? Did I show up on time? Did I say "sorry," "please" and "thank you" the right number of times?*

In the back and forth of emails, texts, and messages that Florence unleashes upon us, four of my new colleagues check in on me. Two offer me places to stay. The one I reach out to on my own never replies.

* * *

As nervous as I am, the uniqueness of my situation isn't lost on me. I, the granddaughter of refugees, am keenly aware that evacuation is its own privilege. Back in 1947, shortly after India gained Independence, both sides of my grandparents were forced out of homes they had lived in for generations. They fled to Calcutta, from what was then East Pakistan, and rebuilt their lives from scratch. But along the way, they lost friends and family, a language or two, and items that had made them who they were in the first place. *We gave away rooms full of books. Hard-bound with gold lettering on the spine.* Their stories of surviving on rice water, of standing in unending lines in hopes of food and shelter, of days spent simply waiting, are as much my inheritance as my language or surname. And still, all through my time with them, my grandparents insisted they were "the lucky ones." They didn't talk much about those who didn't or couldn't evacuate.

* * *

I weigh my options through every lens I own—the good, the bad, the absolutely nonsensical.

I cannot rent a hotel room in Raleigh or Durham, my nearest safe cities. I don't know how long Wilmington will remain unapproachable. I don't know how long I will be able to afford a hotel if recovery extends from a matter of days to weeks.

What will Captain Nemo say? He, my first literary crush; tall, erudite, and bearded; the son of an Indian prince, and the hero of *Twenty Thousand Leagues Under the Sea*? What kind of person insists she is excited by all the marine history surrounding Wilmington, including the fact that were he still alive, the notorious pirate Blackbeard would practically be her neighbor, but runs away at the first sign of trouble?

123

When I call my husband, he is in no mood for discussion. "I am buying you a ticket," he says. We look at prices, and I recoil as if I have been struck. Given the demand and urgency of the situation, tickets are few, and they cost a fortune.

*　*　*

Ultimately, the decision gets made for me.

I call home, meaning, my parents and brother in New Delhi, with the intent to brainstorm. It's my father who answers. In the thirty seconds it takes for Baba's "hello" to travel from the oval dining table of my childhood home to reach the circular dining table I have had since my now-husband and I got together ten years ago, I break down. I howl, as if fear has ballooned inside me and taken over my entire body and mind. I hear panic in Baba's voice, as he frantically calls out to my brother and mother, and puts me on speaker phone.

Right then and there, I make up my mind. I will evacuate to Idaho. I don't need to brainstorm. I know what will happen to my father if I don't try everything I can to keep myself safe. My Baba, who is always strong, who never shows any weakness, unless it's my last day in India, and we are hours from when I am supposed to leave for the airport.

*　*　*

I reread the property managers' email. I move furniture away from doors and windows. I unplug the TV and return it to its box. I fold clothes and put them away in suitcases. I disconnect everything electronic. My husband calls to make sure I haven't changed my mind, then adds, just as I am about to hang up, "Don't forget to bring a jacket. It's cold in Idaho." It doesn't register in my head that everyone everywhere is not in my state of panic. I shake my phone and scream, "No, it's over 80 degrees!"

I look at my belongings, half scattered, half still in boxes. I don't know what to pack, what to squirrel away, what to possibly take to Idaho. My grandfather's memoirs, written at my request in an old diary? Pictures from my childhood that I have carted around in a thick, brown envelope since my first day in the US in August 2009?

I pace from the bedroom to the kitchen to the study. I prepare my backpack for my flight—medicine kit, granola bars, chewing gum, an extra set of clothes and underwear, Bill Bryson's *I Am A Stranger Here Myself*. I refresh the weather app on my phone. The dense, white clot stares right back.

* * *

I take off from Wilmington two days before the airport is shut down. I hold my breath until I land in Atlanta, then breathe a bit in Minneapolis, then in Spokane, and then finally, at home in Moscow. At this point in time, I won't know that Florence will be labeled "a thousand-year storm event" because of the 8 trillion gallons of rain it will pour into North Carolina.

In Moscow, I will revisit the cafes I so missed in Wilmington but I will be too distracted to read or write. I will refresh my email over and over again, not knowing that campus will remain closed not for a week or two, but a month, something that's never happened in the history of the university in spite of Wilmington's long tryst with hurricanes.

I won't know that all over the city, hundreds of trees will fall, in one case, killing a mother and her child inside their home. Some neighborhoods will lose everything, and for days Wilmington will remain cut off from the rest of the world, because all roads leading to it will be under water.

It's only much later that I will learn about the debilitating damage in terms of environmental health. Seven million gallons of waste will spill into the Cape Fear River from hog farms owned by the world's largest pig and pork producer, and located in Duplin and Sampson Counties, about an hour north of Wilmington. *Vox* will report the death of 5,500 pigs and 3.4 million chickens. In *Our State* magazine, my colleague Philip Gerard, will write about these carcasses finding their way into the Cape Fear River, along with tons and tons of toxic coal ash, plus the breaching of the dam surrounding Sutton Lake—the retention pond that cools water for the local power plant—and about unusual activity at the nuclear power plant in Southport. *The New Yorker* will ask, *Could Smithfield Foods Have Prevented the "Rivers of Hog Waste" in North Carolina After Florence?*

In Idaho, I will spend time with friends that I have missed, but I will do so in a state of distraction. I will bristle every time someone will say something like, "What an unexpected vacation for you!" I will think of my students, and wonder if everyone made it out, if their homes are okay, if they and their families are safe. When the roads clear, a colleague will drive past my apartment building and send me pictures of damaged walls, of shingles peeling off the roof. Another will borrow a key from the leasing company, and enter my apartment. "All is well," she will report. I will remain split in the middle, learning, realizing, that you can make yourself a home in a month.

What I Found There: Transcendence Through the Blues and Two Books

Shikha Malaviya

'...back down south, where the water tastes just like cherry wine'
—From *A Man and the Blues* by Buddy Guy

There is a man carrying a suitcase on his head, walking in the middle of the street. He is a thin man with a thick mustache and deep-set eyes. He seems no more than thirty, though it's hard to tell through the car window. This man seems unperturbed by the traffic that swishes by on both sides of him. He alternates between looking ahead and looking at his feet. If this were a man in India or other parts of South Asia, no one would pay him a second glance. Men and women there carry everything on their heads, from suitcases, bricks, pots and pans tied together with string, to baskets of piled fruit, and more, with the ease of a tightrope walker.

But let me begin again. It is 1994. There is a brown man carrying a suitcase on his head in the middle of Bruce B. Downs Boulevard in Tampa, Florida. It is a busy, six-lane suburban street full of restaurants and shops and apartment complexes. Cars flit in and out of parking lots, slowing down enough to rubberneck, but too busy to actually care what's happening on this street flanked with baby palm trees. It is a sultry summer day where even the lizards don't show their tails, hiding in the shade.

My husband and I spot this man on the way back from the Indian grocery store, and are jarred by his presence. He sways as if he is drunk, one hand on his suitcase, walking towards oncoming traffic. His free hand wipes an eye. He is crying.

My husband rolls down the window and asks him if he needs help.

"My wife has thrown me out of the house and I have nowhere to go," he reveals bluntly between sobs.

We ask him a few questions and learn that he has just recently arrived from the south of India to Tampa, Florida, the south of the United States. Suitcase Man and his wife have had a fight. He knows no one and has nowhere to go. We commiserate and guess he hasn't been married too long. Those first-year marriage adjustments can be intense. We know because we've just crossed the one-and-a-half year mark. And here we are in Florida, with only our suitcases, living in an apartment with rented furniture, our own stuff in storage in New Jersey. We barely know anyone here. In a span of twenty months, we've moved twice, from Maryland to New Jersey and then New Jersey to Florida, that too, to a place, ironically, known as Suitcase City, because of its transient nature. If you count my move from Minnesota to Maryland because of my marriage that makes it three moves in less than two years. My heart tugs at this living and breathing harbinger that symbolizes arrival and departure at the same time.

Suitcase Man is our strange welcome to the American South and the best thing we can think of doing without calling the police is to take him back to the Indian store where Patel Bhai will hopefully help him and do some Indian 'jugaad', that magic thing which means in the loosest way possible—adjust, as well as compromise and improvise—all rolled into one. Jugaad is what Indian women are made of, what marriages are made of, what immigrants are made of, and what that poor man with a suitcase on his head was hopefully made of on that sweltering Southern summer day twenty-six years ago.

Did he make up with his wife? Are they still in Florida, happily married with two kids in college now, or did he return to India alone, a broken man—who's to say?

*   *   *

Back in the summer of 1994, Tampa feels like a tropical ghost town and I, its ghost bride. I roam alone among the lush foliage that covers our apartment complex that looks like a resort with its white stucco exterior and red tile roof. No one seems to be around except for reptiles that flash me some skin and tail before disappearing among leaf and green. I go to the gym where the television is on for nobody, blaring HGTV, and cycle for 20 minutes, watching an interior decorator explain how to give your home that special touch. Except that I can't. Our home with its drab grey rental sofa scratched-up glass dining table and overly springy queen bed feels like an old, stuck-in-the-80s room at the Holiday Inn. Nothing belongs to us. Everything reeks of smoke, even though we were promised otherwise. The less time I spend inside our apartment, the better. Each day feels like it's for rent and that we're trying it on for size. The day before, I attempt to pop some corn the old-fashioned way, and my pot catches fire. As I lay the scorched pot on the kitchen floor, it melts a hole in the linoleum, adding to my desolation. I miss my thick-bottomed triple-ply steel pot.

We are at that stage of our marriage where everything is a first and there is a certain romance in each of the objects we acquire because it marks who we are together: a white circular dining table that halves into a semi-circle and fits perfectly against the wall of our first apartment, a studio, where everything is one open room. We buy only two white chairs for the two of us, because that is our current universe and it is all that we can afford. Six months into our marriage and we buy two more. A full-size futon, gifted by an aunt, becomes a sofa by day and our bed by night. An unbreakable Corelle dinner set for four and steel Farberware pots and pans meant to survive a novice bride's first year attempts are gifts from family. All of these are now in New Jersey, waiting in a storage unit, as we dip our toe in Southern waters. I throw down a rug to cover the melted hole, to sweep it under the rug, literally.

129

It's not that I can't cook. I have never popped corn before. I was trying to do something different and hadn't quite succeeded. But I would try again. Marriage can be like that. Moving to a new place can be like that. You have to show up and keep trying. Perhaps that's what we should have said to Suitcase Man, except that we were still in the beta testing phase ourselves.

*　*　*

OPRAH: What is it like being in an arranged marriage? How is it different?
ME: We learn something new about each other every day.
—*The Oprah Winfrey Show*, March 1994

My husband and I learn that we love the blues. We learn this in Tampa when my husband's colleague, a single man originally from Bangladesh, who like us is also newly transplanted here, comes over and has us listen to Buddy Guy. Buddy Guy is that perfect mix of love and longing, of smoldering angst, loss, and anticipation, in which we find the perfect Southern soundtrack to our new life. Buddy Guy tells us that love comes out of nowhere like a hurricane, that Southern water is sweet as cherry wine, that women could be stone crazy and make a man cry. We can't get enough of him and buy our first Buddy Guy CD. How is it that no matter where we are, we tend to gravitate towards our own or what we perceive to be our own, and through our own, we discover things so gloriously different and make them our own? The blues seem the American equivalent of Hindustani Thumri, which evokes love and separation in a meandering sort of way. After marriage, music is one of the things that bring my husband and me closer, which helps us build a bridge between two lives that have fused so quickly, so suddenly. *Babul Mora, naihar chhooto hi jaye. Father of mine, my mother's home slips from me.* For twenty-one years, I am one person, and suddenly I have become another. I recall how many times my grandmother and mother always said, citing themselves as examples, that your husband's family is your family. But around me, I see so many different types of families, different types of bonds. Our Bangladeshi friend has dinner with us often, like a brother, and we discuss blues and jazz. I share how I heard John Coltrane playing on the speaker in a cafe in Minnesota, on campus, and ran almost breathless to the music store to buy Coltrane's album, *My Favorite Things*. It is still one of my favorite albums after all these years. Sometimes you just know. Music, my constant, my anchor in this life of transitions. A song for every occasion.

Growing up, I often pretended to be a singer with an empty toilet paper roll in my hand. The walls of our house always shook with strains of one song or another, and I grew up thinking I would make music my life.

I played the violin, the clarinet, and the saxophone. I sang in choir, solos, and in competitions. In my mind, I was always a musician first and then a writer. Music, that one thing I likened to breathing, that I had always taken for granted, has suddenly fallen to the side. Also my poems. And my studies. Marriage has temporarily displaced all my interests, for suddenly I am someone's wife first and everything else after that. I am no longer just a daughter or a student or a friend. I am now part of another family, one, which seems loving yet not familiar enough, my last name now four syllables instead of three. Thrust into adulthood so suddenly, I am trying to figure out who I am.

One of the other consultants my husband works with, who lives in the same complex as us, invites us over for lunch. He and his wife are from India as well. They, too, recently, have moved to Tampa. They've just had a baby and have been married for almost three years. "You're not planning to have a baby yet?" the wife asks when she learns we've been married for almost two years. "Not yet," I say, holding her daughter, whose eyes are deep black pools of innocence I find myself drowning in. I feel a twinge and wonder if I should consider this. "We're just getting to know each other," I say. Since the time I was twelve, I had dreamt of being a mother. I loved taking care of babies and had honed my skills babysitting a steady stream of cousins in our extended family. The soft sweet milky smell of a baby's breath. Their skin, smooth like dough. I feel my will crumbling. "I still have two quarters of college left. And I'm thinking about graduate school." I say out loud as if to convince myself. "You're lucky," our neighbor says. "They started asking me the day after we got married for some 'good news.'"

* * *

Six months before moving to Florida, my husband and I found ourselves on *The Oprah Winfrey Show*, on an episode about arranged marriages, where we represented the happily arranged married couple. The make-up artist asked me the same question as my Tampa neighbor, but in a much more direct way. "Are you pregnant?" she inquired, lining my eyes and touching up my face with foundation. I went red and stumbled out a no. Within a year of getting married, I had gained more than fifteen pounds. A different sort of freshman fifteen. I was wearing a pleated floral chiffon dress and immediately regretted not choosing a flattering Indian outfit instead. Of course, the make-up artist didn't know any of this. "You're so young and you have that glow," she said. "No baby? How come you got married then?"

131

My husband and I are brought together by my aunt, my father's sister who is married to my husband's first cousin on his father's side. It is an arrangement carefully worked on for four years, starting when I am in eleventh grade. We are told stories that are almost mythical on how intelligent, witty, and bold the other is, along with good looks, of course. My aunt, who I idolized as a child, who I wanted to be just like when I grew up, tells my prospective in-laws who adore her, that "she is exactly like me."

It takes my husband and me exactly three days to decide we will marry each other. I am twenty and he is twenty-four. I was born in the UK and raised in the US and India, while he was born in India and lived there for the first two decades of his life. English is my first language, Hindi is his. His field of study is electrical engineering and computer science, mine is music and literature. In most ways, we are the complete opposite. Both of us have never planned on getting married so early or that it should be arranged. We both believe in free will and the right to choose one's own spouse, among other things.

The first time we meet, it is a rainy December evening, which happens to be my future spouse's birthday. Our family just happens to be passing through Maryland after a family trip to Pennsylvania. My future husband and I exchange two whole sentences. 'Hello! Nice to meet you.' My parents like him while I have no opinion. I promptly forget him until March, when my father informs me that he's invited this prospective groom over for spring break. I fret and fume and say that when he's here, I'll completely ignore him. Instead, the night he arrives, we end up talking until my alarm rings the next morning at 6:30 AM. It turns out that we have a lot in common—that we both love India, that we are spiritual yet not religious, that we are liberal yet family-oriented, intellectual yet not snobbish, that we both have a zest for life, even though we haven't lived it together yet. One date in an Irish bar and cafe, another at a sculpture garden, and we think we are made for each other. What will happen to my BA in creative writing and mass communications? And my plans to go to graduate school and do a Ph.D.? You can complete it after marriage, my parents and future husband say. I will complete it after marriage, I tell myself.

* * *

In Florida, we go searching for India. My parents visit us from the Midwest and we decide to see a Hindi movie in the theater called *Andaz Apna Apna* (everyone has their own style). Two of the three Khan superstars have come together, Amir Khan and Salman Khan, and they are both rivals trying to woo a rich girl. The theater is so packed that we can only find seats in the

132

front. Everything is a blur of bright colors and the dialogues are deliciously cheesy:

Galti se mistake ho gaya (By mistake I made a mistake).

Do dost ek hi pyale mein chai peeyenge, isse dosti badhti hai (Two friends will drink from one cup of tea. This is how friendship deepens).

Could our friendship with this new city deepen in the same way? Could we all drink from the same communal cup and find ourselves among friends? A week later we go to a stadium where a Diwali fair is taking place. Women are dressed in mirrored ghagra cholis holding dandiya sticks as they spin in half circles. I am dizzy from watching and suddenly feel lost. These are my people and yet they aren't. We share the same country, but not the same language, and it's as if I'm in a new country within a country. When we drive down the causeway flanked by water so inky blue, it's as if a million pens have drowned in it, I wonder what it means to belong.

* * *

Days in Tampa seem suspended in treacle. Even the cars seem like they are moving in slow motion with white-haired people behind the wheel. I think about how one day my husband and I might be like that, living in a country and culture where senior citizens either live alone or in old homes. I admire their independence and pity them at the same time. Where are their sons and daughters or other relatives? What will they do if they have an emergency? I keep on thinking of that medical alert device infomercial, where an elderly woman is on the floor, shouting, "Help! I've fallen and I can't get up." In almost every home I know of in India, there is a grandmother, grandfather, or both, living with their sons or daughters. For them, retirement means hours of sitting in the sun, either reading the newspaper or embroidering or chopping vegetables or praying. It seems a leisurely life, where after years of familial devotion and duty, it was now time to turn towards God and hopefully grandchildren. But here, it is a different scene altogether. There are elderly couples everywhere stooped with canes and walkers, assisting one another, holding each other's hand as they cross the street, going to the movies or grocery shopping, driving fifteen miles an hour where it should be thirty-five. Were the constantly blue sky, hot weather, and glimpses of the ocean compensation enough for a life in slo-mo? Of buffets, golf, and bingo? Occasionally, one of the fit, sporty-at-seventy seniors whizzes past us on tandem bicycles or rollerblades. "Hopefully that will be us," I think to myself, though I haven't pushed an actual bike's pedal in ten years. But what of those years in between? What will we make of ourselves? Who am I,

133

who are we? My mind seems to be stuck at fifteen miles an hour, while other minds overtake me.

A bookstore in Tampa comes to my rescue, one whose name I can't recall. As I struggle to remember, I imagine it as a small, obscure independent bookstore, filled with unique books curated by an owner passionate about the earth, women's issues, and voices of color, whose recommendations are handwritten in placards above the shelves. But instead Barnes & Noble flashes through my mind. Which one is it? That is the fallible thing about memory. What I do remember, however, is that poetry sections are often the smallest sections of a bookstore and this one is no exception. Two books leap out at me, almost literally, falling into my hands. One is an anthology sporting a bright red cover with a brown woman wearing a transparent saree through which we glimpse a hill and trees. It is called *Our Feet Walk the Sky: Women of the South Asian Diaspora*. The other book is much more sedate and serious in appearance, mostly white with a blue square in one corner, and the author's name in black all capital letters, the R's in red, bigger than the title itself: ADRIENNE RICH, *What is Found There, Notebooks on Poetry and Politics*. These two books combined turn out to be exactly what I've been looking for in determining my life's work. There is a shiver of recognition and purpose as I flip through these books, folding the corners of pages I know I must come back to, even though I haven't paid for them yet.

In *Our Feet Walk the Sky*, I find community through words. In poems, short stories, and essays, I find a cultural history of witness and introspection; of immigrant lives that are fraught, messy, and yet beautiful. These are the stories I have wanted to read as well as write. These are the stories I have been looking for, but haven't found until now. Seeing a whole anthology dedicated to the South Asian woman immigrant experience and displayed on a shelf in Florida gives me both courage and permission to tell my stories as well, to admit to myself and by extension, the world, that I am indeed a writer, or at least have the heart of one.

In Adrienne Rich's book, I find a vision and manifesto, of how the act of writing poetry is a radical one, even more so if you are a woman. Throughout my childhood and as a newly anointed adult, I had been praised for pursuing poetry, for carrying on the legacy of my father's father who had also been one in India, though he had not made a career of it. Making a living out of poetry would be almost impossible is the message I constantly received from well-meaning family, friends, and even teachers. I decide to close my eyes and randomly open a page in *What is Found There* and see what message this book has to give me. The beginning of chapter seven faces me and the first sentence hits me like a sucker punch: "You must write and read as if your life depended on it." I fold the corner of this page. A few page turns further and "There is happiness in finding *what will work* simultaneously with the discovery of *what it works for*." I fold the corner of this page as well. And then the clincher, which makes me realize I need this book in my life: "Poetry, in its own way, is a carrier of the sparks, because it too comes out of silence, seeking connection with unseen others." This is what I want to do with my life and I will find a way, no matter the obstacles, no matter the naysayers.

That very evening, I decide I must leave Suitcase City; that in six short months, the South has given me a lifetime's purpose. Now that I knew what I wanted to do, I would be off to the Midwest, to complete my studies that I had started four years ago, and begin another journey with renewed purpose. I was going to write, I was going to make some noise, I was going to be a voice that represented my culture. I was going to be more than one thing at a time. As Buddy Guy crooned so soulfully with the hint of a promise, it would be *my time after a while*. Like Suitcase Man, and all those others, carrying the burden of their hopes and dreams, I was departing and arriving at the same time.

Slow Fruiting

Rukmini Kalamangalam

SLOW FRUITING

In times of terrible uncertainty, there are the sure contours of fruit. The immovable knowledge that orange peel kept in the sun will dry, the skin of a Louisiana persimmon will blush and burst open into custard, a pear will yellow and melt in our mouths. It is our gift to ourselves and to whichever God we believe in. It is a source of constancy, the rhythm of my grandparents eating a banana apiece each morning, the counting of golden raisins for paisam.

Gardens are our way of connecting and collecting. Back doors open into yards rich with fruit: heerekai green and ridged, swaying softly when rattled, karela stretching their vines over fences and careful trellises. These are our moments of recreation, where good southern soil and tropical sun allow us to shape a familiar home.

Each gathering, stuffed into a chosen house in a chosen subdivision, is an opportunity to show off and share bounty. Meethi neem cuttings in exchange for a newly rooting tulsi branch. Medicinal herbal secrets are traded, roses are propagated, children are fed the right balance of cooling and heating foods. Women are allowed our space to discuss anything and everything: circles of shimmering saris gathered in the kitchen or by the buffet table.

Across countries, across generations, there are some things that don't change. I ground myself in taste, jewel color. I recognize myself in round, lumpy shapes. I make myself beautiful in juice dripping from my new lips.

Jamun: Bangalore, Karnataka

It's the South. I'm aware of this just like I'm aware the blue house in my peripheral vision is where my father lived in his supposed childhood. A jamun tree provides a patch of uncombed shade. The purple of the fat fruit is almost unreal, the bright faraway feeling of this long kurta billowing around me, the dust gritting into my mouth through my triangled handkerchief. The letters look uneasy here, their squat bodies growing like deformed breasts.

I feel consumed by the space in my salwar kameez, hemmed to my size by a tailor who refused to take my measurements. It's tight around my shoulders and chest, then balloons out over my stomach, down to my knees. The crotch on my leggings starts halfway down my thighs but tightens around my calves until I'm worried about the circulation in my toes, wiggling in my new shoes. Someone bent to slide these white wonders on my feet as if I could order a beheading.

Motorcyclists slow down as they pass us. In Houston, I had gotten used to hungry mouths whistling and honking as my sister and I waited to cross the street. The street noise here is different, warm with summer and

138

unrefrigerated houses. At home, breath drifts out of AC cool cars like ice refusing to melt. This breath is new, thawed, the drip of tea leaves staining a white counter.

Quiet.

It feels like I've designed these eyes myself. They are perfumed until slick, body odor emerging like the flower of fresh ground cumin. A caravan, backwards, where all the mirrors bloom until I drown in a flood of marigolds. A good, holy way to go out.

Not to say that mouths are holy here — I don't know yet. I want to crawl into one and poke around in the blackness between teeth, chewed tobacco and sugar crystals settling into deep cavities. It might be nice to nestle there for a moment, in a still darkness. I have been unable to sleep every night since I got here, headlights painting twisted stories on my wall, dreams I can't remember.

I can't sleep with the lights shifting. I can't outline the shape of myself. I don't close the window because I can't stand the stillness in the room, the fan lazy as a kept dog's tongue. I am growing in ways that cluster and stretch the seams of my clothes. I can't stand the heat, pressing like a tire over the outline of a dead green thing.

When I exhale like a failed whistle, my breath runs hot. Raised bumps tender the inside of my arm. Even upstairs, away from the heat of asphalt licking the sun, I am unsure how to stop the basket of my chest from collecting rotten jamuns, distorting my thin patterned blanket. I am growing into one of the letters that adorn the street signs, something I cannot read.

My ears are ringing with the sound of my father telling stories in loud Kannada. He is in the living room downstairs, but I already know the cloth sofa is bursting with the vibrations of his voice, like a carpet trying to muffle heaviness creeping down late night stairs. The language is as familiar as the light sting of a toothpick on cheek fat, jostling in the space between his teeth.

Kannada circles and echoes in my head, lodges inside until even the slow whip of fan blades is telling me something I can't understand. Swallowed consonants bury themselves in the tangled waves of my hair. My uncle's laughter drifts in and out like a sweet scent, maybe a night-blooming jasmine, or the exhaust of a dryer. If I strain, I can hear the golden thud of their beer glasses as they're sat down on .com coasters. Perhaps I am stuck here, lying half awake with my eyes tracing unsolved patterns in shadows dancing on the walls, because they are using up all the air in the house. A child outside laughs and shrieks and I imagine she is collecting jamuns too, throwing them at a sister already drenched in good purple juice. I am soft as overripe skin, bursting open on contact.

Chikoo: Houston, Texas

It is my first day of school in America, and I am small and brown and spiky. Or it is my first day of sixth grade, and I am not sure what to do with the small spikes of hair I have inherited from my brownness. My leg hair catches the wind like a thousand small sails, or a thousand spiders' legs reaching for new silks to sleep in.

When I take in all these sails one by one in the shower, there is blood that trails into the drain like wind that has nowhere to go, or a silk that has no indented stomach to wrap around. The next day the dance locker room still smells like Japanese Cherry Blossom body mist mixed with sweat and dried hairspray. I have learned to layer my tank tops underneath my shirt so my nipples don't poke through the clean light fabric.

The day I start my period I come home from school with a splinter in my finger from running my hand along the stair-rails leading up to the temporary classrooms. The blood has dripped so far from my finger I am bleeding from places that do not exist.

On my first ever day of school I topple over in my chair and hurt myself in a place that does not exist. When my teacher asks me if I am alright, I point to the spike of the chair leg. That is all I can do, since I do not know how to name this empty space in a language that is not brown.

When I tell my mother after school, she offers me no English to describe this small, hurt piece of me. I will find out later: I should only ask my mother for what she already wants to give. I will find out later: I do not know my mother. I am not small. My brownness is a spike that digs into me like a splinter.

The pouch of my stomach appears soon after I start bleeding. It eyes the glossy jalebis stacked behind the counter at Bombay Sweets, the large chikoo shake that struggles for space in the fridge. I pick the fine fibers of chikoo out of my teeth. It is supposed to make me lose weight, take up space in my stomach so I can't fit more in. It doesn't work: I overeat to feel solid, colored in. When I ask for another plate of food, my mother gifts it to me easily. Her sharp eyes hollow me. I fill my plate. My stomach hangs out of my shirt like a bruise.

Amla: Gainesville, Florida

I am at the dinner table, asking my grandmother how to make pickles because her favorite Mexican dish is lasagna. My sister and I have cooked brunch for her before, tacos with rich black beans and spiced green peppers.

She patted us on the head, ate little except decorative pieces of avocado. She prefers baked vegetables dripping in oil scraped burnt from a stained glass pan. This is America for her: an oven that runs too hot, an eggplant still raw in the middle with the skin falling off.

I try to tell her that here in North Central Florida we kind of only do things in extremes. We have a lightning that strikes the ground and water that floods holy; we remake our creation every hurricane season. She is used to monsoons that sweep by with regality, lingering over the red earth of her front yard in Benares, flooding shaped a kiss.

Our clouds don't love softly. Even now, the winds scream in their useless breasts like our ancient poets longing for a divine lover to fuck them.

I am not eating, but she is remaking cubed potato with the tips of her fingers, nails cut short and practiced. My sister picks leftovers from under her nails, washing them down the garbage disposal. It gurgles, but accepts her meager offering. The rose pink polish is already yellowing from turmeric stains, the sun setting from her cuticle to the tip of her nail.

Over the running water, my grandmother is explaining that she no longer makes long-term pickles. I had forgot I asked her a question. Home cooked pickles rot too quickly. Instead, mango and pink ginger soak quietly in salt water.

I think of patience.

Days cutting strips and drying them in the sun, checking them for rot by poking at them cautiously. I have no patience. I put whole gooseberries in my mouth to feel salt and spice and heat drip down my throat. I can handle all three without choking or coughing, thankyouverymuch. I am brown as wood.

I interview my grandmother after dinner. I tell her it is for a school project, but really I want to ask her to reveal the shape of herself, to take up some space and freeze there, with her lungs full of air and stomach expanded. I want to capture her voice, her story, her thoughts, buried as they are between sofa cushions and someone else's interjection. She is not loud. She shifts restlessly against the sofa and the squeaking makes its way into my recording, her words fuzzing.

Listening to the recording later, I see the outline of her, sharp and known. I see fruit in her hands, the press of a butter knife through the meat of a banana. I see the shape of her thumb stopping a sharp edge in its tracks.

Nartangai: Monroe, Louisiana

The day of our second storm in six weeks, it's already raining, the sky low and grey as school buildings or uncleaned mantels. Ash, dust. Even the yellow of the nartangai hanging into our soggy garden is not bright, but a fake sweetness dull as imitation sugar. We squeeze bottled condensed milk into afternoon tea. This is a hurricane. I am sure somewhere my sister is measuring sugar with her clothes dusted in fine powder . I cannot see her. My hair collects rain glimmering like imitation.

I am a black box in my stiff jacket, moving hot air in between various pockets. Picking nartangai up from the ground. Sitting them carelessly in our various buckets. I am tempted to sink my teeth into one to spoil the unmarred yellow skin, as proof that the wind is still slow and there is feeling beyond the thrash of crepe myrtle branches against a beloved window. Windows become loved when they are beat once every six weeks in the sweating heat of summer. More people sweat a weak beat in a loving summer, by which I mean more heart attacks happen on Daylight Savings day than any other.

I do not know if this is a fact, but my aunt mentioned it as we were driving to get bread and real milk. We learn from our mistakes. We have cooled our hands to better scoop ice without melting it. Mine carry two bags of ice to our car and stuff them into the cool bags my sister and I once made fun of. We used to load groceries we bought from a parrot in a tropical heat. I watch myself like an anchored cloud.

The clouds drift by quickly. They are pushed along at 60 miles an hour. I drive that fast and my hands shake. The winds tremble at their own audacity, at the wide mouth of the bayou and all the dead things rising, clutching at their howling sneakers.

At some point, I hear nothing but Paul Wall saying "drive slow." At some point, the traffic pole is nothing but twisted metal saying "drive slow." At some point, the nartangai have been raked off the bare tree and toweled off into Walmart bags. We drive through slow puddles to leave them at low doorsteps. Rain collects like the beginning of a flood in the slick grey plastic.

Mosambi: Sugarland, Texas

It is late. The elaborate speaker system is still set up but someone turned down the volume so the bass is just a whisper. My stomach hurts like an empty field bursting with compost. Bites swallowed whole swim and kick.

All the shoes that piled up by the door are gone, except for one flattened sandal that manages to be left behind in the long goodbyes. We are the last guests at a wide home that could swallow three of ours. We have hugged once and then again, the door wide open. I hope that in the commotion a baby decorated with sparkly things and thick black kajal purposefully knocked her other sandal into bushes wild with night.

142

Mosquitos drift in and out of our peripheries, little commas bursting into being when they flit under the light. The trash can is overflowing with paper plates and cups, even the extra bag hanging off the pantry door. I already know the lid will barely close over the last bites of vegetable disposed of by sneaky kids, stained napkins from the inevitable spill of muttar paneer and the red of it sinking into the greying carpet.

We are standing too close to the shuddering speaker. Every couple minutes *my desi girl, my desi girl girl girl girl* interrupts our fading conversation like a besharam ladki speaking out of turn. I used to want a Bollywood romance: a field of yellow flowers pressing themselves into me, a truck bed secure beneath my dancing feet. That idea fizzled out pretty quickly. I am no desi girl: my footsteps are heavy and clunky. There was once something gold fluttering in my throat when I talked to God, but my Hindi has dried and left dust under my tongue.

The night is thick with Texas crickets.

When we return home, my father sits quietly in the dark. The sofa is empty except for his mosambi peels, smuggled past customs wrapped in a dozen of some aunty's dupattas. It is only now, with the lamps turned off and the speaker far away, that I see his shoulders unclench. The night has grated on his nerves some, with all the voices that refuse to stay put and the unceasing sequins. Me and him both prefer to channel light through the magnifying glass, drilling small fires into big dry branches.

Every Texas night the sky is clear with stars and the air sharp with smoke. Under my father's fingernails, the oil of mosambi peel sits carefully as he washes the dishes bare-handed. When he comes upstairs to say goodnight, I can still smell it on his palm. Much later, when it's night and he no longer comes, I open the window to let the smoke in.

The Weight of His Bones

Jenny Bhatt

When my son Deepu rushes into the food mart, his face is swollen, and through his torn shirt I see bloody scratches on his body. His downturned gaze and the police officer accompanying him tell me he has done wrong.

I see his defiance rising like a shield that the world will, in time, smash as it has smashed mine, A liquid sourness burns my throat. I can barely pay heed to the police officer as I nod, yes, I am the father. With his pot belly, low-slung belt, and gum-chewing mouth, the officer reminds me of the gutka-chewing, squat-looking Pandu constables who stood at the corner stalls of the Mumbai streets where I grew up.

It's a breezy evening out across North Texas and we've been listening to the periodic tornado watch alerts on the television screen at the far end of the store. But the air inside here is humid, close, stale. After another long day that began with hauling boxes in the back room, I'm getting ready to close shop and head over to Amit's place. I had not been expecting Deepu. Each time he storms out, he stays away longer. Who knows where he goes or sleeps. He comes back, eventually, like a dog with rabid eyes and loping strides. This police escort is a first. Still, they've let him come here, so it can't be serious.

Pandu starts talking, fat face bobbing from side to side, one arm swinging about. His blue pants stay fastened tight below that belly and his shirt is missing a button. Deepu had "aggressively touched" a teenage girl at the nearby community park. The girl and her friends had called the cops on him. His supervisor had wanted to lock the boy up. But he had intervened out of pity.

He whacks Deepu's back with a meaty palm. "Same age as my son," he says, raising his nasal tones like he's giving a speech to the four-five people wandering about the aisles.

When Pandu stops to spit his gum into the trash can, I look again at Deepu, who has edged into the corner shadows—away from us and the mock-filled eyes of our customers. A buzzing fly has settled on the cut lip, where the blood is still not dry. I want him to deny the accusation, hit the man back, swat the insect away, do or say something, anything, that I can then put a stop to. He remains rocklike.

The police officer starts on me next. Tells me I need to teach the boy to stick with our kind, make him understand that touching girls like that is wrong, make him do an honest day's work. He wrinkles his nose as if his white-man shit doesn't smell like ours. When he slaps Deepu's back again on his way out, I feel the sting on mine. His unsaid parting thought echoes in my ears: "You can wash coal as much as you like; it will never turn white."

Once Pandu has turned the corner, I tell the gawking motherfuckers pretending to browse to get lost if they don't want their teeth handed to them.

146

They mutter and laugh till I casually lift my Glock 19 semi-automatic from under the counter and place it on top. They leave their shopping baskets and disperse quickly.

Turning the Closed sign to the front, I lock the entrance. Then, I grab Deepu's neck and throw him down. My kicks land on his shoulders. He knows to turn his face away. He crouches, bracing for more. Finally, I lean against the counter and slide down, taking in a gasp of cool air. Slowly, he moves over to squat at the far end, near the ice-cream freezers. For all the world, we might just be a father and son sitting in easy companionship.

A little black girl stares at us with large shiny eyes from the other side of the glass door, fidgeting with the hem of her pink and purple dress. Thick smoke and spicy meat odors drift from the Bangladeshi restaurant next door, filling our nostrils, making our stomachs rumble and our eyes water. In that silence, I recall my mother's usual yelling, crying, and cursing when I used to come home drunk at Deepu's age. Deepu has never known a woman who cared as much about him.

Seeing how he's shifting uneasily every few moments, I say, quieter than I want to: "Next time, don't come here. Let them lock you up, beat you up. What did you think, touching that girl? That she would go with you?"

He stares ahead and it angers me more that his small ears, hooked nose, and jutting chin are so like mine.

Curse his slut mother for leaving when he was only two months old. In those early, rough days in the city, she wept every night while I struggled to find ways to make money. All these years, I, alone, have carried him, feeling the constant weight of his bones bearing down on me.

The first time he disappeared, I thought I'd lost him forever. During the 2016 police officer shootings, I'd been loading newspaper trucks with the *Dallas Morning News*. When they shut the city down, I dropped everything and ran for him. He wasn't even a teenager then. Couldn't find him for hours.

People said he was gone. A fist of pain had squeezed my chest as I had roamed the curfewed streets. The next day, he had shown up as if nothing had happened.

After that, I never look for him when he disappears. That fist inside me has hardened to stone.

I get up and put the Glock 19 back. "Go to *Guddi Dolls* if you want it so bad."

At last, he speaks, voice guttural and harsh: "Pay for it like you, you pathetic fucker?"

He may resemble me, yet how is he my blood? I walk over and kick him again.

Losing balance, he topples and rolls himself into a ball. I step away,

147

shaking my head.

A scream spins me around. He's swaying in front of the door, knees buckling, hands clutching his head. That unnatural sound from his wide-open mouth makes my insides ache.

The girl, watching all the while through the glass, bursts into tears and runs off.

Opening the door, I push him out. Then, I lock it and walk away.

* * *

Amit and I arrive at *Guddi Dolls* after midnight and two half-empty bottles of Teacher's. Ramiya's sitting on the pink couch with a girl pressing her feet. She looks us over and says, "You've got your drink. I suppose you're hungry now."

Behind her, past the flimsy curtain, we glimpse humping backs and bare limbs. Some regulars pay just for the live shows. For most others, privacy is an unaffordable extra.

Amit drops beside her, takes her hand, kisses it. "Ramiya," he slobbers, "You know my *dil* and *jaan* are yours forever. I cannot even look at another. Not one of your dolls here can match up to you."

She slaps his face away, laughing, "Ja, you filthy cur. You just want a free ride."

I pay for both of us. She calls out a couple of girls. Ramiya keeps a clean house. I've been coming many years and never had cause to complain. But it seems the girls keep getting younger. Or I'm getting older. No matter. A man has an itch, he needs to scratch it. No need to go grabbing what is not on sale or freely offered. That boy deserved what came to him.

Ramiya points to the scrawny one and says to me, "She's new—fresh from Vittalnagar. Thought an experienced man like you best to break her in."

I know what that means. We go to the only room with a door. No one is allowed here other than girls who need to rest. New ones like this one often do, especially when I'm done with them. More so if they try to fight. This one doesn't—crumpling into a bloody, naked heap in minutes. "Look at me, Vittalnagar," I pull her head up by her hair. No facial marks, which is a relief as that puts Ramiya in a horn-tossing mood.

* * *

Back at the store, Deepu hasn't returned yet again. A smoggy grey dawn is trying to smother the pitch-dark night. I lie down in the back room to rest. But that old stone-fist begins grinding heavily inside me, its jagged edges ripping me apart.

Then I know I'm being watched. "Deepu?" I whisper.

He breathes out and a half-sob escapes. I close my eyes to his pain, which drips like hot wax from a burning candle. A few minutes pass and I am drawn into that familiar, welcome heaviness before sleep descends. When a cold grasp tightens around my throat, I gasp for air. His weight bears down on me, pinning me to the mattress. I drown in my son's tears as they rain down like stinging acid.

They will likely say I was killed by some petty thug who came to rob the store. They'll look for Deepu and find him, eventually, jugging and jawing in a parking lot south of LBJ Freeway, off Skillman Street. Out where the buses don't run. He'll do that half-smile of his on hearing that his old man is dead and being told to go back where he came from. "I'm from here," he'll laugh at the night sky, "Texas born and bred, just like all y'all."

Laxman Sir in America

Khem K. Aryal

On entering the two-bedroom apartment at Emerald Pointe in East Memphis, Laxman Acharya felt let down for a second or two. Mira wore a pair of jeans and an elbow-sleeved maroon top instead of the sari that he had in mind when he called her before leaving the Amazon fulfillment center, where he worked. Their two sons had on "I Love USA" t-shirts—"love" marked by a heart-shaped US flag—over six-dollar trousers bought at Walmart.

"You want water? Something?" Mira asked him, and turned to the brothers, who kept crashing their Hot Wheels cars together. "Pack them up, boys."

Laxman sat on a floral couch, his palms pressed between his thighs. He didn't mean to gawk, but his eyes followed Mira's petite figure as she walked to the kitchen. In a sari she looked much taller. And much more decent. She would be "Mira Miss." Just like he would be "Laxman Sir" in his ironed cotton trousers and bleached white shirt.

"We are ready," said Mira, handing him a glass of water. "Where are we going?"

Laxman emptied the glass slowly, as if it were a chore. "Where?" he said in his usual monotone, grinning. "Can you wear a sari?"

"Who?" Mira as visibly confused. "Me?"

She had been embarrassed, as had been Laxman, when she first wore jeans, even though they'd been mentally prepared for this change in America. She'd been brought up in a Brahmin family in a village, and after her marriage she mostly wore a sari, occasionally switching to a kurtha-salwar, as was expected of a decent woman in the family. When she started teaching at a private school in Kathmandu, and thus became Mira Miss, there were no other ways she would dress up. Laxman himself had never worn jeans in Nepal. He had been a teacher, a Nepali teacher at that, with a degree in Sanskrit. Ditching his creased trousers and white dress shirts had not been easy for him. But that was history, now.

Why would he want her to wear a sari suddenly? Mira asked, the empty glass in her hand. "Is there a Nepali gathering?" She complained he should have told her in advance if there was one; wearing a sari wasn't like slipping into a pair of jeans. "Are you serious?" she asked. "You look secretive today."

"It's okay, just saying," said Laxman, walking past the younger boy, who acknowledged his presence by saying he'd already done his homework.

In the bedroom, he put on a pair of cotton trousers and a white dress shirt that had been left unused since last Dashain, when the family attended a gathering at a university hall where Nepali students had organized an event to celebrate the biggest festival. He tucked the shirt into the trousers, and stood in front of a five-dollar Walmart mirror. This old avatar of himself made Laxman miss his teaching days desperately.

When he walked back into the living room, Mira stepped back in disbelief. "Are you serious?" she asked. "You really want me to wear a sari? Give me ten minutes."

He insisted she was okay. This was nothing special.

"I don't understand you," said Mira, herding the boys out.

Laxman smoothed the shirtsleeves as they walked to the car.

"But I keep telling you," Mira said, "you look much better in those clothes."

"Do we have a party, Baba?" asked the older boy, who was nine.

"No," Laxman replied, and he chortled at his own predicament. He wore clothes like these every day in Kathmandu, not only when he went to teach but even when he went to Baneshwor Chowk to stroll, to scan through the newspapers that the vendors spread on the pavement, to talk about politics with whoever happened to be ready for it, and to disparage the left parties that never tired of staging protests. Putting on a finely creased shirt, cotton trousers, and black leather shoes didn't require an occasion back then. It was who he had been, back in his country, before his wife won a diversity lottery visa and they began to pursue the American dream.

"Where are we even going?" demanded Mira after a few minutes of the aimless drive. "This is crazy."

He had no answer. He released a barely audible murmur, to the effect that there was no particular place he wanted to take them. It was as if he were trying to keep his family in suspense, in anticipation of a surprise reward. The whole time, though, he kept telling himself that he was not just wearing those clothes; he was "Laxman Sir," a teacher.

No one had called him "Laxman Sir" in America, except some Nepalis, and that didn't count. (They called even a bus driver "guru-ji" back in Nepal.) Why would any American call him "Laxman Sir?" He'd come to America as a lottery winner, and he could have been any of those DV-wallahs who had neither a present nor a future in Nepal. When his family had landed in St. Louis two years before, he was a nobody, let alone a teacher, and he had been forced to begin his American life as a dishwasher at a restaurant called House of India. (He'd also been offered work at Everest Café and Bar, but the thought of washing dishes at the Nepali restaurant had petrified him. How could Laxman Sir wash dishes at a restaurant in the first place? What would his colleagues back home think?) It had been particularly hard for him to find a better job because of his poor English. Back in his early days, he'd regarded English as the "cow-eating" language, like everyone else in his circle. He was a holy pundit's son.

Who would have thought that one day he'd come to America? The first three months had been the worst in his life. He'd told Mira every day that

153

he wanted to return to Nepal. He was ready to spend the rest of his life as a schoolteacher, while also doing politics at his level, instead of living such an insult in America. But Mira Miss had found that wearing jeans and a top was much more comfortable than whatever she wore back home. There were no relatives for her to serve, no curmudgeonly in-laws to take care of, no constant flow of villagers coming for a stay as they visited Kathmandu to cure their chronic gastritis.

More importantly, there were their sons. They had already picked up the new language, and they loved their "I Love USA" t-shirts. Their happiness trumped everything. Laxman Sir had swallowed his pride and smoothed his jeans. When his English had improved, he'd moved to Memphis to join the Amazon fulfillment center as a picker.

How would he have any idea back then that his boss at the Amazon, a process assistant, would call him "Laxman Sir?"

Laxman's ears had burned suddenly, and he'd looked at the young man in his early twenties in amazement. It was true that he had called him "Lax-man Sir"—but still it was "Laxman Sir." He was a teacher. Everyone who knew him in Nepal called him "Laxman Sir." That's what it meant to be a teacher.

"My boss called me Laxman Sir today," he revealed to his wife, without turning to her.

Mira turned to him, her right leg dashed forward, and waited for him to explain.

"Yeah, yeah," Laxman had replied to the young man, without even worrying to comprehend the message. The term "Laxman Sir" had made every other bit of the conversation irrelevant, while he'd in fact been cautioned that he was too slow as a picker, and if he didn't improve in performance, he could get his first warning letter soon; two more letters and he'd be fired. The warning had seeped into his pores, finally reaching his mind, giving him an electric shock. That had made his longing for "Laxman Sir" even more intense.

"So?" asked Mira with a mixture of surprise, sympathy, and regret.

"Do you think he knows I was a teacher in Nepal?" he asked his wife during the dinner they ended up eating at India Palace, after making a trip to the pyramid on the bank of the Mississippi River.

"Why would he call you 'Laxman Sir,' otherwise?" said Mira. No wonder she liked his "Laxman Sir" avatar.

"How are you, sir?" the younger boy, who seemed minding only his business at the table, asked his brother and giggled.

154

* * *

The following day, Laxman wore a similar ironed shirt and cotton trousers to go to work. Mira laughed, reminding him that he was no more Laxman Sir. "Thank your boss or whoever it is and continue wearing your jeans!" she said as a practical woman. But she also added that he finally looked like somebody going to a proper office.

What was the point of coming to America if he had to degrade himself into being a third-class laborer? Laxman thought on his way to work. Had he stayed back, he'd secure a pension in the next few years, and that would allow him to live the rest of his life doing nothing but politics in his district. He could one day stand for election, and become a lawmaker. Why not? He had connections; he had already gotten a hold on the village party. The communists were failing—they had undermined the Sanatana heritage of the country; they had fallen prey to foreign powers and Christian missionaries—and so the conservatives were sure to get back into power.

Wasn't that what they said in America, too? President Trump was great. It was great that many other countries seemed to follow conservative ideas. What was that thing—men marrying men? Women marrying women? Those so-called liberals were going too far. Anyway, he'd already become somebody back in his country. His coming to America and working at Amazon didn't mean that he had to dress up like a village goon in those faded jeans.

During the stand-up meeting that morning, he stood close to the process assistant. This young man had well-carved arms, and his long blonde hair was neatly cropped around his neck. He spoke with extraordinary inflection, making it musical to hear but hard for Laxman to understand. He instructed his associates with confidence, no matter how old and senior-looking those associates were.

"Hands up!" yelled the young man, whose name was Leonard White.

Laxman spread his legs wide and raised his hands, touching them in the Namaste pose, his version of a jumping jack. The white shirt tucked into his trousers came loose. When Leonard instructed the next move, Laxman was fighting the shirt that would not stay tucked.

"Lex!" yelled Leonard. "Are you okay?"

Lex! Who's Lex? What Lex? There's no Lex! Laxman had revolting thoughts.

"Stretch!" instructed Leonard.

He was not Lex, Laxman told himself. He was Laxman Sir. What did those people think of themselves? You introduce yourself as Laxman, and they instantly call you Lax, or Lex. "Can I call you Lex?" Leonard had asked him the first day they had met, and he'd said, "Yeah, yeah!" But that didn't feel quite right, now. Didn't he call him "Laxman Sir" only yesterday? You

155

call somebody "Laxman Sir" today and "Lex" tomorrow? That was not only insulting but also confusing.

During the brief lunch break, they happened to line up together for coffee.

"I like your shirt," said Leonard.

"I like your t-shirt," Laxman responded. Then he realized it made no sense. Leonard had been wearing the same t-shirt since they'd first met, or at least that was how Laxman felt about it, and there was nothing special about the t-shirt. "I wore this shirt when I went to teach," he added quickly, as if to amend his impulsive compliment.

"You taught?" Leonard was amazed. "Were you a teacher?"

"Yeah, yeah," said Laxman proudly, and grinned widely.

"That is impressive," said Leonard with his usual inflection.

Laxman sighed, looking away. He was not just a picker at the Amazon fulfillment center. He was a teacher first, Laxman Sir. It felt good that the young man was impressed.

"I always wanted to be a teacher," said Leonard. "I like helping people."

As they sat with their food, Leonard asked, "Why did you come to America?"

Laxman's heart was filled with pride. Yes, why did he come to America? As a DV winner, at that? He felt like hugging Leonard.

He didn't have to come to America.

Laxman spent the next couple of days rejoicing at the question "Why did you come to America?" and looking for an opportunity to share with somebody, not just his wife, what he'd been asked by his boss. When the Nepali families met over potluck, every one of them boasted of their success in securing a U.S. visa. They seemed to believe that one's worth in life was measured by their ability to enter the U.S. But for him Nepal was a superior place. Why did he come to America?

* * *

A few days later, the family attended a birthday party of an eleven-year-old boy whose parents had moved to the States when the father, a government official, faced a corruption charge over the tender of fertilizer. Laxman listened quietly as the men boasted of the hours they managed to accumulate a week, the dollars they made and the businesses they built, drinking Franzia, Heineken, Johnnie Walker. One Ramesh Bhatta had just bought a gas station on Elvis Presley Boulevard. Shankardev had gotten a new job at a software company. Dipendra was buying a new hybrid SUV. The women, busy wrapping chicken momos on the kitchen floor, chewed over jewelry they wanted brought from Nepal the next time somebody they could ask traveled to the country. At his first chance to speak, Laxman, who wouldn't drink alcohol, of course, blurted out, "I have a boss who asked me the other day why I came to America."

It seemed that his slow, monotone statement took a while to reach the audience and register in their consciousness. But when it did, they all crowed dismissively, "He asked you why you came to America?"

Of course he did! Why would he not?

Laxman felt defensive. After all, he was a well-respected teacher and a political man, and for him Nepal was not bad. He wasn't like the host, who had fled the county at the fear of being locked up; he was not even like Ramesh, who'd come to America via Mexico, spending a full six months on his way. Fine, he'd gotten a DV, but neither he nor his wife had had to apply for it in the first place. Laxman had no answer for those who were too complacent to understand.

"That stupid ass!" said one Govindaraj. "Fly him to Nepal for a week, ask him to labor for a dollar a day. Okay, five dollars."

Everyone laughed in unison.

"And say he falls sick," said another.

"And he needs to deal with government officials to get something done."

"And the so-called leaders."

"Will he eat mud when he doesn't find any work?"

Laxman had not bargained for this. It seemed the men hated everything about the country they'd left behind. They hated the leaders, they hated the lack of opportunities, they hated the hardship in the villages, they hated the traffic in Kathmandu, they hated the government employees, they hated airport officials, they hated businesspeople. They hated everything.

"That stupid ass!" Ramesh groaned and swigged his wine. "Why come to America?"

"These people don't know anything," said Dipendra, who claimed to have been forced to flee Nepal because of the Maoist rebellion.

"Not only that, friends," joined the host. "This is racist. How can he ask why we come here?"

"Yes, racist," said Shyam Prasad, who called himself a journalist because he used to be a newspaper reporter in Nepal. "Is he white?"

Laxman had not thought about that. "He asked me with good intentions," he said of Leonard White.

"Good intentions!" mimicked the host. "How can one ask it with good intentions? Is it only their country? Were they not immigrants, too, not so long ago? He's a racist pig."

"Xenophobe," said Shyam Prasad.

157

"He must be a Trumpist," said Dipendra and laughed proudly, baring his teeth as he got an overwhelming response.

Laxman felt that he'd been manipulated. He didn't mean to jeopardize the young man's reputation. He simply wanted to assert that he had no business coming to America—to himself, more than to anybody else. He was a teacher, a well-respected teacher, everyone's Laxman Sir, and he wanted an affirmation, if possible, that he had no reason to come to America as a DV winner to work at Amazon as a picker.

"But Laxman-ji supports Trump," said Ramesh. "Don't you?"

Suddenly Laxman suspected that he was trapped with liberals, no matter what their political affiliations back in Nepal.

"Do you support his wall, Laxman-ji?" Ramesh pushed further, before Laxman could formulate his response.

Laxman lacked the time and necessary knowledge to engage in politics in America. He had, however, taken it for granted as a conservative party worker back in Nepal that supporting the Republican Party would be the most natural thing for him to do. He saw value in religion. He still believed that the caste system had a point. It embarrassed him when the liberals talked about gay marriages, women's rights, undocumented immigrants, and this and that. *Just like the communists in Nepal*, he'd say to himself of the liberals. Wouldn't a conservative Nepali Congress Party member who came to America naturally become a Republican ally?

"I see nothing wrong with the wall, sir," he replied. "Don't we want a strong border between Nepal and India?"

"But this is America," roared the crowd.

He'd considered it safe to express his support for the wall because it was the liberals, those communists, who wanted border walls between Nepal and India. But look! He reminded himself of the contradictions of the left. He'd debated them in Kathmandu and he'd debated them in his village many times. They said one thing and did another. They said they fought for the people, and amassed wealth for themselves. They instigated young people to tear down schools in the name of revolution, and sent their children to Nainital and America to study.

"Laxman-ji is already in America," Govindaraj said. "It won't bother him a bit even if Trump cancels the DV." He raised his glass. "Ki Kaso ho sathi ho?" *Am I wrong, friends?*

Laxman knelt, as if preparing for serious business. "Teso hoina, sir; teso hoina!" he said, raising a hand. *That's not the point!* "I won't mind if he sends me back."

"Ohohoho!" went their collective dismissal.

"Oi, Mira Bhauju, listen!" Dipendra yelled to Laxman's wife, who was busy in the kitchen with the other women. "Listen, Laxman Sir won't mind Trump sending him back to Nepal. Are you ready to return?"

"Ohohoho!" the women responded in disbelief.

"Are you ready?" more of the men asked.

"Send your brother, if he wants to go back," said Mira, wrapping momos, and everyone laughed like it was a good joke.

Nothing could be more ridiculous than claiming that one wouldn't mind returning to Nepal in the current environment. People were dying to come to America, spending tens of thousands of dollars and risking their lives as they took illegal routes to the Mexican border via Guatemala.

"America is not everything," declared Laxman, and began to fold his shirtsleeves.

"America is everything," resisted Shyam Prasad.

The debate quickly morphed into a shower of questions. If you were so happy in Nepal, why did you come to America? If you believed so much you had a more dignified life in Nepal, why did you come to America? If you trusted the leaders so much, why did you come to America? If you valued your heritage so much, why did you come to America? If you believed so much your kids would do fantastic in Nepal, why did you come to America? If you loved Nepal so much, why did you come to America? Why did you come to America? Why did you come to America?

"I'm not asking anyone to go back, sir!" Laxman bleated once the host played mediator, and he remained quiet for the rest of the rowdy evening.

* * *

Leonard White had not called him "Laxman Sir" again, not even "Sir," but only "Lex." Was anything going to trigger the young man to call Lex "Laxman Sir" again? Did Leonard really respect him so much as to call him "Laxman Sir?"

The next time he had a chance to speak with Leonard White, Laxman said without being prompted that he didn't disagree with everything Trump said.

"What?" asked Leonard.

Laxman wanted to make sure that Leonard knew Laxman Sir was aware of politics. If asked, he'd happily talk about his party affiliation in Nepal. "I mean President Trump," he said. "Like he wants to build the wall."

"What? You support that moron?" asked Leonard.

"Yeah, yeah!"

"He calls immigrants drug dealers and rapists. Are you sure, sir?"

Laxman suddenly felt betrayed. This young man named Leonard White wasn't only named White. He *was* white. So white. How could he not support

Trump? he wondered.

Everything in America seemed complicated. He'd heard the news that the president had called immigrants drug dealers and rapists, but he'd never thought he could be said to be one of them. First, he was not from Latin America, and second, he'd entered America legally. There was no way he could be one of those whom the president disparaged.

"You were a teacher, right?" asked Leonard.

"Yeah," said Laxman. "I'm thinking of returning to Nepal."

"I can see that this work doesn't suit you, Lex," said Leonard.

The following day, Laxman got his first warning letter. Two more cases of unmet targets and he'd be fired.

Whatever, he thought, and waited impatiently for the sun to go down. As soon as he believed that the people in Kathmandu must have gotten up, he dialed one of his colleagues, walking around the apartment complex.

"Oho, sir, you remembered us from America?" said the friend as Laxman announced himself on the phone.

Laxman didn't have the enthusiasm to match his friend's. "I always remember you, Dhanraj Sir," he said flatly.

"We miss you here, sir," said the friend. "We're often short of a member for *dahalmara*."

Dahalmara! The collect-the-tens card game that they played on weekends, in the sun on the rooftop. What fun it was! *What's here in America? Work for hours every day, come home and sleep, go work for them, pay your bills, and at the end you have nothing. No friends, no society, no fun. Nobody recognizes you; there's no dignity.*

"I miss dahalmara," he said, and waited. "I may return," he announced. "Tell Head Sir."

"Come back, sir, come! We should play dahalmara again. We had a lot of fun together.

"Nepal is Nepal, Laxman Sir," Dhanraj added after a silence. "What's there in America? Ghanta hanne ta ho hami jastale!" *People like us only get to work by the hour!* "A person like you shouldn't have fled to America in the first place."

When they hung up, Laxman felt he'd taken a heavy load off his chest. He was lucky there still was a space for him in Nepal. Even if he'd left his country, his country had not left him. He'd earned colleagues who waited eagerly to welcome him back at any moment.

Laxman spent the next couple of days calling many of his colleagues he believed could encourage him to return to Nepal. Some of them said they were happy he had not forgotten the country. Some said he was making the right decision—there was not much in America for a person like him; he was

160

doing well in Nepal already. Others said they doubted he'd ever return, but that it was the right decision. All of them said they would have fun together when he returned.

Despite his sudden longing to play dahalmara, on top of the craving to be "Laxman Sir," it didn't take him long to question why he'd told so many people in Nepal that he was returning. He knew none of them believed him, no matter how they'd responded. By the end of the week, he decided to not even talk to his wife about returning. He had not been able to muster the courage so far, and there was hardly any chance that he'd be able to do it now. He felt lost.

*　*　*

That Friday, he was watching the news on CNN, not so much for the news but for distraction, when his wife hollered from the kitchen. "Do you hear me?" she said. "Jannavi called me this morning."

He'd forgotten who Jannavi was. His wife called him "buddhu," for having forgotten her friend so soon, then he recalled. Oh, yes, she was Dhanraj's wife, the Dhanraj he'd called a few days before and who'd been enthusiastic about playing dahalmara together again.

"So?" he asked. "Dhanraj wants me to return to Nepal," he said before she replied.

She didn't acknowledge the sharing. Instead she explained that her friend was asking if they could send them some money. Their kids' school fees were insanely expensive, and so was the rent in Kathmandu; her husband had had a surgery recently, and so they wanted some help, she explained.

"Had a surgery?" said Laxman. "He didn't tell me anything when we spoke a few days ago."

"Wish we could help them come to America," continued Mira. "They've been applying for a DV forever, no luck yet."

Laxman focused on the television. Wait! What did the president say? He flicked the television off and turned on his Dell. There he found, as he'd suspected, that even Nepali sites carried with emphasis the news that the president of the United States had said that the ones who went to America on the diversity visa were dimwitted people, worthy of trash cans. No country would send America great people through the DV lottery, and so the scheme needed to go away, said the orange-haired man.

Some online portals rejoiced at his claim. They said the DV-wallahs would now be taught what it meant to ditch their country. They called them "bhagaudas," *runaways*, and wished them good luck in the new America that treated them like trash.

161

"Do you hear me?" Mira asked, joining him. "You know how hard it is to survive on a teacher's salary in Kathmandu. Can't we lend them $1,000 for a few months? He is an honest man, your friend. They'll pay us back."

"Have you read the news?" Laxman asked in reply.

They stared at the screen together for a long time. "Who cares?" Mira broke the silence. "Is he the one who brought us here? We came here by winning a lottery. It's our luck! My luck!"

"I never applied for a DV lottery," Laxman said, defeated.

"I knew you'd never do it," his wife said. "That's why I applied. Think how we could be asking a friend for help, like Jannavi, to send our sons to school if I hadn't applied for a DV."

He wanted to say he was happier in Nepal. He was a government teacher. He lived with dignity. He had connections. He understood politics. He wished she had not brought their friend into their debate; everyone has their own obligations. "I still have the job in Nepal," he ended up saying.

Mira said he was free to return if he wanted. She was able to take care of her two sons. "For the love of your job," she mocked him, "that pays you 15,000 rupees a month."

*   *   *

Laxman told Leonard the following Monday that he used to earn an equivalent of $150 a month.

"Are you kidding me?" Leonard sounded like he was singing a funny song.

"Life is hard in Nepal," said Laxman, picking an item. "It's expensive to send kids to school. A lot of corruption."

"I see!" said Leonard. He became pensive for a few seconds, and said he was sorry for what his president had said about immigrants. "I apologize for him, Lex," he said. "He called immigrants animals! I mean, give me a *break*."

Laxman didn't like Leonard White. Didn't he just tell him that as a teacher he earned $150 a month back in Nepal?

That evening, he decided not to check on the Nepali news about the new information that the orange-haired man had called people like Laxman animals. What was the point of verifying the information? His family was already in America; his sons loved the "I Love USA" t-shirts, and now they were already making their wish lists for Christmas. "And Dhanraj Sir needs my help," he murmured to himself. "How much money was she asking for?" he asked Mira.

The following morning, he wore his jeans and t-shirt. It felt good to be able to keep up with the rest of the team members during the stand-up

162

meeting—stretching and squatting and jumping—especially with the process assistant, Leonard White. *Such a kind-hearted man!* Laxman thought. Once he caught the tenor of the meeting, he thought about sending money from Walmart to his friend on his way home.

He'd call Dhanraj Sir afterward. He'd ask him about dahalmara, too.

Writing the Immigrant Southern in the *New* New South

Soniah Kamal

Southern literary giant Ernest Gaines was born in 1933 in pre–Civil Rights Louisiana. There was no high school for him to attend there and, at the time, in the segregated South, few public libraries were available to African Americans outside of major cities. In 1948, Gaines would leave for California in order to attend high school, and he would also go to the library for the first time. In California, Gaines would later publish his first two stories and go on to receive a Wallace Stegner Writing Fellowship and also a Guggenheim. That fifteen-year-old boy who couldn't attend a library in Louisiana had found his literary feet and success in California, and yet he said, "My physical body had gone west to California but my soul stayed [in Louisiana]." Gaines would return to Louisiana in 1981 and would remain there until his death in 2019.

And so in Gaines we find a nod to the world of setting beyond mere place. Instead we see a setting divided into physical geography and emotional geography. Can one be in two places at the same time? As writers we know that we can be in a million places simultaneously and that it is in the coalescing and colliding of all these places within us that our unique stories are birthed. I doubt many writers decide their stories' location(s) with a throw of a dart at a map. Even fictitious locations are based in some reality, be it Gaines's Bayonne, William Faulkner's Yoknapatawpha County, R. K. Narayan's Malgudi, or in my novel *Unmarriageable*, Dilipabad, which is modeled on many small towns in Pakistan. All of Gaines's eight novels are set in Louisiana. Did he try to write about California? If yes, why? And if not, why not? What is it about certain locations that captures the thematic heart of a writer's imagination?

But perhaps more vital than physical location are a writer's emotional coordinates. When I say "Paris, Karachi, New York, San Juan, Mogadishu, Warsaw, London, Beijing, Istanbul, Damascus, Gainesville," surely all of you have an emotional reaction, even if it is apathy. When I say "the American South," what comes to your mind? For me it's kudzu, which I noticed for the first time as my family drove into Georgia, a U-Haul attached to the back of our car. It was raining hard, and the gleaming Georgia freeway was edged with trees that had walls of vine growing around their trunks. It looked like something out of "Sleeping Beauty." I thought it was beautiful. I did not see it in suburbia, and it would be months before I'd ask a neighbor, who was into gardening, if he knew what that vine could be. Kudzu, he said. He wasn't sure how to pronounce it. But, he added, it's not native to Georgia. I looked up the pronunciation online: *kud-zoo*. According to online sources, "Kudzu is native to Japan. It came to the U.S. in 1876 as an ornamental and a forage crop plant. Southern farmers planted kudzu to reduce soil erosion. Kudzu grows at an incredible speed. It is edible. Leaves, flowers, roots, everything except the vines."

I told my neighbor all this. He shrugged. Indifferent, really, though he did say he was not interested in eating that stuff.

* * *

How many years does it take for a place to become home? How many years should it take? What is so important about having a home, feeling at home, being at home? Is home just an equation of time plus an address? While readers may well seek stories in order to search for answers to these questions, as writers we know that sometimes, oftentimes, there are no answers, there are just stories about lives lived in places and stories about hearts yearning for elsewhere.

One definition of *immigrant* is "a person who comes to live permanently in a foreign country." When does the country stop being foreign? Does the foreigner ever see himself as native? Does your self-definition count more than how someone else may define you? Did Ernest Gaines see himself as a foreigner, a stranger, in California? What impact may Gaines's years in California have had on the people he met there? On his writing? Even if his heart was in Louisiana, his body was yet walking and talking through California, buying California-grown groceries to prepare Southern meals— or, to be more specific, because as writers we know specificity is everything— the Southern meals of Louisiana. In food, at least, his physical and emotional selves would have met.

I have been living in Georgia for years and years, and my mother's Kashmiri dish of mustard greens now uses Georgia-grown collard greens; my father's favorite dish of daal chawal, yellow lentils and rice, is a creamy substitute for black-eyed peas and rice; cornbread is simply makki ki roti, a flat round bread made of corn; and sweet potatoes so happily turn into aloo tikkis, meaning potato cutlets. What is foreign for one is home for another, and when the two combine, it turns out it's just a hot nourishing meal on the table, and this is writing the immigrant Southern in the New South.

The South does not know how very responsible I hold it for my marriage. During the spring break of my junior year of college in D.C., I visit an aunt living in Marietta, Georgia, where a proposal is foisted upon me. I'm told a family is driving in from Florida to take a look at me to see if I'm a suitable girl for their boy, and this is how I find out that Florida and Georgia are neighboring states. The family arrives with a bag full of Florida-grown oranges, and suddenly I'm on a quest to find Georgia-grown peaches, but it is 1995 and, despite all the roads named Peachtree, not a peach tree or a peach is in sight. The boy likes the look of me and so do his parents (as a girl, no one cares whether I like the look of them). The next day he takes me out to lunch, where, in a desperate bid to banish him, I rely on a statement Pakistani girls are too often told, which is "do whatever you want after marriage," and announce that my dream in life is to become a stripper. It works. He flees. I will go on to administer the "stripper test" to subsequent suitors. One man will finally pass and I will marry him. So it is that my marriage story begins in Florida and Georgia, and this is my first personal instance of the immigrant Southern in the New South.

*　*　*

One of my favorite short stories, "Everyday Use," is by Alice Walker, whose Pulitzer Prize-winning novel *The Color Purple* is set in Georgia. Alice Walker is an American author. Alice Walker is a Southern author. Alice Walker is an author from Georgia. The story "Everyday Use" is set in the rural Deep South. It is about an heirloom quilt and whether Mama will give that quilt to her quiet daughter Maggie, who has never left home and plans to one day use the quilt to keep herself warm, or to daughter Dee, who has long left home and renamed herself Wangaro and is back for a visit with her boyfriend, who greets them with "Asalamalakim"; Dee-Wangaro wants the quilt in order to hang it on her wall.

The first time I read this story, I put my hand over my heart. "Everyday Use" was about home and family and distances and legacy and memory and commemoration. I was "Everyday Use" and "Everyday Use" was me. Alice Walker is an American author. She is a Southern author. An author from Georgia. All of that matters. None of that matters. She was from everywhere and nowhere, which is not true, because we are all from somewhere. She was story and she was light and life and enlightenment. And so I learn: There is no single story, but there are stories that can show us we are all one.

Alice Walker led me to Zora Neale Hurston and Walker's essay "In Search of Zora Neale Hurston." Zora Neale Hurston was born in 1891 in Eatonville, Florida, and would die in a welfare home in Fort Pierce, Florida, with no funds for a funeral. Hurston was a leading writer of the Harlem Renaissance in New York as well as of the South, meaning she'd covered lots of ground and territory and came and went and had a fluid identity with physical and emotional geography. The church people in Hurston's hometown thought she was "pretty loose." I have a thing for fellow women labeled "pretty loose." The good folk of my hometown thought I was pretty loose too and probably still do, and I still don't give a screw.

Hurston died in obscurity until Alice Walker, in a quest to find Hurston's unmarked grave, walked across snake-infested fields in search of it, found it, installed a tombstone, and wrote an essay about it. Perhaps I was inspired by

168

Walker's journey, but years later, I would finally go in search of Pakistani icon Saadat Hasan Manto's home in Lahore, Pakistan. I had an idea of the general vicinity, but cities change and memories fade, and it was after hours of driving up and down roads one gray Sunday morning that I would find his home by sheer fluke, one of those coincidences that if you put into fiction people will simply not believe. I would find a semicircle of flats and beside double doors a blue nameplate: *Saadat Hasan Manto / Short Story Writer / 1912–1955*. Like Ernest Gaines, whose Southern roots informed his whole life, one could safely say that Manto was a writer split into two by the 1947 partition of the Subcontinent into Pakistan and India, his body in Lahore, Pakistan, but his heart beating in Bombay, India. Manto would die of a broken heart. Perhaps he considered himself homeless. But here was his home, and I entered.

Two years later, I would revisit Manto's home. Pakistan not being up there on preservation of cultural heritage, his home had recently been sold to a cell phone company, but the blue nameplate was still there. I would beseech the company employees to request the owner never take it down. I stressed the importance of Manto, of home, of history, of memory, of commemoration. They assured me that the building could fall but the nameplate would remain. The next year, when I visited yet again, the nameplate was gone, and I remember instantly thinking of Alice Walker and Zora Neale Hurston and a grave that now had a tombstone. This is writing the immigrant Southern in the New South.

* * *

When I think of a film that teaches the most about the South, I do not think of *Driving Miss Daisy*, or *Steel Magnolias*, or *Fried Green Tomatoes at the Whistle Stop Café*. Instead, I think of *My Cousin Vinny*, that joyful farce about "no place like home," in which strangers come to town and are forever changed and neither is the town left the same. Perhaps I should have started out by asking what it even means to be *Southern* in the South? Many years ago, having newly arrived in Georgia and eager to find literary community, I volunteered at the inaugural Decatur Book Festival, where I attended the panel "What Does It Mean to Be a Southern Writer?" The panelists could not decide. Old South was slavery and pre-Civil War. New South was industrialization and post-Civil War, as well as Civil Rights. Magnolias came up, steel and otherwise; so did moonlight and moonshine and the shifting of place and legacy in a South between old and new. The discussion centered on a white South and a black South, their combined South; immigrants did not come up at all.

Writing and publishing came up and with it the indignant "*they* want to keep the South South" as panelists discussed the meaning of "Southern" for

New York publishers and how New York editors did not want fresh stories, but rather insisted on certain tales and tropes. I scribbled notes: *Old South, New South, South South, New York, expectations, stereotypes, clichés.*

A few years on, my literary journalism would have me reviewing books set in the South and interviewing the authors, and I would get a sense of the hackneyed: haints; ghosts; Southern hospitality; Prohibition; bootlegging; frilly debutantes and their frippery; drunks and naïve fools; rural kids who despite useless parents fend for themselves; a wise old woman or man; unhappy love stories involving gentleman callers with rogue souls and hearts of gold; black vs. white; getting along; not getting along; fearless Martin Luther King, Jr.; brave Rosa Parks; broken Zelda Fitzgerald; never-to-be-broken Scarlet O'Hara; mint juleps clutching aged pearls; bored young housewives drinking one too many in the afternoon as they said mean things about neighbors in roundabout ways; and "why don't you sit down and keep quiet, dear"—Blanche DuBois' perfume hanging over everything. But it wasn't until a few more years later, when one of my many literary agents would be trying to sell my debut novel, *An Isolated Incident*, to New York publishers and one of the rejections we got said, "Would a Pakistani family in the U.S. really be eating so much pizza?" that I not only got the "*they* want to keep the South South" but saw the connection between stereotypes, whether expected of a Southern writer or an immigrant writer.

That got me thinking of what might be expected of the Immigrant-Southern, the immigrant writer of the South, by which I mean all the clichés of the South combined with all the clichés of immigrant life, in my case a South Asian/Desi Diaspora/Pakistani/Muslim immigrant experience. What preset notions of immigrant angst, assimilation adventures, model minorities, generational culture clashes, fresh-off-the-boat tropes, mangos-monkeys-mystics-masalas, and other presumptions might I be expected to include in my work? Let alone publishing gatekeepers, even everyday neighborly encounters come with assumptions: "Where are you *really* from? Why is *your* English so good? But don't *you all* have arranged marriages?" I do not fit the narrative and—bless my heart—I refuse to squeeze into a preset shape. This too is writing the immigrant Southern in the New South.

It was at that panel that I first heard the term *New South* and I mistook it to mean a South that immigrants were making new and vibrant with their diversity and cultures, thinking that the New South was beyond black and white, that the New South was a place with room for everyone. I thought of it as the *New* New South. In Georgia you will find Americans who are originally from Mexico, Pakistan, Bangladesh, India, Ethiopia, Vietnam, South Korea, China, Syria, and more. In fact the city of Clarkston in DeKalb County, Georgia, is called "the most diverse square mile in America" and "the Ellis

170

Island of the South." A few years ago at an event celebrating Clarkston, I was invited to read a poem, "Face this Face," about how my face seems to fit the contours of so many countries. In the poem, I mention the white man in my local Starbucks who continued to greet with me a merry "Namaste" even after I told him I was not from India, and neither was I Hindu, and that if he was fond of greeting people who looked unlike him with something other than a "hi," then he needed to greet me with "aslamailaikum." He did, all of once, and then returned to Namaste. I started to call him "Starbucks Uncle," Uncle being the term in Pakistan one uses for elderly gentlemen, and otherwise. This too is writing the immigrant Southern in the *New* New South.

* * *

When California saw Louisiana transplant Ernest Gaines, who did it see? *Transplant* is an interesting world for a migrant who moves from one state to another state; did Gaines see himself as a "transplant," plucked from one soil, planted into another, surviving, thriving? When I look at the South, I see familiarity in old-school traditions in which good girls are not tomboys and the best good girls are demure and dainty and behave themselves and want little more from life than a husband, home, and children, and if they do want more it's only after a ring on their finger declares their duty done and that most important of labels won: *Mrs. Wife*.

* * *

However, when the South sees me, what and who does it see? The answer would probably depend on which South I was looking at, Old South, New South, *New* New South, a religious South, an irreligious South. I think of representation, gatekeepers, power, inclusion, neighborhoods, girls with hyphenated names like Sue-Ellen and Sarah-Beth, and identities that are hyphenated, like Southern-hyphen-American and Pakistani-hyphen-American and Pakistani-hyphen-Southern-hyphen-American. I think of that reading I attended where an elderly white woman with blue-tinged silver hair spoke up from the audience to tell the white novelist on tour whose novel was set in the South and who considered herself a Southerner that she was not Southern at all. Then the elderly woman turned to a black writer in the audience, whose husband was from Mexico, who had earlier shared that she was a decades-ago transplant from the North to the South and that her children were all born in the South. *No*, the elderly woman said firmly, they'd never qualify as Southern, it wasn't going to happen, never ever, poor dears.

* * *

Some instances of Southern hospitality when I moved to Georgia:

"Don't leave the perimeter after dark. They shoot people who look like you."

"I tried to become a member of this country club back in the sixties, but they had a no-Jews-allowed policy then. They wouldn't have let you in either."

"Go back where you came from. And take your kids with you too. We don't want the likes of you here."

* * *

But also:

The immigrant Southern in the *New* New South is your neighbor at dusk calling her children in an Indian accent, "Y'all need to come in now."

The immigrant Southern in the *New* New South is to be mesmerized by the character of Whitley in the TV show *A Different World*, not because of her Southern accent but because in her character I see so clearly Pakistan.

The immigrant Southern in the *New* New South is learning that the Atlanta suburb I live in was once just farmland and that to think back then that there would be a grocery store selling halal meat just down the road would have been as absurd a notion as walking on the moon must have once seemed.

The immigrant Southern in the *New* New South is being at Barnes and Noble, hearing the announcement that the African American Book Club is about to start its monthly meeting, hesitantly arriving at the table and foolishly informing the ladies gathered that you are not black, and their saying that they can see that and inviting you to sit down. You do sit down for the next several years.

The immigrant Southern in the *New* New South is your daughter craving BBQ, green beans, and biscuits, by which she means round soft pillowy buttery layered bread, even as your British-educated brain equates biscuits with cookies, which I would have with hot chai and she would have with iced tea.

Geography can come to you through joy. And sometimes, geography becomes home through grief. My four-month-old fetus, my baby, my child, named Khyber, was conceived here and died inside of me here and was miscarried into my hands here. Whatever life he lived was lived in Georgia, and if he is not of the South then what is he? There are no answers to these questions. Perhaps the questions are the answers themselves. Here is the email I received about the graveyard that houses him:

Friday, October 12, 2007, 6:28 p.m.: <*pnl@atlanta.com*> wrote:

Directions to Stone Mountain Cemetery: The cemetery is located in old town Stone Mountain at the corner of Ponce de Leon Avenue and James B. Rivers Drive. As you drive into the cemetery, take the road on your right. You will pass some Confederate soldier markers. Make the 2nd right, which will dead end into another small road. The plot where the babies are buried is the site on the right across the road in front of you.

Through this fetus/baby/child my heart is tied to Georgia forever, and this is writing the immigrant Southern in the *New* New South, the emotional story buried in me and the physical story buried in Georgia. (That a part of me is connected to Stone Mountain, a town known as the birthplace of the modern Ku Klux Klan, is a bad ill feeling, and this too is the immigrant Southern in the *New* New South.)

* * *

The immigrant Southern in the *New* New South is to go to a public library, where a fellow patron tells you and yours to get out of America; is to decide to become a citizen; is to go to that very same library to take a class on the citizenship test, in which one hundred questions will be taught, out of which ten random questions will be asked, out of which you have to get six correct or you will fail; is to realize this is worse than any driver's license test; is to pass the citizenship test; is to arrive at the Ceremonial Courthouse in downtown Atlanta; is to state the name of the country you are coming from with 150 new fellow citizens with whom you then recite the pledge of allegiance; is to receive your United States Citizenship Certificate; is to shake the judge's hand: "Welcome to America."

And sometimes *a place will claim you as its own*: to eight years later be invited, the first writer and novelist to deliver the keynote welcome address at the Atlanta Ceremonial Courthouse Citizenship Oath Ceremony; is to find yourself in that very same building in that very same room where you once sat waiting to receive your certificate; is to deliver your address to 150 new citizens; is to be asked to hand out the 150 Certificates of Citizenship and welcome citizens to their new home as you were once welcomed to the United States of America and the State of Georgia; is to shake each and every one of those 150 hands and look each new citizen in the eye: "Welcome to America. Welcome home."

To the immigrant Southern writing the *New* New South, to the immigrant writing America, to any writer anywhere writing a new world, the following questions are forever present: What does literature from somewhere even mean? Does it mean where the author was born, or brought up, or their

173

current domicile, or topic?

A decade-plus ago, when my husband's job relocated our family to Georgia, I didn't know much about this state I was going to be calling home. Perhaps the only literary fact I knew about Georgia was that it was where Margaret Mitchell wrote her opus *Gone with the Wind*. I had read *Gone with the Wind* one teenage summer when I set out to read other books whose lengths made me cringe, such as Alex Haley's *Roots*, Tolstoy's *Anna Karenina*, and Dickens's *Oliver Twist*—but read them I did. I had grouped these books together for sheer length, but that tween perspective aside, these novelists from these different countries and various cultures—American, Russian, British—had themes in common too: politics, slavery, economic welfare, emotional survival, serfdom, debtor's prison, and of course love. In other words, no matter the country or the culture these works were set in, their concerns mirrored my intellectual interest, and so this British story, this Russian story, this American story belonged to me; it became a Pakistani story.

The world is vast and when you get on a plane—or train, automobile, bicycle, ship, horse-drawn carriage—it magically shrinks. I was born in Karachi. When I was six months old, my parents moved us to England. When I was nine, we moved again, this time to Jeddah, Saudi Arabia, where we would live until my teenage years, at which time we returned to Pakistan. Now had I grown up in only England and Pakistan, the chances are that I would have only read the usual British classics and authors of whom, back in the day, the writer Enid Blyton was the most prolific, with more than five hundred books for children. In contemporary terms, imagine going to a bookstore and for the most part the only author on the shelves is J. K. Rowling. However, the school I attended in Jeddah was designated as International and, as such, the library housed not just books from British authors, but also Canadian ones, such as L. M. Montgomery's *Anne of Green Gables*; and Australian, such as Colleen McCullough's *The Thorn Birds*; and there was the *Diary of Anne Frank*; and there were also American authors.

*　*　*

Books by American authors were on shelf after shelf, and had I grown up only in America, I would have only read authors such as Judy Blume, and Marcia Martin who wrote the Donna Parker series, and Francine Pascal with the Sweet Valley High series, and Helen Wells with her tales of stewardess Vicki Barr and her nurse Cherry Ames. What my school's library may have lacked, schoolmates from all over the world—this international school's student body resembled a mini United Nations—brought with them, from

Japan tales of Momotarō the "Peach Boy"; and from Russia tales of the witch Baba Yaga; from the African continent tales of trickster Anansi, who could turn into a spider, and crocodiles that looked like rocks, and stories of the sun and origins of the earth; and from India the comics *Amar Chitra Katha*, based on tales from the Ramayana; and from Norway tales set in Valhalla and of Vikings. And though the following weren't in books but on tv, dramatized stories from the Quran, such as a spiderweb saving Prophet Muhammed's life, and an army of elephants bowing before the Kaaba in Mecca instead of charging to destroy it even as birds appeared overhead with stones to deter the assaulters.

This then was the world I grew up in, a world where no matter how terrible the day, stories and my school library were a sanctuary. However, despite this cornucopia of stories from everywhere, there was one kind of story missing, and those were stories written in English but set in Pakistan. As a consequence, I naturally started to remap or reorient as I read, and therefore scones turned into samosas, bonnets into dupattas, and locations such as Farbrook, New Jersey, where lived author Judy Blume's adolescent Margaret Simon from *Are You There God? It's Me, Margaret* into the city of Lahore and particularly the area of Gulberg where I seemed to be destined, as an immigrant kid, to spend every one of my summer vacations. And so there I was, with scones, bonnets, and anywhere and everywhere in the world equaling samosas, dupattas, and Lahore. Without realizing it, I had made the leap into recognizing the universalities in literature across cultures.

Because I could not find representation within the pages I was reading, I began to re-create my own representation. It was hardly a stretch for me then when, upon reading Jane Austen's *Pride and Prejudice* for the first time at around age sixteen, the story of a marriage-obsessed mother whose career it is to get her five daughters married off, regardless of what the daughters may want, seemed a quintessentially Pakistani story. For me Jane Austen was Pakistani, though she did not know this two hundred years ago in Regency England, nor that a lost young girl from Pakistan would start calling her "Jane Khala"—Aunt Jane. My teenage self decided that one day I would write and set *Pride and Prejudice* in Pakistan.

It wasn't until adulthood that I came across colonizer Thomas Babington Macaulay's address to British Parliament in 1835, in which he recommends the British Empire replace the colonies' languages with English in order to create "a person brown in color but white in sensibilities." To see the nefarious roots of the language I speak and thereby British education I'd received was disorienting, to say the least (after the 1947 partition of the Subcontinent, Pakistan became an independent country and made English one of its official languages). In order to reorient myself, to remap and reclaim identity, it became vital and necessary for me to write *Unmarriageable*. Professor Nalini Iyer has called *Unmarriageable* "Macaulay's worst nightmare," and I suppose it is, because, you see, the colonized are always only meant to admire all things empire and never aspire to it or take it on as equal.

In a 1981 speech, Toni Morrison stated, "If there's a book that you want to read but it hasn't been written yet, then you must write it." So I did. In writing *Unmarriageable* I've transformed the British classic into all-Pakistani. This is why *Unmarriageable* is a "parallel retelling," by which I mean it includes every plot point as well as character from the original, rather than an "inspired by" or a "sequel." It is a postcolonial retelling and as such literally *Pride and Prejudice* in Pakistan. There is a long legacy of authors who have known to write themselves from invisible to visible. Ernest Gaines said, "Back in '48, '49 . . . there were hardly any books there by or about blacks in those libraries. . . . I read literature of the other writers, the Russian writers and the British writers and the American writers, of course. But when I didn't see me there, it was then that I thought I'd start writing, try to write."

*   *   *

There are so many American authors whose stories have spoken to me: Langston Hughes, especially his poem "Harlem," though I had no idea in the eighth grade that Harlem was an African American district in New York City. All I knew was this poem with its lines "What happens to a dream deferred? / Does it dry up / like a raisin in the sun? / Or fester like a sore— / And then run?" meant a lot to me. After all, I had been around twelve years old when my anesthesiologist mother returned from the hospital one afternoon and I greeted her by telling her that I wanted to be an actress and she replied by giving me a swift reprimand. Apparently at the time, it was not a respectable dream to have, because it would leave me unmarriageable, and by association my sister and cousins and no one in Pakistan would get married, and what a tragedy that would be. I even received film and tv offers, but I was denied this dream by my father. Reluctantly and resentfully, I became a writer instead. Hughes's question—what happens to a dream deferred—stays with me always because it can apply to lost potential and regrets caused by restrictions of *every* sort.

And then there were Flannery O'Connor's short stories, in particular "Good Country People," "Everything That Rises Must Converge," and "The Life You Save May Be Your Own." At the time I read them, I had zero idea that I would one day reside in Georgia and visit O'Connor's homes in Savannah and Milledgeville and see her farm's peacocks, which were just like peacocks in Pakistan with the same appetite for gobbling up snakes, and the Bible she kept by her bedside as would be kept any Quran, and her crutches, which could just as easily have been anyone's anywhere in the world. O'Connor's outspoken yet naïve characters resonated deeply with me as did her Southern society, all too reflective of Pakistani society with its emphasis on keeping up appearances and good reputations. Who is to blame for our downfalls, O'Connor seems to be asking, the flaws within us? Or the flawed systems outside of us?

There was Shirley Jackson and "The Lottery," which hammered into me the cruelty of fate, or chance, that could sacrifice a life for the so-called greater good so very randomly. Fate, chance, bad luck—Tennessee Williams's protagonist Blanche DuBois in *A Streetcar Named Desire* and Jessie Redmon Fausett's Angela Murray in her novel *Plum Bun* and Alice Walker's Maggie in "Everyday Use" showed me how fickle even the best of intentions can be unless good luck comes to your rescue. There is Leslie Marmon Silko's short story "Lullaby," in which Native American Indigenous children are taken from their tribes, homes, and language to become someone other than who they were born—a story whose themes of linguistic colonialism and imperialism haunts me. And writers Kate Chopin, Jamaica Kincaid, Paule Marshall, Amy Tan, Americans all, whose immigrant tales illustrate living and surviving and thriving in multiple cultures and across hyphenated identities and simply being American.

In the world of storytelling we are all immigrants then, coming and going and going and coming and settling and resettling and making homes and saying goodbyes and carrying memories. Books make us belong everywhere; we belong in every book and in the stories we read and in the stories we write. Books are the one place where physical geography and emotional geography merge. When you pass through a book, your fingertips turning the pages, the words imprinting on your soul, you are home, and that home becomes part of you. You carry it wherever you go.

"My physical body had gone west to California but my soul stayed [in Louisiana]," said Ernest Gaines. And yet he was of both places and both places were touched by him. As writers we know how minutely the latitude and longitude of geography both external and internal make us, how we live and breathe and combine and write the coordinates of place, and that our geographies, all of them, are the stories we have read and the stories we are destined to tell. And so it is that here I stand delivering a keynote at a conference named after Georgia's red clay. This is writing the immigrant Southern in the *New* New South, or at least a version of it, my particular reality, where connections are made between cultures and places and where the physical and the soul meet and belong on the page and beyond the page.

177

CONTRIBUTORS

Khem K. Aryal is a writer, editor, and translator, originally from Nepal. His work has appeared in such journals as *The Pinch, New Writing, Isthmus, Pangyrus, Warscapes, Hawai'i Pacific Review* and *Valley Voices*. His short story collection, *The In-Betweeners*, is forthcoming from Braddock Avenue Books (2023). He is an associate professor of English at Arkansas State University, where he also serves as Creative Materials Editor of *Arkansas Review*. He has a PhD in English (Creative Writing, and Composition) from the University of Missouri.

Sindya Bhanoo is the author of the short story collection, *Seeking Fortune Elsewhere* (Catapult). Her fiction has appeared in *Granta, New England Review, Glimmer Train*, and elsewhere. She is the recipient of an O. Henry Award, the Disquiet Literary Prize, and Elizabeth George Foundation grant and scholarships from the Bread Loaf and Sewanee writers conferences. A longtime newspaper reporter, Sindya has worked for *The New York Times* and *The Washington Post*, where she is still a frequent contributor.

Jenny Bhatt is a writer, literary translator, and book critic. She is the founder of Desi Books and teaches creative writing at Writing Workshops Dallas. Her debut story collection, *Each of Us Killers: Stories* (7.13 Books; Sep 2020) won a 2020 Foreword INDIES award in the Short Stories category and was a finalist in the Multicultural Adult Fiction category. Her literary translation, *Ratno Dholi: Dhumketu's Best Short Stories* (HarperCollins India; Oct 2020) was shortlisted for the 2021 PFC-VoW Book Awards for English Translation from Regional Languages and will be out in the US in 2022. Her writing has appeared in various venues including *The Atlantic, NPR, BBC Culture, The Washington Post, Publishers Weekly, Los Angeles Review of Books, Dallas Morning News, Literary Hub, Longreads, Poets & Writers, Guernica, Electric Literature*, and more. Having lived and worked her way around India, England, Germany, Scotland, and various parts of the US, she now lives in a suburb of Dallas, Texas.

Born in Calcutta and raised in New Delhi, **Sayantani Dasgupta** received her MFA in Creative Writing from the University of Idaho. She is an Assistant Professor of Creative Writing at the University of North Carolina Wilmington. Her most recent book is the short story collection *Women Who Misbehave*. She is also the author of *Fire Girl: Essays on India, America, & the In-Between*—a Finalist for the Foreword Indies Awards for Creative Nonfiction—and the chapbook *The House of Nails: Memories of a New Delhi Childhood*. Her essays and short stories have appeared in *The Rumpus, Hunger Mountain, Southern Humanities Review, The Hindu, Scroll*, and others. Besides the US, she has also taught writing in India, Italy, and Mexico.

Anjali Enjeti has lived most of her life in the Deep South. She's an award-winning journalist, activist, and author of two books, the collection *Southbound: Essays on Identity, Inheritance, and Social Change*, and the novel *The Parted Earth*. Her other writing has appeared in *The Oxford American, Harper's Bazaar, Poets & Writers, Boston Globe, The Nation, Washington Post*, and elsewhere. A former board member of the National Books Critics Circle, she teaches creative writing in the MFA program at Reinhardt University. In 2019, she co-founded the Georgia chapter of They See Blue, an organization for South Asian Democrats. She lives with her family outside of Atlanta.

Ali Eteraz is the author of the debut novel, *Native Believer*, a *NYTimes Book Review* Editors' Choice selection. Eteraz is also the author of the critically acclaimed memoir *Children of Dust*. It was selected as a New Statesman Book of the Year and was featured on PBS with Tavis Smiley, NPR with Terry Gross, C-SPAN2, and numerous international outlets. *O, The Oprah Magazine*, called it "a picaresque journey" and the book was long-listed for the Asian American Writer's Workshop Award. Previously, he wrote the short story collection *Falsipedies and Fibsiennes*. Other short stories have appeared in *Adirondack Review, storySouth, Chicago Quarterly Review*, and *Forge Journal*.

Tarfia Faizullah is the author of two poetry collections, *Registers of Illuminated Villages* and *Seam*, and essays. The recipient of a Fulbright fellowship, three Pushcart prizes, and other honors, Tarfia has been featured in periodicals, magazines, and anthologies both here and abroad. Tarfia presents work at institutions and organizations worldwide, and collaborations include photographers, producers, composers, filmmakers, musicians, and visual artists, resulting in several interdisciplinary projects. In 2016, Tarfia was recognized by Harvard Law School as one of 50 Women Inspiring Change. Tarfia is a 2019 United States Artists Fellow.

Nepal-born **Anuja Ghimire** writes poetry, flash fiction and creative nonfiction. She is the author of poetry chapbook *Kathmandu, fable-weavers* and two poetry books in Nepali. She is a Best of the Net and Pushcart nominee. By day, she works as a senior publisher in an online learning company. She reads poetry for *Up the Staircase Quarterly*. She enjoys teaching poetry to children in summer camps. Her work found home in *Glass: A journal of poetry, Orbis: London, EcoTheo Review, UCity Review*, and *Crack the Spine*, among others. She lives near Dallas, Texas with her husband and two children.

Rukmini Kalamangalam is a proud South Asian American with roots in Houston, Texas and across the South. In the past, Rukmini has worked advocating for marginalized women of color, from survivors of violence to at-promise girls. She is passionate about envisioning an equitable future using the framework of abolition and is committed to building community power around Southern and Asian identities. In 2018, she was named Youth

Poet Laureate of the Southwest as well as Houston Youth Poet Laureate. Her poem, "After Harvey," was set to music by the Houston Grand Opera. She currently lives and works in Atlanta, GA.

Soniah Kamal is an award winning novelist, essayist and public speaker. Her novel, *Unmarriageable: Pride & Prejudice in Pakistan*, is a *Financial Times* Readers' Best Book of 2019, a NPR Code Switch Summer Read Selection, a *People's Magazine* and a New York Public Library pick, received starred reviews from *Publishers Weekly, Library Journal* and *Shelf Awareness* and more. *Unmarriageable* is a 'Books All Georgians Should Read', a Georgia Author of the Year for Literary Fiction nominee and shortlisted for the Townsend Award for Fiction. Soniah's TED talk is about second chances, and she has delivered numerous keynotes at Writers Conferences as well as 'We are the Ink', at a U.S. Citizenship Oath Ceremony about immigrants and the real American Dreams and her keynote at the Jane Austen Festival is about universality across time and cultures. Soniah's work has appeared in critically acclaimed anthologies and publications including *The New York Times, The Guardian, The Georgia Review, The Bitter Southerner, Catapult, The Normal School, Apartment Therapy* and more. She has taught creative writing at Emory University, Oglethorpe University and Reinhardt University.

Aruni Kashyap is a writer and translator. He is the author of *His Father's Disease* and the novel *The House With a Thousand Stories*. He has also translated from Assamese and introduced celebrated Indian writer Indira Goswami's last work of fiction, *The Bronze Sword of Thengphakhri Tehsildar*. He won the Charles Wallace India Trust Scholarship for Creative Writing to the University of Edinburgh, and his poetry collection, *There is No Good Time for Bad News* was a finalist for the 2018 Marsh Hawk Press Poetry Prize and 2018 Four Way Books Levis Award in Poetry. His short stories, poems, and essays have appeared in *Catapult, Bitch Media, The Boston Review, Electric Literature, The Oxford Anthology of Writings from Northeast, The Kenyon Review, The New York Times, The Guardian UK*, and others. He is an assistant professor of Creative Writing at the University of Georgia, Athens. He also writes in Assamese, and his first Assamese novel is *Noikhon Etia Duroit*.

Shikha Malaviya is a poet, writer and publisher. She is co-founder of The (Great) Indian Poetry Collective, a mentorship model press publishing powerful voices from India and the Indian diaspora. Her poetry has been nominated for the Pushcart Prize and featured in *PLUME, Chicago Quarterly Review, Prairie Schooner* and other fine publications. Shikha was a featured TEDx speaker in GolfLinks, Bangalore, in 2013, where she gave a talk on poetry. She was selected as Poet Laureate of San Ramon, California, 2016. Shikha is a five-time AWP poetry mentor and the 2020 poetry judge for AWP's Kurt Brown Prize. Currently, she is a Mosaic Silicon Valley Fellow, committed to cultural diversity and artistic excellence in the San Francisco Bay Area. Her book of poems is *Geography of Tongues*.

Kirtan Nautiyal is a practicing hematologist and oncologist near Houston, TX. His essays have been published in *Guernica, Crazyhorse, The Southern Review, Boulevard, McSweeney's Internet Tendency, Longreads*, and elsewhere; "Down to the Marrow of Our Bones," published in *Mount Hope,* was recognized as notable in the *Best American Essays* 2019. He is at work on a collection.

Chaitali Sen is the author of the novel *The Pathless Sky* (Europa Editions, 2015) and the story collection *A New Race of Men from Heaven* (Sarabande Books, 2023), which was selected by Danielle Evans as the winner of the 2021 Mary McCarthy Prize for Short Fiction. She is a graduate of the Hunter College MFA program in Fiction, and founder of the interview series Borderless: Conversations on Art, Action, and Justice. She lives in Smithville, Texas with her family.

Hasanthika Sirisena's short story collection *The Other One* won the Juniper Prize for Fiction and was released in 2016. Her essay collection *Dark Tourist* won the Gournay Prize and has been published from The Ohio State University Press/Mad Creek Books (2021).

Jaya Wagle immigrated to America in 2001 and currently lives in Dallas, Texas with her husband and 16-year old son. Her fiction and non-fiction work centers around her immigrant experience. Her work has been published or is forthcoming in *Barrell House, Maudlin House, Hobart, Rumpus, Sweet, Bending Genres, Pithead Chapel* and elsewhere. She teaches English Literature and Technical Writing at University of North Texas.

ACKNOWLEDGMENTS

Khem K. Aryal: "Laxman Sir in America" originally appeared in *Valley Voices* 21.1, Spring 2021.

Sindya Bhanoo: "Nature Exchange" from *Seeking Fortune Elsewhere*: Stories. ©2022 by Sindya Bhanoo. Reprinted with the permission of The Permissions Company, LLC on behalf of Catapult LLC, www.catapult.co.

Jenny Bhatt: "The Weight of His Bones" originally appeared, in an earlier version, in *The Nottingham Review* (March, 2017.)

Sayantani Dasgupta: "Rinse, Repeat" originally appeared in *Chautauqua Journal*, Water Issue, 2021.

Anjali Enjeti: "Drinking Chai to Savannah" originally appeared in *Longreads*, January 24, 2017.

Ali Eteraz: "Encased" originally appeared in *Forge* 7.2, October 2013.

Tarfia Faizullah: "Necessary Failure" originally appeared in *Oxford American*, September 2014.

Soniah Kamal: "Writing the Immigrant in the *New* New South" originally appeared in *Georgia Review*, Spring 2020.

Aruni Kashyap: "Nafisa Ali's Life, Love, and Friendships, Before and After the Travel Ban" originally appeared in *Oakland Review*, Spring 2021.

Kirtan Nautiyal: "Gettysburg" originally appeared in *Guernica Online*, October 27, 2021.

Chaitali Sen: "The Immigrant" originally appeared in *The Colorado Review*, Vol. 40, #2, Summer 2013.

Hasanthika Sirisena: "Pine" originally appeared in *The Other One* (UMass Press, 2016).

Jaya Wagle: "Fresh Off the Plane" originally published as part of Citizenship and Its Discontents Folio for *Anomaly Lit*, October 2020.